Old
Romantics

For Katie, Frank and Grace

Old
Romantics

Maggie Armstrong

TRAMPPRESS

First published in 2024 by Tramp Press
www.tramppress.com

'The Dublin Marriage' was first published in *Banshee*
(Issue 15 Spring/Summer 2023)
'Old Romantics' was first published as 'A Critic At
Large' in the *Dublin Review* (Issue 82 Spring 2021)
An early version of 'Baked Alaska' was first published
as 'Getting Away' in *Cassandra Voices* (30 Dec 2021)
An early version of 'Trouble' was first published in
the *Stinging Fly* (Issue 44 Vol. 2 Summer 2021)
'My Mistake' was first published in the
Belfield Literary Review (Issue 2 Spring 2022)
'Two Nice People' was first published in the
Dublin Review (Issue 85 Winter 2021)

A CIP record for this title is available
from the British Library.

1 3 5 7 9 8 6 4 2

Tramp Press gratefully acknowledges the
financial assistance of the Arts Council.

Trade Paperback ISBN 978-1-915290-13-7
eBook ISBN 978-1-915290-14-4

Thank you for supporting independent publishing.

Set in Palatino by Marsha Swan
Printed by L&C Printing Group, Poland

Contents

Number One

It was as simple as deciding to go outside and walk two streets north to the sandwich bar. Normally she stayed in the canteen, but the day was fine, and she felt like something different. She'd recently been hired on a traineeship programme and she 'loved every minute of it' and 'hadn't a clue' as she might try to convince an aunt or a friend, and they would roll their eyes, because she was very bright, well cut out for it. She worked hard and saved everything up, rarely drew attention to herself. And if she had known where this would lead she would not, in her right mind, have left the office that particular lunch hour.

The heat inside the sandwich place was unbearable. It was cramped and the queue was always completely disorganised. But the trainee liked their grilled four-cheese sandwich.

He was standing right at her sleeve, and when she moved, he moved with her. She thought she knew his face from somewhere – he'd worked behind a bar, or maybe he'd been in an Irish film. Or it was just one of those faces.

She moved again, and his shoulder wheeled ahead, reinstating his position. She saw what he was doing. He was neatly built and strong, a very physical person, with a golden tan scorched on the back of his neck. He got ahead of her in the queue, and she stood looking at him, aghast.

He left with a grilled four-cheese sandwich wrapped up under his arm. She was next. She asked for the four-cheese, but the serving lady shook her head: they were all out. The trainee got a salad that did not excite her. She intended to walk back to her office right away, but then she noticed him on the bench outside the shop.

Her pencil skirt made it awkward to sit and her blouse clung to her flesh in the heat. At the other end of the bench, he ate her sandwich. She noted the animal way he attacked her sandwich. How, when he was finished, he balled up the paper and left it there between them on the bench to unball. He was very nice-looking, with a symmetrical face, like the face of the prince in the pantomime she had seen as a little girl and become obsessed with. She would one day use the word 'savage' to describe his body, in an email he never replied to. When she had finished her salad, she opened a new pack of cigarettes and asked him for a lighter. "Fraid not,' he said, but he'd take a cigarette. She waited. 'Oh look!' she said, and she saw he didn't believe she hadn't known there was a lighter in her handbag all along.

They smoked and watched the street. They watched as a cyclist's wheel got caught in the tram track and the cyclist was thrown to the ground. Two people rushed in to help him, and the trainee stood braced. She had a first-aid certificate, her name was on a list in the kitchenette at work. She carried an organ donor card, she'd tried to give blood. She was ready.

'No point everyone helping him, look, he's alright,' the guy reasoned.

But the cyclist wasn't alright. By the time the ambulance drove off, the trainee felt that they had both seen something they should not move along from too hastily. She looked up. 'Could I ask you, have we met before?' It turned out they had, maybe once, in a bar. They had been college students; it was a dive. 'What a filthy dive,' she said, wincing and laughing. 'Never very salubrious,' he agreed. 'What about you,' she said. 'Do you work around here?' 'My work is varied,' he said, 'but I have a flat over there.' He glanced up the narrow jumble of shops, pubs, massage parlours, bubble tea houses, take-aways. 'You should come visit.' And though her chest tightened like a fist, she knew that she would go through with it, and she wrote his address on a business card in her wallet; his phone wasn't working.

She wondered was this it. For a long time, she had treasured this uniqueness of hers, but the thing had gone rusty on her, and she guessed that getting rid of it would be painful but forgettable, a quick job. After work, she went to the pharmacy.

There were two rows of buzzers. None was obviously his, so she tried every one of them. The door opened and she pushed it with difficulty, finding a floor mat thickly piled with fliers and unopened bills. The building was creaky and stale, not the kind of place she would go for any other reason. She took the stairs to the second floor, where he met her, shoeless, wide-eyed.

Inside, she waited as he made himself a cup of instant coffee, carefully adding milk, then two spoons of sugar. He lit a joint and put something harsh and jungly on the CD player – all this happened some time ago. Their kisses, on the grotty sofa, were tender, and he removed all her clothes without delay. She wasn't sure what to do, but he seemed to think she was no idiot. 'Do you like this,' he said, 'is this OK?' 'Yeah,' she said. 'Go on.' But she was distracted. They moved to the floor, and she pushed him away suddenly. She said, 'Are you even going to offer me a drink? Like was that coffee just for you?'

He said, 'Whoops. I was looking after number one.'

'Same as when you skipped me in the queue?'

He looked affronted – this was hardly the time to talk about – he had to concentrate here.

'You did! You know it.'

'It must be my eyesight,' he said. 'Depth perception. That and that I couldn't be bothered with fucking rules.'

She laughed. 'Didn't they teach you any manners in – where?'

'In the country,' he said, taking her by the hips. 'I'm from the country.'

'I'm a virgin!' she said. 'And be careful!' She had waited for the moment to declaim her truth and now it was gone.

'Really?'

'Yes.'

'Oh dear,' he said, stroking himself. 'Come here.'

'No, you come here.' She got up and found a small crackly towel, and she lay on it and handed him a condom. She tried not to look at him as he put it on, it was all too bizarre. She pushed away a can and a couple of DVDs with men all over the covers. She wouldn't like to make too much of it afterwards, to overthink it, but the flinty glare of Tom Cruise was the last thing she saw before he bored into her, a snout digging in the placid earth.

'Should I stop,' he said.

'No,' she said. 'Just get inside, get it over with.'

Once he had got it over with, she sat up and, astride of his white thighs, cried out, furious, also satisfied with the pain. 'That hurts!' she said.

The room and the street beyond were very quiet as she waited for him on the sofa, wrapped in the towel. She was faintly elated. She quizzed him on his friends, nodded when he mentioned their names and nicknames.

Before she left she put the towel inside the drum of the washing machine. She stood at the door in her work clothes, watching him lick three Rizlas together. 'What's your rent like?' she asked, and she was disappointed when he told her it wasn't his place.

He had taken care, just before they parted, to tell her that he would be in touch when he got a replacement phone. For the next two weeks she heard nothing from him. She could only wait, and she hadn't imagined the degree of longing and need she would have to contend with. She searched online, but there was no trace of him. She asked college friends, who only half-remembered him, and they weren't sure. She went to the sandwich place every lunchtime, she detoured past it on her way home. She scoured the faces, which felt bold, transgressive, though it wasn't, really.

One evening her screen flashed with a number. It took him a while to state his purpose. He cleared his throat as if absent-minded, or ill. 'I was thinking of inviting you to dinner,' he said finally.

She said she would love this. It was boomtime in the country, new places were opening, everyone splashed out.

'Seeing as things are so expensive in town,' he said, 'I was gonna make you dinner.'

'That would be nice,' she said. They agreed to meet at the market, Saturday, four o'clock, to select all the ingredients.

She found him on a wall, eating a brightly stuffed falafel wrap out of tinfoil. He offered her a bite, but continued chatting with a man selling flowers, whom she half-knew. A Polish woman had waxed her vagina to the standards of a doll; she'd fasted since morning and washed her hair and blow-dried it; she'd lain back and studied between her legs with a pocket mirror. She had butterflies in her stomach, she had no appetite.

They sat in a general silence while he finished his falafel wrap. The fish man chopped up fish with a big knife. The vegetable grower in skirt and apron tossed salad leaves in baskets with strong hands. He said nothing – he was a man of few words but, the trainee assumed, a very deep mind. She was nervous, she despaired of the daylight, she couldn't think of anything to do except get into bed with him.

They both gazed up at the clouds, which were grey and billowing. When raindrops started hitting their faces, he suggested a pint.

In the pub he ordered himself a pint. For a moment she let it slide. Then she said, 'You bought yourself a pint.'

He glanced up, mid-sip. 'Oops,' he said, 'I'm looking after number one again.'

She was annoyed for a moment, but relaxed when he signalled to the barman. When her drink was coming she took out her wallet, waving him away. 'Phew,' he said, 'I'm on my last—' and rubbed his fingertips together.

They drank beer and cider for the afternoon. Because they had so little to say to one another they talked to the barman, and to the regular customers. The trainee laughed and threw a bouncy ball with a little girl, though she knew she was too drunk to be around a child.

They found a Chinese restaurant and once seated, he ordered a glass of red wine for himself and a portion of crispy duck spring rolls with egg-fried rice. He sat up very straight as he ate, gripping with a neat confidence his knife and fork – he admitted he had been to boarding school, sent away at seven. When he eyed her prawn toast, she let him help himself. She only wanted to be alone with him again. The first time, it hadn't been satisfactory, and nothing could prevent her now from finding out where exactly this was going.

His friend's flat looked different, its air of squalor more startling under the artificial light. Empty cans and shopping bags indicated people were often in and out. This time they went straight into the bedroom. It was shuttered, stuffy, the floor on one side covered with clothes, electrical things, an open suitcase, bus tickets and plectrums. Madeira cakes spilling from their packet. She averted her eyes and kissed him; she intended to scrub this place from her mind.

'Are you OK?' he asked, a little later, his cheek against hers, breath hot in her ear. 'You're doing very well.'

She could only nod. The pain surprised her, at this stage; she told him to stop.

'We'll try again later,' he whispered.

They tried again in the night, and without her even realising, it no longer hurt. She would do this with no one else. She would fall in love with him. He loved her so much and adored her. She was adored. It ended abruptly and he shouted, 'Sorry!' Once he'd lain next to her for a while, once he brought his hand between her legs, he said he would like to see her come. He was very good at making her come, he had done this with lots of others. Or she was good at coming, she was the best – it didn't matter. She felt proud of herself, active and invincible – incredible, lucky, adored – as she came wrapped around him.

In the morning they had sex again, and this time it lasted maybe an hour. She had no idea. She'd learned very quickly how pleasure would be possible with another person, and while she didn't fight for her own this time, she wanted to see his and to feel it moving through her, for herself to be the source – this made her so proud. She thought she could live with him, forgive him everything, if she got to do this with him any time they liked.

'You little—!' He berated her from above, reprimanded her, finishing, exhausted, inside her willing body. They lay on the streaked and damp sheets, and she day-dreamed, coverless, exposed and singed with bliss at having found him.

She watched, admiring him, as he tidied up and went to get coffee for her. What she did not notice among the scraps he took away was a condom that had torn right through.

On the way to get the abortion pills she told him to take her to lunch afterwards; she felt that would be appropriate. She'd researched the options on her laptop at home, spoken to a woman, and been assured it was safe. On the antique-furniture street they went up a flight of stairs to a nail bar. She'd taken the precaution of walking the street the day before and was not alarmed. But he was restless. He wiped sweat from his face and said, 'Just – how much are they going to charge?'

'I already told you how much it would be,' she said.

Less than a fucking baby costs, she thought.

He paced the cluttered salon, eyeing walls of glitzy gadgets, tins of life-enhancing potions and human hair in packets – he flapped his t-shirt with the stress of it.

'Would it be an idea', he said, 'to split the cost?'

'Whatever,' she said.

A woman in a black suit jacket came in and handed her a packet. 'You can take them at home,' she said. 'But we don't mind if you want to take the first one here.'

The woman served her a plastic cup of water. She put a hand on her wrist, and it felt soft and caring. 'You might feel sick today and tomorrow,' she said, and handed her an A4 page of printed material. And that was all. 'One-twenty with consultation,' the receptionist in the hot-pink wig said.

In the pizza restaurant they ordered two margheritas. He rolled up each slice of pizza from its tip like a pancake and swallowed, apparently without chewing, then pushed his empty plate away from him and asked for a Bloody Mary. She was mute and jittery. They had nothing to say to each other, they never had anything to say. This concerned but also interested her as she thought they must be in a deep place, finding their way to some echoing mysterious truth. He sipped his cocktail. Already, she was spilling blood. She reached a hand underneath her jeans, she touched the vinyl chair cover. Just her imagination. She smiled. He slashed a celery stick with the side of his mouth, like a horse. When the bill came, he put some money on the plate, leaned back and flexed himself all over. What she understood from his contribution was that she should now read through the bill herself.

2 x Pizza Margherita €34

TOTAL €34

Service not included. Thank you for your visit.

She pointed out that his drink wasn't on the bill. The guy put a finger to his lips. When she opened her wallet she found she was out of cash. 'Sorry,' she said. 'I'll pay you back.'

At his doorstep, they kissed and said goodbye. The unopened post and leaflets were still on the floor and she really wanted to stack and sort them. As she lingered, he felt in his pockets, and held her stare.

'Your money,' she said, remembering. 'I'll get it.'

'Oh, yeah,' he said, 'that would be great.'

He went on upstairs. She walked down the street to a bank machine, and after that to Centra for change. The man at the till told her she would have to buy something in order for him to open the till, so she bought a bar of Dairy Milk. Her uterus, by now, was very present to her; she worried she had got dangerous pills and would die.

'Here,' she said, back in his bedroom.

'I'm making money off you,' he joked, sliding the note into his wallet. 'It was only thirty-four euro.'

'I know, but the tip. You left a tip?'

He said he never actually tipped. 'Those people earn so much more than us,' he said. 'I mean, more than me.

You're doing alright for yourself, aren't you, you little upstart.'

She found out through a mutual connection he was the son of a lord. 'That makes you, what, Honourable somebody? A count?' she said. 'A viscount?' 'More of a vagrant,' he said, puffing on his rollie. 'A knight of the road.'

She spent all her free time with him, confused, in love. They had really nothing at all in common. She came from a provincial town. His family had land and he knew about country things, breeding and killing and hanging, and riding horses. He had nothing much to say about his family – 'They think I'm a wanker, and I think they're all wankers,' was all.

He seemed indifferent to new people, and his tastes were strange and introverted. He liked cheap cuts of meat, herbal highs, free things. She wondered had he ever read a book in full, ever been inside a bank. He was very good in bed, becoming, in their nakedness, someone shy and giving. His passions and desires were sequestered in a mind that was often stoned, a mind to which she no longer really wanted access. Silence was acceptable, after her long days. He had an old van, a horsebox. Apart from the land owned by his estranged Lord and Lady parents he had no fixed address, no steady job, though he got excited about small ventures, crazy projects that could become serious ways of life. He slept in his van and got keys to friends' flats, and he only really talked to her when he was inside her.

She rented her own place, and he stayed there until some time after she had decided that she did not want him to be her boyfriend. She decided it quietly, and endeavoured, through a coldness, to repel him. But he just kept showing up, tired. Then he would go away, then come back for a long weekend, or five days, wearing leather sandals flattened at the heel, sunburned, with a red beard on his face that made him very dislike-able to her. He wore glasses now, with cheap frames to which he hadn't given any thought. He had no notion about when he smelled, no intention of washing even when she told him it was what he had to do. He didn't say please. He didn't say thank you unless she told him to – manners, he said, were forced on him as a child. He ran out of phone credit, he borrowed phones to send texts. One time, he made her a compilation CD – it had no case, no list of songs, but the music would pour in her ears as she unwound. For her birthday, he wrapped up an old diving suit he'd never really used and gave it to her with a card he had made himself with pastels. But he was very good-looking.

Mornings were when he made vague plans. He sent circular emails about spit-roasting a pig, he talked about paella, fantasised about festivals. He still cooked for her in strange apartments. She arrived to see pots of pota-toes with lumps of butter thrown in, and he didn't give her any cutlery, just served himself and started eating because – fuck – he was looking after number one. 'Sorry, my dear,' he said, and then they would go to bed, and he would talk. 'Yes, that's good for you, you little vixen, hold on there, hold it out, you little fucking vixen.' She loved when he talked, and she would shout at him: 'You better be nicer to me, d'you hear?' She felt great, she felt power-less in these ecstatic moments. But in the morning, having coffee, she went back to an accommodating silence.

They were sitting in another market when she told him it was all over between them. She had a bigger role now, she had a nameplate and an underground parking space. She wore stiff outfits. Once, they'd made love in her office toilets, and it only bothered her afterwards.

He sighed, fidgeted, when she told him. 'Well that's just great,' he said. There were his summer plans, wrecked. He had nowhere to stay, her home was his, so he stayed on in the flat a week more, made granola in his y-fronts, left the oven on. He would disappear and return with a rucksack, a bag of food. The supple, needy air of a lost cat. She told him he could stay until he found his own place but that they were no longer *in a relationship*. So she would split the bed in two with an invisible line they both understood, and he would lay his sleeping bag out, and she would get under her duvet and they would lie on their different sides; but they always woke up in the night having sex with each other. She cared less and less about what he thought. There had been others, one or two, but only he knew how to touch her and she knew, in the aftermath of each burst of bliss that she needed to go far away from him.

It wasn't long before she got a year-long opportunity with the European Group. In Madrid, she made new friends and joined a gym. As the months dragged on, she found she would be willing to see him once again, here, where it would be different and hot. She'd found no one to replace him, and she missed him. She phoned him up. 'You did ask me not to contact you,' he said, but he booked a flight. She filled her fridge with good things; he didn't turn up. She stood in the empty bus station, ringing every number that had to do with him. He arrived the next day at the wrong station. She'd thought he was dead. He was tired from travel. He was empty-handed and sorry about that. But they had a good time. He had made some money working on an organic farm in Leitrim, and he treated her to nice things until that money was gone. They took trips out of the city, out to Segovia, to Ávila. In a tapas bar on the Plaza Mayor he cleared his throat and said, 'You, eh, still owe me for the—' 'The bus ticket,' she said. 'Right,' he said. The bill came, and as she paid he put the mints in his pocket, his other arm tucked around her waist.

She liked Madrid, but she heard through a girl back home that he had slept with a girl who had the same name as her. 'Seriously,' she shouted, on the phone, 'I didn't even know there was another Margaret in Dublin.' Although she had let him go, although he did not belong to her, it was unacceptable. She wanted him so much more now that there was another Margaret.

Back in Dublin, she met him for a drink, and she confronted him about the other Margaret. 'You're annoyed,' he said, nodding. He wanted to tell her, though, that he had tickets to a lovely little garden festival. 'Why should I go to some festival,' she said, and he said, 'Yeah, I understand.' She found something to wear and met him in town. They were going by bus because his van had been returned to his uncle, and they had no mutual friends to call upon, no social scene. One of his upper teeth to the back was missing, and one arm of his glasses was held on with several layers of Sellotape.

In the beer tent, she demanded wine. He spilled a fistful of coins on the bar table, which the barman then had to sweep, coin by coin, into his palm. She added mental notes to those that sat thick in an imaginary pull-out drawer in her mind, which one day she would empty out and shred until destroyed. It got dark out and she took a weird pill that made her feel sick and caffeinated.

She would get out of here now, soon enough, and take a bus home early. And she was really leaving when he said, 'Look who it is!'

There were three old schoolfriends, and their three slender girlfriends, standing still as chess pieces. The guys were happy to see him and interested in her. They all hung out. One started grinning into his phone. 'Look,' he said, 'it says it right here: the Count is three-hundred-and-seventy-second in line for the throne! What do you make of that, three-hundred-and-seventy-second!' She tried to gauge the spirit in which this information had been offered, to humour them.

'I'm a commoner,' she said.

'You're an ambitious woman,' another countered, and they all laughed, and she wanted to die. They slapped her boyfriend's back: 'Your round, it's your round, don't cheat!' 'Hey now, the Count would like the honour of buying these, come partake in the Count's bounty!' She poured a plastic cup of Pinot Noir down her throat and decided she could handle this and that it was never too late to become a completely different person.

On the bus home she stood, suddenly, and asked the bus driver to please stop, and she climbed down off the bus to vomit on the roadside. She didn't feel at all better after bending over in the ditch. She was aware that the bus driver and the people on the bus could see her retching. She got back on, clutching the seats.

He was still asleep, his Discman in his ears.

The bus dumped them on O'Connell Street. She sat limp on the pavement, her head in her folded arms. 'Come on,' he said. 'Get me a taxi,' she said. 'Get up, come on. Fresh air,' he said.

The street outside the General Post Office was in a state of crisis, children hopping around, men and women queueing for paper plates of food. Police sirens rang along the shoddy boulevard. A man in a ragged tracksuit with big blue eyes and a handsome face approached them. 'Howyas both, I'm homeless,' he said. 'Can you help me?' They both said, 'No, sorry.' 'Please,' he said. 'If I were you,' he said, 'and I met someone in my position, I would help them.'

'No, sorry.'

Nothing would ever be right again. When they reached Burger King, she ran upstairs and threw up again in the toilets.

He was waiting for her on the steps of the Daniel O'Connell statue, eating a bag of chips. When he saw her, he offered her one.

In the morning, he slept on. She made coffee and eggs and carried it all out to the balcony table. He picked up a spoon, sliced the top off his boiled egg and sighed and put the spoon down. He rubbed his eyes. The yolk was hard because she had overcooked it, again. For the whole afternoon, he lay across the length of the balcony, wearing sunglasses over his ordinary glasses.

She had allowed a month to pass since her return from Madrid before she let him back into her apartment. In her messed-up bedroom, Sunday very slowly developed into Monday. She had told him multiple times that his beard did not suit him, that it repelled her and offended everything she had worked hard to achieve. Now, watching him in the hard morning light, she wished she could shave it off, and that it could be a joke between them rather than an expression of rage.

She left him sleeping and went to work.

At her desk again, in the glassy space, she felt peace return. One thing she loved was how clean it always was inside this fishbowl. She clicked on emails, she replied with a crisp and bright efficiency to the little queries of the hapless trainees in the new intake. She clicked on the Probate folder, opened her document, and pinned her gaze at the wording:

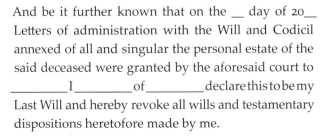

She'd make a career out of doing this, helping people to die with a shrewd dispersal of assets. And she would one day form her own practice, she knew it.

They had arranged to meet for a sandwich, and they sat on the boardwalk facing the river and the glass office blocks. It smelled of the sea out here, where the gulls called for food, the ripples glistened and the buses churned, interrupting the scene. Beside him she was tired, suddenly, wistful. She found she yawned a lot around him these days. He was busy on his phone, and this was not good either.

She asked him: 'Do you think you would have wanted to keep the baby if that's what I'd wanted?'

He sighed. She had brought this up before, and he never gave her the answer she was looking for.

'I think you would be a good mother,' he said. 'But I'm pretty sure I should spare this world another offspring.'

She had nothing to say to this. Her chest banged like a broken toy, and after he lit a cigarette and placed his hand upon her thigh the feeling overtook her.

'I don't think I want to be with you anymore,' she told him.

He'd heard this before as well.

'Sorry,' she added.

'Right,' he said.

He sat up slowly, sucking up the last crackles of his cigarette. 'I understand – it makes sense.'

'Really?'

They talked for a few moments about it. They would always be friends. They looked into each other's eyes, they held hands, and they embraced. So it felt like nothing to conclude it all. A minor disruption, a small dent in her working day. She had a busy week ahead, and she needed to remove herself from the bench.

'Give me a smoke, would you,' she said. All these years she was still trying to give up, and when she asked this, he slid the pack from his jacket pocket, and held it under his eyes, like a hand of cards.

She laughed. 'Do you only have one left?'

'Yeah,' he said, relieved.

'Give me it, now.' She took the pack from him. Three cigarettes jumped around inside it. She took one, and then she emptied the other two onto the filthy ground, with the pack too, and stamped her heel on them.

'Goodbye,' she said, eyes shining, and did not turn to look at him left there.

She married, and he settled down with a woman in the countryside, and made cheese and yoghurt. And because she didn't form her own practice in the end, he still called in sometimes for a cup of tea. One time he brought her a fridge magnet with his new gardening services logo and phone number on it – Strimming, Landscaping, Weeding, Tree-felling, Full Organic Waste Removal. The phone number was missing a digit, which he'd written in with biro. Then he got into seafoods. He'd arrive on a bicycle, and hold his finger on the doorbell and, once invited in, say he had three nets of mussels and if she cooked them today, they'd be fine. Her little boy would run to the door, wrap his arms around her leg; and the man would look past him. She opened wine; he handed her a bag of green olives, and they drank the wine and ate the olives and then he took the rest of the olives away with him. But he still called to her – he still calls, so I hear.

The problem is, in the years of mothering and cleaning up, she often feels like company. She often wishes an outside force would intrude. She can be histrionic and unfair. She will make piercing noises of frustration from behind her shut lips. And from nowhere, as if summoned, he will send her a message. The doorbell will ring. Her girls will eye him, and she'll make toast and proper Earl Grey tea for the poor drifter, with his reusable bags, his litter of receipts, the smashed stock cubes melting in his wallet, the white beard growing under his eyes. 'He's our friend,' her older girl says, after he leaves, and the mother stands and watches him receding in his heavy anorak. Friend, she thinks. Yes, he is our friend.

She even tells him, same way she tells her little boy: 'You know, you should really say thanks to people.' He just says, 'Right,' and nods eagerly. 'Right.'

The Dublin Marriage

I met my husband at a house viewing one Saturday in the spring when we were young. I was locking my bike to a pole when he came towards me, squinting through his thick black cartoon-hero glasses.

'Daniel?' I said.

'Margaret?'

A mutual friend had introduced us over email, suggesting that we find a place together since we'd both been searching for so long. We joined the queue to view the property on that pleasant redbrick terrace in The Liberties, up to the doorway where an estate agent with a clipboard was casting friendly glances at the crowd.

I was never exactly physically attracted to Dan, though I remember him with an obstinate tenderness even now. His bright, startled-animal eyes behind the frames, black Shavian beard growing thickly around his features, bobbling navy duffel coat with the buttons done up around what looked like an expansion of waistline. Walking around the rooms with him, I underwent an enormous inner transformation. I became completely new and shy and full of possibility, lingering at a bedroom door, or nodding at the ersatz bronze claw feet of the bathtub, which still merited eager nodding, for being claw-foot.

Soft light stole in; I sank into the bathtub while he made a pair of cocktails. He marinated chicken pieces, diced cucumber for salads – he was a bon viveur, uxorious, everything he did was for my benefit. I was a wife, productive, dominant, beloved. He never missed a day of work, but I missed a lifetime, going back to bed to write my little stories between sheets that needed putting in the wash. That morning I met Dan I started to imagine things, believing they were real. There was no threshold between the disparate realms, between the now and wished for, just a breezy opening into what was better, what was happiness, what was the very least you could expect from being born.

We didn't get the plastic claw-foot bathtub house, but Dan and I kept searching, exchanging charged-up emails, desperate that we were. Dan was sleeping on his office sofa, while I had overstayed a pretty long-drawn-out childhood at my parents'. I had anxiety and depression, or whatever you might call that form of turmoil that makes you picture, regularly, in shocking previews, your most lonely death. I'd been to the GP for a prescription, paid a woman weekly for her hour of listening; now I needed reasons to sustain me here.

When we found the little two-bed redbrick cottage in the Guinness heartlands, neither of us noticed on first glance the rot and lies pervading everything. In an atmosphere of beating hearts we told the landlady we were both professionals. She took a wad of fifties from my hand, and Dan and I stood on the doorstep, housemates.

There was a shoddy, bogus feel to this house in which we fell in love. Across the way stood an industrial plant, lined with tall spiked barbed-wire railings and a metal sign that read NO DUMPING / COSC AR DHUMPÁIL. The redbrick was a purple shade of imitation period veneer that looked like you could peel it off. Dark, bare living spaces; plain, lifeless bedrooms furnished in bland biscuit shades. The street was just one street – nothing opposite, adjacent or behind, only this one strip of residential glaring windows, as if whoever drew the plans got bored five minutes in and thought of something else to do. There were four houses and a landfill – a house with walls and windows like our house, only weeds and thistles in the place of rooms, and bags of rubbish blowing.

That first evening I was emptying my books and vinyl from their boxes onto the floor, because there was no shelf to put them on, when a knock came on the door and there he stood, a morose shape with suitcases.

'Thanks, Margaret!' Dan said, and took the key I'd had cut for him. It turned out neither of us had eaten, so we walked out to get a takeaway, and back home carrying steaming paper bags. And we sat, that night, together at the kitchen table, a sudden couple, making conversation over tofu curries with fried rice. Dan used chopsticks fluently; I used plastic cutlery as if I'd never held a fork before or sat up at a table. I was rattled to my twisted insides. The kitchen light was crude and low over our heads, making stark the new and troubling eventuality that we would sit together like this all the rest of our lives. We talked of coffee shops and books and albums not everyone knew about, but we did. Bob Dylan, *John Wesley Harding*. Knut Hamsun, *Hunger*. And I can't think of any others, but whatever, our sensibilities were tied as if by some invisible design. I tried keeping my emotions to myself; Dan did this naturally, dark horse. He was always curious – he asked careful questions, pushed his glasses up his nose. He had a slightly wary, fearful disposition when he looked into my eyes, as if preparing for the very worst.

That night, I knew for certain I would marry him and leave the rest behind. And with the thrill of knowing that my search was up came disappointment. Sorrow – oppressed feeling. I could foresee it all. The rickety, squat house, rambling back garden – the barbeques, the skewered meats, the citronella candles, then one by one, our two wild little children, our freelance problems. The fast-arriving drudgery, the claustrophobia within a love sustained by friendship and respect.

Dan sat appreciatively while I washed and stacked the cartons and the cutlery and chopsticks for recycling. 'Thanks!' he said, in his puzzled, gracious way, and then separately, we went upstairs, into the separate double bedrooms that faced each other on the landing. We each had our own en suite, so we would never need to run into one another in the night. The next morning, he was gone when I woke up and I sat down to work on my short story.

All this time I thought myself a writer. I had a salvaged school desk, and a street view, and sitting at this eyrie – words like this I would have liberally used – I could see across the street into the plant, or turning left, into the landfill, the house they never built, its pit of plastic bags and dead grey weeds.

I didn't have direction as a writer, or any publications, yet, though I had ambition, could execute a rushed idea. I was well capable of banging out long passionate accounts of hot desire, rejection and revenge – screechy autofictions which I would expunge on A4 paper before abandoning them one by one.

This was the trouble with it all. So much tension gathered in me when I sat down to work, because I doubted I had any talent whatsoever. I knew exactly where this would end up. Of all the sentences I'd written, crossed out and rewritten, they'd all gone in the bin, or were left to disappear in boxes for eventual removal to the attic where my parents said I shouldn't put things anymore. All endeavour had been useless, but I did it anyway, slashed away each morning, with a cramping finger grip. I could do eight foolscap pages at a sitting, staple them together, but could never bear to look at them again.

That first day I opened up my emails, and wrote down a list of restaurants I'd a hankering to visit. Underneath that, a list of brands for clothing, shoes and earrings. He'd like that I'm assertive when it comes to taste. I saved the email in my drafts. The street dulled my thoughts.

NO DUMPING / COSC AR DHUMPÁIL
OFFENDERS PROSECUTED

Morning time with him at work was solitary, productive. I wrote many lists. We were building our first home – I called the gas and electricity, compared price plans for broadband, set up a bin account. I walked streets, past

Victorian redbricks, and the air had a thick and smoky, hoppy flavour, unless I am embellishing. The cupboards needed to be filled so I went up to Smithfield, and came back with all the best things: rooibos tea and coffee beans, dark chocolate, peanut butter, Maldon salt, white miso paste, Spanish tuna and paprika almonds. I packed the tiny fridge with delicacies too good to open: Black Forest panna cotta, raw cow's milk from the farm, Swiss mountain cheese, and pumpernickel bread, and cornichons, and quince jam. And I put on a record and just sat.

It was late that night and I was half-asleep upstairs when I heard Dan come in, and in the morning he was gone again. Tuesday was the same. And so I took to staying up and waiting for him, heart racing, energetic, like a feral spaniel who can't find their owner. I just couldn't rest. He never did come home, my husband – he saw his clients in the evenings, in the pub I think, pushing it, timewise. I poured a glass of wine, put almonds in a little bowl – stuck on a record, a solitary waltz, and crumpled on the sofa in the manner of a tragic woman being painted. I waited, resentfully, my feet reclined, and no one to top up my wine.

Dreaming – manufacturing scenarios – is what you end up doing, when you've nothing special to amuse yourself with, I guess! On the Friday evening I could hear the clink of bottles in a plastic bag. Dan removed his sombre coat, and we both stood talking, in the front room, as if our house was just an emptied venue and we were acquaintances. My blood boiled through my chest. 'Have a beer,' he said. There were two fake leather sofas in that living room. The sofas were too big for one, but definitely too small to seat two, so that your choice of where to sit was like a declaration of the heart. The sofas huddled on the floor pathetically. We took one each and sipped our frosted microbrews, and talked about the Dylan record I had picked to spark a conversation. Once his beer was gone, Dan yawned, and said he had an early start.

In the morning he was gone.

When I rose, I hoovered up and tidied all our things into their places. I called the broadband company, made more lists, went out with shopping bags, came home with breaking bags containing all my purchases: light bulbs; cutlery organiser; door hook for our keys; jug for olive oil; Kilner jar for sundries; soap dish for the good soap, for if there were guests. I busied around our various feng shui to give it life. Between the two of us we owned: a typewriter with a broken mangled ribbon I would get repaired one day; a small locked treasure chest whose only key had been misplaced, and I knew one day I would find it; a gramophone (we would have called it that); two boxes of LPs; a chessboard with carved-ivory bone pieces, missing both its castles but overrun with pawns; a film projector for which Dan said he'd get a cable; two Italian coffee pots in pistachio and coral red; two old hipster bikes.

On his bike, the front wheel was buckled so he left it in the yard. On my bike, a beautiful white racer, the wheels needed a good pumping, nothing more. So I made the practical suggestion he should ride my bike – as long as he should need to. I wanted to furnish him in life and pave his way, and I wasn't cycling so much owing to a dislocated kneecap long ago. The bike was his.

One Friday evening in the month of June, we sat a little later than was normal for us, on our sofas. We had become shy together, all smiles and Fair Isle jumpers brushing by the gramophone. Tonight he was exhausted from his work designing book jackets and homeware catalogues; he took off his glasses, slumped back, opened one button on his floral motif shirt. His hair had grown around his ears, his beard was thick and unkempt, like the drawing of the husband in *The Joy of Sex*. When I got up to pour another glass of whiskey, I stood beside his sofa until he moved to make some room for me.

Squished together, we continued our discussion as if oblivious. Oblivious to the sudden warmth caused by the constriction of the space between us. I sipped my whiskey at a restless pace and I dreaded everything. What if we didn't know how we should kiss? How would he be with all his clothes removed? How would he cope with how he felt? He felt humiliated, at risk of self-exposure. The experience of just being there was so uncomfortable as to paralyse my will to budge and put an end to it. I saw our happiness, our doom. The little house again, two scruffy children, pagan wedding, homemade veggie burgers. I hadn't seen it happening so soon, so quickly and conveniently, with so little fight. No more pining, striving, no exhaustive abject quest to share your life with someone, because here they were, bespectacled, hirsute, with a timid posture. I lost my sense of time attempting to look in his eyes, which were small and catlike, with a filmy glisten that held back some fear, or subtle plea, some faraway *please don't*. Don't what, I couldn't figure out.

He stood up and yawned: 'Well Marg.' He stacked his bottles by the door. I climbed at his heels, and watched him disappear again. We didn't fall in love as quickly as I'd thought two people should when they are young and perfectly compatible.

—

It rained throughout July and when it rained the dogshit in the yard behind the kitchen began to form the makings of a muddy stream. The landlady was selling, and things started to not matter. Our pregnant neighbour, padding by, looked at the yard and raised her head. 'I'm going to clean that up,' she said, and flicked her cigarette on top of it, and closed the door behind her.

Very soon we had to clear out for the viewings at particular times of day, and the estate agents were forever rearranging my spices into pointless rows. Besides this, I'd started to not like some little things I noticed about Dan. His empty water glasses by the sink, and the way, if I offered him a square of chocolate or a nut or a dried mango slice, he always took it. The way he never bought a single piece of fruit. I felt sometimes I'd been an idiot, a fantasist, fixated on some fairy tale. I'd lusted after things I didn't even want, lied to myself. And yet I always felt that I was much more interesting than evidently perceived by those who had deserted me; I felt that they had missed something, or seen it all just as presented but without its cloud of magic. This was pretty disenchanting, to not have managed to enthral someone, since everything they saw was to the highest standard I could meet. To have been so charming and so interesting, then been looked through, was basically nullifying. Because this was all I had to offer, there was nothing in reserve.

Sitting down to do my work was not without its complications. The mere paperwork of just being here, just waking up and breathing, had become colossal. My tax affairs were not in order and now there were emails that I needed to provide, Forms 19 and 22, receipts to prove the shoes I bought were shoes you'd wear to work.

Nice things would have been welcomed: on a Monday morning in July, I opened up my laptop, and compiled a list of wines that we should stock up on, using pictures of the wine labels I had photographed. This was presumptuous I admit, but also helped avoid the possibility that he would buy a wine I didn't like the taste of.

We would need to get a house together, something permanent to stick a root in, so to simplify the process of the search I gave him my dad's phone number. One day they could have conversations that would point us to a more suburban realm, no doubt, with local primary schools, then just tell me where to put my signature – I'd have no spare hands. The babies, when they came along, would want accessories, mounds of baby kit – I'd need him to source the pram, the car seat and car-seat adapters, the little parasol, the Velcro baby mirror for the car, the cradle and the bedding for the cradle, the bouncers and the baby zoo, the bumper packs of everything imaginable.

The house would need new floors – he'd measure, do his homework, send away for samples. Paints, too, in any shade or finish, didn't matter, just as long as nothing in particular came back to me and no one sought opinions. New floors, tiles, grout, new grass to grow with seeds, and picnic benches to assemble. Then art. One thing I could supply was modest works of art collected from around the place but he'd have to do the framing, hammering, or use the stick-on hooks. Plants, shelving units, dinner sets, rugs, water filters – how was I supposed to know how to replace the charcoal inserts in the complicated water filters? Everything to do with cars, insurance, tax disks, permits, parking apps, and holiday car rentals, he'd be on top of – I left some papers at his bedroom door, stacked with the forms to fill. Picking out the car and filling it with fuel while I put a little supper on and looked after the children – I know this sounds traditional, old-fashioned, but that still works for those of us whose place is well and truly in the home.

Bills, utilities, for gas and electricity and ultimately bins as well, and motor tax and car insurance, everything, would be transferred to him, would flow through him like water, invisible to me. Living life unfortunately could mean as well a lot of costly medical appointments and since he dealt with health insurance he would need receipts. I knew I should be reimbursed where possible, but wasn't sure how to begin this project. I kept all baffling paperwork in a shoebox labelled, in black marker: 'Marg Health'.

Since he wasn't coming home most evenings and the dirt was very visible to me I devised a cleaning rota, and texted it to him:

> Week 1: Marg's week
> Week 2: Dan's week

When my week came I cleaned the rooms, and left a tealight in a jam jar by the downstairs window. When his week came he didn't clean. But I wanted the place clean, so I cleaned the place on his behalf. The next week, officially my week but now he owed me a week, he didn't clean, again. Another week passed – he'd had a crisis in his work, he texted back. It was August. I took a weekend in a hotel, sat by a swimming pool, lay in bed at night with my short-story binder. I thought of Dan – or maybe didn't think at all, but saw Dan, summoned him, felt him climb inside me and the kind of wet, self-pitying surrender I was starting to expect from him.

—

When I got home from holidays the place was in a mess. The empty craft beer bottles by the sofa, the sofa grooves a trail mix of old nuts and crumbs. The floor, heel-printed with rainwater, the bins, patiently awaiting my return. The kitchen, bare of anything to eat. Fairy Liquid thinning to a neon line. I cleaned the house, brought out the recycling. Obstacles had formed between us. The problem was the confines of our situation. The shoddy space, benighted digs – we couldn't be ourselves. Couldn't finish what we'd started. That's how one evening, in a headrush of excitable despair, I suggested breakfast in a café.

The café I picked was on a dull and busy thoroughfare of speeding cars, between the quays and Thomas Street. A café where the people at the tables never have to talk to one another. Hard hats lined the countertops, and men sat in fours. Not that I'd have noticed many details. I hoped we wouldn't have to talk at all that day, myself and Dan. I sat at the Formica counter with my back to the door so that he would see me first. I had suggested 8am, and it was 8.05. I opened my A4 pad, and beheld my paragraph again.

It was a lightweight story I was working on, to do with infantile and everyday desires, a slow descent into disappointment, with attempted anal penetration at the close. Most likely, I'd abandon this one too, trash everything, produce a child within twelve months. It mattered little really, when you met someone you really loved, what dreams you had to drop. The pleasure of adoring him was a pleasure only I on earth would ever have.

At 8.15am, I swivelled around my chair. It was raining harshly on the shop window and the pavements swam. I knew he would be drenched in rain and I felt guilty about that, embarrassed to have put him to the trouble. The fantasy sketched on the page was turning out to be so very dull. I found the sight of such bland sentences distressing – they all began with I, and ended me – and slammed the notepad shut as if its contents had offended me. Ten minutes passed. Fifteen. Without the silhouette of Dan cycling my bike, without the café door swung open to a sight of Dan, tossed by weather.

If forty minutes passed, I'd ring him. The rain slapped viciously on the glass outside, the cold air snuck in through the door where it was flapping open. This gratuitous kind of cold upset me, rain wrecked everybody's morning. Forty minutes was considerably late, if you really cared for somebody, and forty minutes it had been.

I pressed his number on my phone, incanting to myself how I'd reproach him, planning to maintain an exaggerated stern, my face already hot. His voice – his cheerful voice – came swimming in my ear. 'Dan here, leave a message.' His answering-machine voice. I ordered toast.

The toast was sliced-pan toast, cut in flimsy triangles. I sipped the dregs of coffee, which was weak and bitter tasting. I was dangling towards the window glass by now. The road glistened, wet and dank, the city had no season. My toast was cold and chewy. At 9am I wrote to Dan that I was leaving. The pleasure of adoring him was a pleasure that had not been set aside for me, in the overarching, unseen plan, that morning.

Dan had overslept, and when he woke and saw how late it was, he decided it was too late to have gone at all – too late also to explain to me why he'd been late. It was just so late by then, he would have ended up even more late, and he had clients. He wrote this in the reply that I received that evening at the sink while washing up my single plate and fork.

I'd almost given up, when walking around the balmy streets towards the end of summer I got a text. 'Just seeing, will you be home later?' His words ran through me like a party drug, my limbs were flooded with their potency. I walked faster, nowhere. Moments like this one should be suspended for as long as possible. I walked for half an hour, stopping off in Fresh to buy some craft beer, soft cheese, strawberries and cream.

'Home soon. Why do you ask?'

'Cool,' came the enigmatic signal.

When I opened the front door I didn't say hello to Dan immediately. I stood dazed, because it looked as though I'd come into another house. One sofa had been pushed against a wall. Against the other wall a movie was projecting and on the sofa, Dan and a woman watched it. Dan gathered himself up, and pressed pause on the laptop.

'Marg!' he said with overfriendliness. 'Would you like a beer? This is Eleanor.'

She had wavy, carefree hair cut in a bob. She smiled and raised a mug of tea with, I supposed, my milk in it. Worst was that I didn't go to bed alone then. I watched *No Country for Old Men* with my husband and his wife.

The shitty fake Victorian houses were bought up by a group of Dutch investors, perhaps they're still for rent. Madam Landlady said we'd been great tenants while she evicted us and I assured her we were more than ready to move on. She handed us our full deposit, which we split over the kitchen table, before he heaved his suitcases out the door, waving me a glum and amiable 'Goodbye,' and disappeared.

In the winter of the same year I went to my GP to see would they increase the dose, or change it altogether. And, I swear it, the doctor looked across at me and asked, 'Do you want a slow and agonizing end? Or would you fancy a near-lethal cocktail?'

'I'll take the extra-strong one, for my sins,' I said and snatched the script out of his hands. I take the poison every day, and it floors me. Makes me see things that are real. Makes me long for times I was unhappiest. But I don't picture not existing anymore – no need, when so much has been stamped out as it is, closed off, put out of bounds.

Though once, just once, passing through town, I strayed so far I got to Cork Street, and I saw him, coming down the hill. He was cycling – of course he was – my shining bike. I took the left turn past the funeral home and headed towards Christ Church. There he was, astride my bike, leaning forwards, gripping at the handlebars, dark mane in the wind, going at it with a purpose. I stood at the corner of Marrowbone Lane and Cork Street and watched him soar on up in one determined line, and I had to admire how he made such good use of something that was mine.

'Fuck you!' I told the street.

'I never liked you anyway!' I told my husband, told him angrily, and brightened with the discharge of this rage. Where there was a man I saw a unicorn. A splendid unicorn went by, dark mane lifting in the wind, white flanks draped in robes of pink and gold, and spirals shimmering on their horn – I shut my eyes.

All the Boys

The fishmonger was out of fish. Everybody got there first and now, on the crushed ice display, just two shivering grey prawns curled into one another, a deathly big-eyed creature, and two fat pink slabs of trout nobody wanted. My friend pointed at the trout – he asked, 'Is it Irish? Locally caught?' as if any of it made a difference. He stood fixed and determined as the fishmonger wrapped what he had left and took the payment from him – without giving us the two prawns for free, I noted, though it was closing time on Saturday. I just couldn't help but take a note of the omission of the gesture.

Then we cycled in the direction of his parents' house to light the barbeque. Weeks he had been talking about this, weeks, only sometimes, here and there, enough to make me want to run from the whole plan, it was so perfect. His parents would be gone, we would get the best fish and drink the right kind of wine with the place all to ourselves. The streets out by the sea were wide and empty, houses tall and private, with mighty walls, and as we forced our way up through the rain, there was absolutely nothing left to say.

On Main Street we passed a group of men, some in straw boaters, and a woman in a high-necked dress of Virgin Mary blue with frilly sleeves. Earlier, having a pint up in the village, I had hoped to find some meaning in it being Bloomsday. Some poetry in the air, some racy abandon to make fun of perhaps. I was disappointed we had not found anything much to comment on, around the little pub, the publican in the monocle. We had not run into anyone we knew. The rain splattered loudly through the village and it drenched our clothing as we pressed uphill.

It was April I first noticed him, then became distracted by him, at his work in the expensive grocer's up the road from where my parents lived. He wore a neat white shirt and his biceps and his back muscles rolled as he moved around, lifting boxes, admiring jars of honey before curating them on a wooden shelf. He adjusted wine bottles, smiled at the labels, and I aspired to drink a lot of wine that summer, superior wine. 'Do you have any Sauvignon Blanc?' I asked him, and felt less stupid, about saying *Blanc*, when he pointed to my book and said, 'Is that Prowst?' 'That's Proust,' I said – the grocer's, it had little tables where you could sit and read your book, see, and I did just that on my days off. I would sip a frothy coffee with my block of literature open and eye him and observe him as best I could without seeming to be mad. '*Proust*,' he repeated now. 'I'm on the second book,' I told him at the till as he rang up my purchase. This was truthful. He nodded eagerly. 'You should read *In Search of Lost Time*, I think you'd like it.' This was a wild guess. But the effect was as desired as he told me with a kind of dreamy passion in his eyes that he read a lot of Chekhov. 'The, eh, Russian short-story writer.' I nodded quickly. I felt as if I'd met him in another life. He was dark haired with a face of shadows and pale, desolated green eyes that glowed at you like stained glass. His eyes were portals and I found it almost harrowing to look into them. I felt he'd been sent here from some lost world, some supernatural universe. My delusions were harmless, almost, as I could tell that he was equally susceptible to the whole thing. Visions of the ideal, the fantastic. 'Would you like to have a drink with me?' I asked him on the next occasion. Burning pink, though I'd planned it out. 'Yes,' he said. And I wondered, what was wrong with him? There must be something really wrong.

He was waiting in the pub on South Anne Street, his mother having driven him to town. We took a floral booth. The writers were chequered around us in their picture frames, Beckett, Joyce, O'Casey, Behan, all the boys. We were on our second pint of beer when he told me quietly there was something I should know.

'Oh?' I sat up, wondering what bargain I would need to make.

'There is a reason I've been stacking shelves, still living with my mum and dad. I've been a hopeless mess.' I concentrated on nodding.

'I've kind of lost out on it all you know, the growing up stage. I'm sorry, I – I don't want to horrify you, I just want to be—'

'No, it's OK!' I said. 'I understand. What have you got?'

'Do you really want to know?'

'I'm interested.'

'Manic depression, ups and downs. Life-shattering downs.' He told me, in hushful tones, about the stay in hospital, the psychiatrists, the strict regime. Cycling, yoga, group therapy. Meditation, meds. I listened with a face you would entirely trust. His gaze travelled into mine and pulled me into outer space; the beer was going to my head, but I wanted to prolong this. 'So that's it. Out of my mind!' He laughed. We both laughed, but I straightened up again. It was my turn now, and I couldn't wait to tell him.

'It must have been awful,' I said. 'It must be so challenging. My heart goes out to you. But I do understand. It hasn't happened for a while but, do you know about intrusive thoughts? Recurring bad thoughts you bring upon yourself, they aren't quite voices – it's your own voice – and it basically torments you—'

I wasn't finished with the symptoms, struggles, co-morbidities, but he just looked so disappointed to be interrupted, so crushed. And I was a well person now, I had a job, I was a success. I was here to listen now. It was his turn once again.

'It's the anxiety that's killing me.' He seemed to ask the crowded bar for quiet before continuing. 'I mean, I am recovering very well. I'm tapering from a cocktail of narcotics – one day I hope I'll go to college, have a family, but I wanted you to know in any case – so we can begin this with an honesty, and with a truth.'

I decided that it would be best if I went home. Instead of going home, I signalled at the barman for two more. He was in the middle of a story when I shifted towards him, scanned his body up and down and pressed upon him my bewilderment. He closed a hand around my waist and drew me in and kissed me.

We met up in the long evenings after work, in the pub or in a pizzeria, or we cycled to a park and ate a bag of vinegar-soaked chips, or we walked on beaches, Sandymount, Killiney, or drove to the diving point and took it in turns to mind the other's things while we each plunged, in turn, into a freezing ocean perforated with raindrops. Few things interested me other than pleasure. Few things other than having a tremendous time. My work was uninteresting and every day I struggled at my desk to think of something better we could do. Something more fulfilling, rare, defining. A better park, a more refreshing drink, a more interesting film, a football match, yes – we sat in the stadium and cheered on the boys in green when they still had a hope of qualifying for the World Cup. We drank specifically craft beer and old-world wine with miniature cheese wheels, and anything French in a jar. I wanted to wash away the evenings with him, to be fully young those endless evenings. And when it got late, he would come home with me, and we would kiss and strip our clothes away. And we tried, all of the times. But couldn't. He was too self-conscious, with my parents sleeping down the hallway. Or we had drunk too much. It didn't matter that it hadn't worked yet, we were becoming friends. Sometimes he took out *The Essential Tales of Anton Chekhov* and read to me. He read his favourite stories, 'The Lady with the Dog' or 'The Huntsman', and I would drift off to sleep listening to his gentle voice fill with characters and then hear him rustling, as he would always get up and let himself out.

He didn't want his mother wondering where he was, because she worried about him all the time.

There were no obstacles between us, no lovers, no countries. Not a single real material obstacle stood between us. It seemed like we might fall in love. It gave him hope that I had recovered so efficiently from my problems at the same time as I felt so healthy and so strong because he was so sick. He would tell me he was feeling inauthentic – 'I'm feeling just a little inauthentic,' he would confide, queuing for the rock at the Forty Foot or sheltering from the rain under the hanging branches in the Dodder path, or staring tragically into the ketchup packets on the pub table. 'I think I'm going to die young. It's a feeling that I have, I don't know. Do you not think I'll die young?' It occurred to me that somebody had done this to him, inflicted damage on him. Somebody had been unkind to him.

'I feel too attached,' he'd tell me. 'I feel too attached to earthly possessions—' and I'd think, shut the hell up. We continued though, towards the rainy night in June that found us unlocking the front door of his turreted house on the quiet cul-de-sac. He Chubb locked the door, switched the alarm to Home.

The house was clean and ordered, polished to a chilly shimmer. I felt I shouldn't touch anything. He took off his shoes and went to find a towel for me. I studied the names on the envelopes piled on the table in the hall, then opened the frosted-glass door into a living room with a patent black piano. You could see that his father, the health insurance CEO and his mother, the retired PE teacher and ladies' golf president, had worked hard to secure for their two sons the most appropriate markers

of a rounded education. On the shelves and mantel-
piece were school pictures of the boys in velvet frames,
and small inconsequential trophies. Second place in
Athletics, 1992. Third place in some golf championship,
1997. The cabinet twinkled with the Waterford crystal
vase and sets of silver spoons displayed in opened silk-
lined boxes. I circled the room and found him framed
inside in his Junior Infants picture, stiff-haired and petrified even then.

In the dark and marbled kitchen he unpacked fish
and wine and bread and lemons, talking excitably.
'It's always very tidy here, don't worry though, make
yourself at home – you can just sprawl out with the
newspapers. What am I forgetting now?' He handed me
a folded towel and poured a glass full to the top with ice-
cold wine before disappearing outside. The wine was
Portuguese. The rain tip-tapped all over the patio, the
glass weighed down my wrist as I looked into space, into
the refrigerator, to the note clinging to the refrigerator:

Lithium morning
Temazepam evening
Ziprasidone KEEP NEAR IN CASE

I went to the fridge and read the note again. The instructions were held with a magnet of a smiling vintage 1950s
housewife in a spotted apron bending towards a table
of jellies, creams, iced buns, pink squares of cake. His
mother's handwriting was stern and tall with an indis-
putable authority.

Outside, he aimed a remote control and an awning
came down over us. He fitted a gas cylinder to the side
of the barbeque. The lawn was cut, the barbeque was
forest-green enamel, kept expertly clean or hardly used

at all. Behind us a fountain clattered water into a lily pond, intensifying the feel of deluge. He put the hood down on the smoking fish and refilled my wine glass, then his own. With the size of the glasses, we could get the whole bottle inside in no time and I gulped it thirstily, to kill all misgiving, silence all the qualms and feel just how you're meant to. He carried platefuls of food into the kitchen, and when we pulled out our chairs I saw that the sheet of paper had been taken down off the fridge, put out of sight.

'Is everything alright?' he asked.

'Nothing's ever perfect, but this is all very intoxicating, thank you.'

He was talking about his recovery. 'I'm in a tangle of emotions – there is so much joy and then despair, then insight followed by bouts of utter hopelessness. It feels like the bolts that are holding this construct of darkness and anxiety are creaking under the strain – hold on, is that cooked enough? Oh no.' He took away my plate, rose to his feet, and opened the back door again. The rainy air blew in. I drank and flicked through the weekend supplements while he stood in the storm, jabbing at the grill with an arched brown brow. I could be reading literature, I used to think, when I was far from home. I could be reading all seven volumes of Proust this whole entire squandered time. I could finish *Ulysses*. I could be filled and bettered with great literature. I poured the white wine down my throat and my eye moved, again and again, to the bare fridge door.

We ate the blackened trout. 'Bloomsday,' he said. He waited for me to say something, and I stared back at him. I was ashamed of my contempt for him but it didn't stop it coming.

'We should have gone to the Martello tower,' he said. 'We should have eaten Gorgonzola sandwiches with Burgundy.'

'Nobody eats Gorgonzola in a sandwich,' I said. 'And 16th June 1904, it's just the day Nora Barnacle gave James Joyce a handjob on the beach. But everybody knows that already.'

'Of course, yes, I remember now.'

But he didn't remember; he was making that up. I had a wish for different company. For someone new and different to land in at our table and amuse and educate us. We were vacuous bores. We were dummies. Cutlery moved with an excruciating self-importance. The blank fridge stared and dread rose like a heat in my body as the words returned, fully articulated, to my void. Lithium morning. Temazepam evening. Ziprasidone KEEP NEAR. I sipped and sipped, and he opened a new bottle and refilled my glass. When were we going to get this over with, so I could be released? The sky moved, and thunder broke through the rain outside. 'Did you hear that?' he asked, smiling with amazement, as if he'd thought of everything tonight.

We were facing each other, rain lashing at the sliding doors. I leaned in and kissed him with an ardour that was necessary to express in light of everything. He reached his hand up my dress into my back and his light grasp melted in my skin as I felt for the strength around his thigh. I sought it out, his physical strength.

'What do you want do to?' he asked.

'I don't know, it's your house.'

His was a twin room with two single beds set against opposing walls. Each bed had a locker, a steel bookshelf drilled into the wall between them. So few books lined the shelf I wanted to go home immediately. *A Confederacy of Dunces. Flourishing. Chekhov,* fuck sake. I sat and removed my sandals. He stood above me, picking up and letting go of handfuls of my hair. His palm brushed and cradled my cheek. I breathed in his skin. Outside the wind swept the ivy in that overgrown suburb, which had covered his bedroom windows in lush wet greenness. Lithium. Ziprasidone. Temazepam. Lithium. Ziprasidone. Temazepam. Don't think about it. He is nothing but a person. Not one of us is our problem. Better make use of our disgraceful privilege. I reached for my wine. I reached for him, and the room drifted around me, closing in with all the items of a life caught inside the nets of time. The burgundy electric guitar, the amplifier, the Doors poster. The beanbag.

'How long have you slept in this room?'

'Forever, I guess.'

'Who slept in the other bed?'

'My brother.' Married now in London, I remembered. Child on the way. He joined me on the bed, and we both sat to the wall, toes pointed to the ceiling.

'Do you read books on that beanbag?'

'Sometimes.'

'But when was the last time?'

'Yesterday,' he laughed. He mentioned an author I hadn't read but very much intended to, and showed me the copy by his bed. He even quoted from a line. This invigorated the room, the whole person and his past. I turned to face him.

'What else do you do in here?'

'I hang out. I relax. I watch videos on the internet.'

'Oh. Where do you masturbate?'

'I mean, I watch music videos – the Beatles, Kinks.'

'But where do you jerk off?' He nodded sideways to his neat pillows.

'Just over that corner. Don't worry, I use an old t-shirt.'

'Oh. Do you put it in the wash? It's not that I care, I'm just curious about your routine. I've never been a boy.'

'Once in a while. Every two weeks or so.'

'Does your mother wash your filthy garments?'

He smiled back. His eyes dreamed upon mine, and I reached for him, felt he was becoming hard.

'What about your routine?' he asked.

'Oh I couldn't say anything about that! Much too repressed, too shy.'

'Really? I'd like you to tell me.'

'I'll never need to touch myself again now I have you.' We moved into each other's arms. Our lips met, our tongues. He lifted my dress over my head. I stepped out of my pants, kicked them away, and stayed very still while he unclasped my bra – he'd got better at this trick and I was pleased for him, could see that he himself was pleased to be proficient. He got off his shorts and his erection sprang into my open hand. I held it, moving my hand along his cock. He wrapped his hand around mine, and moved it with mine. We had never been as close as this before, we were never so alone, his skin never felt so soft. Take Lithium. Ziprasidone. Temazepam. Ziprasidone. Temazepam.

No. He kissed my neck, he bent down and kissed my breasts. Lithium. Ziprasidone. Temazepam. No. We both held his cock. We held his cock, protectively and stupidly, as if it were an ornament we weren't sure where to place. He took my flank, took my ass, brought me to him, and his fingers moved softly underneath me. He found the hole, my hole was wet and open, waiting for him. His fingers moved around the rough under-growth of hair and inside the dewy tunnel.

'I don't know what I'm doing,' he said.

'You're fine,' I said. Ziprasidone. Lithium. Temaze-pam IN CASE! What in hell – I kissed him some more, but it didn't work, and I had left the room again.

'Do you want another glass of wine?' he asked, parting from me.

'Absolutely not, no.'

We lay like packed mackerel on his single bed and looked at the ceiling. An overplayed song by somebody was drumming on his MP3.

'Are you feeling well?' I asked him.

'I feel really good right now and really calm in myself,' he said.

Lithium. Ziprasidone. Temazepam KEEP NEAR IN CASE!

Sweat was radiating from his back as it rose and fell. Thunder crackled on the leaf-clad bedroom on the cul-de-sac. A lightening flash – though, I wondered had it happened, or did I just fancy lightening. Cul-de-sac, I thought, sliding underneath his pelvis – dead end, end of the bag, no more to see here. Ziprasidone. Temazepam. Cul-de-sac. No.

'You're so nice,' I said.

'So are you!'

'I like you so much.'

We were going to keep on going with this. Zipra-sidone. Temazepam. Lithium, Lithium.

'Your mother!' I said.

'My mother?'

'Yes.' I held his robust body at an arm's length. We were both out of breath.

'Yes – she.'

'She what?'

'Your mother – your mother did an excellent job of you. Yes. Look at you.'

He closed his eyes as the compliment sank in. It made him go harder for a while, it made him shut his eyes and lose himself.

'Do you think so,' he murmured.

'Yes, I do.'

And harder, with a catastrophic urgency, but then less hard. And not so hard at all. Soon it was just a case of hanging on. We were trying, tightly joined, for longer than seemed reasonable. Trying to find the right sensation, the intended conclusion, and as I fought against him, now on top of him, I was a pearl diver who might never find her way back to the surface, who might perish striving for the buried ocean jewel. Ziprasidone. Temazepam. And Lithium, lithium, lithium. I broke away and gasped.

'Sorry just a bit tired!'

But he wasn't completely tired. He wasn't, so I sat up and finished off the job for him. To be his saviour and his nurse, this bestowed a kind of honour. It took a while, a long while before the moment came that I could let go and watch him shake with his eyes crumpled shut as he reached that exquisite loneliness in which another human soul has no place.

He got up to clean himself.

'You didn't—' he said, back on his pillow, his eyes glazed.

'It's fine.'

I stood up and walked to the curtain to peer out on the dark enclave. I went to use the bathroom, and

lingered in the bathroom mirror. I pushed the rose-co-
loured soap from the dispenser bottle. Behind me, in
the mirror, a fluffy female bathrobe hulked around the
door. The white cabinet was fixed above the sink. I took
the handle of the bathroom cabinet and went to open it,
as normally I would in a strange house, but decided this
time to leave it closed. Walking back to him, I picked up
the *Essential Chekhov* to find the perfect story. His arm
fell around me.

'Ivan Yegoritch Krasnyhin, a fourth-rate journalist ...'
I read, and checked over my shoulder. He was already
asleep. I put the book away.

I woke a couple of hours later on his brother's bed.
Asleep, we must have been unable to bear the feel of
one other. The rain had stopped, and when I lifted up
the curtain the street glistened. From the floor I picked
up a skimpy dress, a cardigan, still damp. He didn't stir.
Downstairs I slid the chain along the bolt and shut the
door behind me – an alarm bell started, and may have
woken him. I cycled away from the dinging bells.

Old Romantics

It's not like I never left this place, oh no. Adventure time, I've had my fill.

I was young, I thought, and Walls, let's just call him, produced the best holidays from his imagination. Sudden trips: châteaux, rectories, hunting lodges, revamped lighthouses, abandoned coastguard stations – he'd get the last-minute deals and haggle them down, then sweep us off, lose no time; and once we'd got away he'd insist on unending diversions. We had good times, and although there were wrong turns, missed flights and funks and outright crack-ups, we always came home invigorated, flattened, with stories to tell.

Walls loved the States, and I had never been. 'Everything is just so big, so outsized and disgraceful!' he'd say, waving hands. It was summer, and he wanted a whole month. I had a bit of money saved from my terminated publishing job and my axed restaurant column, and he had wads of cash – *wads* – his golden fifty-euro notes flickered at me like the pages of a book he could rip from at will – where did the money come from? I can't go into it.

At Dublin Airport, a woman told us we had missed our flight. 'It's gone. Plane's gone – you're two hours late,' she said with an amusement she made no attempt to hide. We could try for standby seats tomorrow, or fly from Shannon on Wednesday? For the shortest second I thought it was a sign: America, not meant to be. But Walls didn't think like that; the missed flight made him reckless and creative. We stood at a bus stop with our bags in the rain. 'Torrential, absolutely heartbreaking, but probably the challenge that makes us, gorgeous, so let's get some seaside in, let's go to Skerries, let's go to Rush, let's go to Lusk – let's minimise our misery here, gorgeousness.' His luscious pet names had a sedative effect on me, I was very much in love.

The bus took us to an empty north Dublin fishing village where, over mugs of beer and Scampi Fries, I opened a tabloid newspaper looking for my final restaurant column. I read eagerly. Sitting there, I was so absorbed in the pleasure of reading my own printed, published sentences I didn't notice he'd gone quiet and jerky, how his face was pale and clenched.

'Right, you're not listening. Oh you are? What did I just say then?' Walls pushed his chair away from the table and left the little bar. I wondered, looking at a desolate shoreline, how it was going to be possible to continue the holiday. Got up and ran after him on the flinty grey beach, in the swampy rain, lunging over rockpools, begging him to understand. Thinking, this is my summer holiday – everyone deserves a holiday.

The next morning, we failed to board a flight again. 'The standby seats are not available, no,' said another woman, one with no sense of humour. The only option was Shannon. We got on a bus to Limerick, and afterwards another bus, and found a room in an expensive hotel where I crawled up to his face and breathed, 'You know I am so excited to be here with you.'

The taxi ride from JFK was long and sweltering. I gazed at the line of skyscrapers and tried to form original impressions of the famous shapes. I did wonder, what's so special about going anywhere, when everything looks so much better in pictures anyway. And why are my legs so blotchy. Why am I so spoilt and inward all the time, why can't I be grateful?

The hotel was big and brash and in-your-face, but he'd had a good time there with his ex-wife, and I was easy. At reception the attractive tall woman explained it to us.

'Sir, it was a no-show, we were obliged to give up your room.'

'But we called. We called,' Walls told this tall, calm, sympathetic woman. 'Didn't we, gorgeous? You all seem very confused. This is a major booking we are talking about, you will have to make this right. I'll stand here until you ...' Eventually another woman came to say that she was so sorry, the hotel was taking care of this. After that they upgraded us to a Triple King Deluxe Room with park views.

The sixth-floor room was furnished in metallic drapes and rugs, and it was alright. I knew there were better rooms they hadn't set aside for us. The giant bed had a soft pink bedspread that licked the room like a frothing

tongue. There was a golden table, two flutes of champagne and two chocolate brownies, glazed with chocolate
sauce and decorated with a little pair of American flags
on cocktail sticks. The window overlooked the trees of
Central Park. Walls beheld the view with outstretched
arms and cracked his back, which ached from days of
travel. I tore off my clothes, picked a cocktail stick out
of a brownie, sucked the chocolate off and took a long
sip of the plonk. In the morning, soft from the shower,
I felt something pierce my heel. I screamed and rocked
on the floor clutching my foot, then pulled out the cocktail stick by its miniature star-spangled banner.

We went to Central Park, Walls ran and I panted after
him in my thriftstore frock and love-heart sunglasses.
'Don't lag, don't embarrass yourself now,' he blared.
I was desperately unfit and my foot still hurt, but Walls
had plans to tick off and adrenaline to expend. We went
into Bloomingdale's and Macy's and haunted the glass
outside Tiffany's. I walked around half-conscious in
his protective shadow, thrilling in the air he breathed.
He was handsome like an overgrown Hollywood star,
with a sheepish air, a cruel sense of humour, unpredict-
able energies. A reddish, swirling cowlick. Flamboyant
hands. He wore, those days, a crushed-linen suit jacket
buttoned too tight, striped Brooks Brothers shirts,
bronze corduroys and bulky white unbranded tennis
shoes. With him, it was enough to merely stand there
and exist, a relief to know that his was personality
enough for two.

We went to Williamsburg to visit a restaurant I'd
read about in a magazine, but we couldn't find the right
street and we were weak with jetlag. We walked for three

hours under the burning sun, nodding at Puerto Rican men selling fruit and hardware. I limped, and on the side of the street Walls doused my heel with alcohol then put the bandage on wrong. When we found the restaurant, it looked small and decrepit, like a shack. A frosty waitress seated us on a terrace surrounded by plants, with twinkling lights woven in the ivy. Next to us three very slim athletic people were talking about interiors over rosé and crostini. Everyone glanced at each other, up and down. They probably didn't take me for Walls' daughter, not quite, but I still liked the curiosity in their saucy eyes. Cocktails arrived, infused with ingredients like elderflower and dandelion. I read the menu.

'Wow!' I said.

'Wow for you,' he said. 'What about me? There's nothing for me here.'

'Summer sausage with labneh and almonds?' I scanned the menu for meat dishes. Brick chicken, three types of oyster. Soppressata?

'What about oysters?' I hedged. 'Do you eat oysters?'

'Do I eat cunts?' he said and I knew that it was happening again. His face was very white and only his mouth moved. 'It's all about you, isn't it?' His head trembled very faintly and one eye popped out as he explained in what precise way I had upset, again, the most basic ways a person should behave.

We walked silently to Rick's Cheese Steak, and that night I slept on the sofa in the hotel room while Walls took the deluxe king-size bed.

We mostly took our rest in diners after that. Or we ate roast-beef sandwiches on benches and the tall, sliced meat toppled onto the ground in red piles to be plucked at by pigeons. Or we ate family bags of crisps.

I got takeaway Starbucks iced lattes with whipped cream and cinnamon sugar on top, and paraded this candy-floss through the streets. My foot oozed a little and every night I iced it back at the hotel, or painted my fungal toenail with a medical varnish while Walls switched news channels, crushed newspapers in outstretched arms, played with his phone, catnapped, made relaxed phone calls to his son, finally waiting at the door for me – come on, let's get out of here, Manhattan's waiting, life's short.

He said I should see Ellis Island and the Statue of Liberty and booked a special tour boat around Manhattan Island. Seated with the tour group, I wrote the day's date on a fresh blank page. I'd bought a Kate Spade notebook from a Macy's display and I planned to write down everything we saw. Now I wondered what to eat for lunch. I thought, look, there's the Statue of Liberty, and look, I have nothing to say about it.

The tour began. We couldn't hear the tour guide over the boat's engine. 'Can you hear anything?' Walls asked me. 'Can any of you hear anything?' he asked the people sitting behind us.

'Not so much,' said an agreeable tourist, maybe Dutch.

'Swindle,' he said. 'We are playing thirty dollars each, that's sixty I've dropped.' He fidgeted and thrashed in his seat. He went to the man with the microphone, then teetered back to me.

'Full volume, not good enough I'm afraid. This is— Hey—' to the calm Dutch tourist and others in the plastic seats around, 'Hey, can you hear that guy? Can you hear that guy? Yeah, it's annoying, right? You know, there's enough of us to do something about this.'

'Mutiny?' suggested the agreeable Dutch tourist, smiling.

'He's not serious,' I said, but Walls was gone again, now leaning gigantically into the tour guide.

He marched back. 'We can get a group of us together, let's not stand for it,' he said, and I gazed out at the ocean, imagined submerging. I faced into the surf as one being rocked from Ellis Island after uncertain years; write something, I thought. THINK, I thought. DON'T SCRIMP ON DETAIL. I burned inside for something other than this, thought, I could just say goodbye. Looked down, past the blowing pages of my blank notebook, touched my sandalled foot with its peeling, filth-gathering bandage – it could be now, I thought, no time like now. Afterwards we rented bikes.

We found ourselves standing next to the Metropolitan Museum of Art, so we went in, laughing. One of the guards asked Walls not to lean against a wall. 'Says who? I can lean against a publicly provided wall.' The guard, suddenly nervous, requested we make our way out since the museum was closing anyway. 'Sir, move along,' said the guard, and Walls said, 'You're saying we can't look at these things? Where is the sign saying we can't look at these things?' 'Move along, sir,' the guard said. 'Hold on now,' said Walls and my internal organs shrivelled. 'What time is closing? Seven pm – we have thirty minutes. We can look at artefacts until seven pm, we paid for all this, we paid for this little, this little clay pipe or this little pestle or this nice little tool, this Ice Age spear, out of our pocket, I'm just looking at this nice little primitive spear. These are nice ancient things belonging to the people, not your personal fossil collection, my girlfriend and I would like to take a good look at this probably violently seized imperial loot, we're on our holidays!' And he walked slowly, crablike, through the great hallway, his eyes pinned on the glass boxes, glancing at me to share the joke, brows arched, and the flashing eyeball.

All the way back to the hotel we shouted at each other with an abandon that was new. None of these people will ever see us again, I told myself. In the room, I iced my heel and we shouted, Walls at the foot of the bed stretching his hamstrings in an impromptu warm-up with his head lancing back and forth. We watched CNN, then dinner was proposed. We got dressed up.

In my restaurant reviews, I used to try to write in a philosophical tone about the ritual of dining. I wrote that you could be happy in a restaurant whatever your state of mind, because of the time-honoured contract: knowing that the cooks and serving people will restore you with fortifying dishes as you bring forth your earnings and best self. To eat out is to choose to be alive, to face each other as citizens of the same earth. We sit up straight and use cutlery and watch the subtle theatre loosen and unwind, all of us flawed and equal, and wine pours through our veins making talk light and fun.

The hotel bar had a bland modern feel, phenomenal prices.

'Hamburger,' he said.

I took out my notebook and wrote down his order. I still thought of myself as a critic, I suppose, and intended to document everything. Walls asked what I was doing and then pulled back his chair. 'Right,' he said. 'Right then.'

We sat at a distance, boiling rapidly under our skins. We fought in our seats, with gimlet eyes, at a rising pitch.

'Everyone is looking at us!' I said.

Food came, a robbery on plates. A platinum-blonde lady with a facelift, dangling her martini glass, looked at us with true disturbance in her eyes. She called over a waiter, and they spoke in each other's ears. Another waiter came, and took her glass and plate. They were moving her to a different table.

I can say goodbye, I thought, waking later that night to see him lurch through the bedroom making animal sounds – I can pack up and go. This can end here.

'I'm sorry it didn't work out,' I said the next morning, pulling my suitcase out the door while he got dressed. And I sat in the dim-lit WiFi zone by the reception of a hotel that, to this day, sends me promotional emails.

So it was over. I could hardly believe it.

I sat on my suitcase, insufferable chill-out muzak in my ears. I had a first cousin living on the Upper West Side. I wrote my cousin an email, edited the email, and left it in drafts. There was no explaining what had happened, not even to myself, and to invent something would be just pathetic. I also wished now that it hadn't actually happened. I wished to retract my goodbye and good riddance. So I took the elevator back up again, right up to the sixth floor, went down the corridor and opened the door with my carefully retained room card.

Walls was gone. Even the complimentary bottles of shampoo and shower gel were gone.

So it was over. On the hot street, I stared into the whipped cream of my Starbucks. I ate a fingerful of cream, then set off towards Central Park. A stone sculpture of Alice in Wonderland sitting on a toadstool yielded no answers. I hauled my suitcase into the subway and then around the Lower East Side. I bumped it up a stairway to try to bargain for a room that was creepy, then changed my mind, and bumped it back down again, and sweated over to a hostel whose bedrooms were the size of toilet cubicles. They had rooms. I spent three nights in one of these sleep coffins, woken at eight every morning by a low smartphone alarm that sounded gently up the walls for an hour or more. From the deodorant-rank room, I wrote a text message to Walls. 'I hope you are happy wherever you are.'

He wrote back. 'I'm right here.'

He was staying with a friend up at Bowery. At Katz's Deli we ate pastrami on rye, which cost fifty-six dollars plus a tip. We stood on Times Square, shocked by the lights and possibilities, consulted ticket prices, and walked away again. We trailed around Greenwich Village – I wanted to see a folk band, but he met a guy scalping tickets to Louis C.K. 'Louis C.K! He's huge! What an opportunity!' he said. I said I didn't like stand-up comedy. It's not funny, I suggested, because every joke has been workshopped and rehearsed with such a cold commercial focus, how could that end up being funny? He said I just wasn't much fun, wasn't game. 'You're about as fun as a table,' he said. 'You're about as fun', he riffed, 'as the guy who discards the banana skin that the funny guy slips on. As fun as the guy who gets the cream pie thrown on his face!' I sucked up the dregs of my Starbucks coffee making a harsh hoovering sound with the straw, which I knew was something a kid does. What I did like, at the end of the long days, was that he did the talking, the explaining, he made me laugh – how we laughed, you really had to be there.

We rented bikes again. We did Coney Island, the fairground. We looked out the window on the overground train home, then we looked for the bikes, we couldn't find the bikes and had to walk back to our hotel. We lost those bikes. My heel stung where the toothpick wound had re-opened, and each time I took a step a gritty pain seemed to crack up through my body, all the way to my right shoulder. His weight pounded me in the toilet-cubicle hotel and he murmured, 'What a privilege. What a nice thing.' He was nice after all. He was funny. I accepted the mistake we would now make. To rent a car, go south – a factored-in mistake, too grand a plan to try to dodge at this late stage. I didn't want to ever be boring. I wrote things down with a mind to one day tell stories, entertain, but all I really wanted was to be entertained.

Our last evening in New York City we sat on the floor of a crowded bus station with tired mothers, small children and babies who screamed. Something had gone wrong with the rental car and he objected to the price of booking a new one at the last minute. The bus to Richmond departed at midnight and we slept hardly at all. In the waking city, we rented a room for a day, pulled the stiff cool sheets over our faces and slept like a two-headed ghost.

We got a car in Richmond. Walls took the driver's seat, adjusting every setting, too big for this world, and he turned the engine on.

He smiled: 'Sure you can trust your tormenter?'

Normally, Walls did the driving. I was better with a map. I used the *Michelin Road Atlas of the USA, Canada and Mexico*, drawing a line with a biro along the proposed route and always at pains to hold the map the right way. There was no particular destination, other than an idea about the South, its lost romance. The car was bulky and unglamorous and he drove very fast, looking at the fancy media screen, beating his finger on the news channels. Drove great distances, stopping only to refuel, at diners and waffle houses and pancake huts.

On Virginia Beach, bobbing in the pale sea, he asked me to please not pass him the yeast infection from my genitals I'd complained of. In Colonial Williamsburg, having a beer, he told me I had the face of a prawn.

We drove and drove. We drove until my legs went jumpy and his back got locked into painful positions. We drove and the grey life zoomed away from us in sheets upon sheets of road like a roll of grey tape unwound accidentally. Late one night, we stopped at a motel advertising a swimming pool on a sign flashing red and yellow. We parked the car, walked up and pressed a buzzer. The curtain scraped open, and a shock went through me. A girl stood in a glass box a metre over us, teeth splayed every which way, all different shades and textures – jagged, serrated, discoloured. Teeth from an internet picture, from a book of freaks. The girl was skinny, with big earrings, and blue flowers painted on her long fake nails. A sign requested patrons to declare their weapons. We asked for a room and she nodded, chewing her chin as she took our dollars through the slot.

She led us past a line of grim apartments and a benighted swimming pool. What troubled me, as I lay down, was the thought that the teeth were the reason this girl was here, in the dead of night, letting potentially armed strangers into an enclosure with her, while I rode free, and never had to put my life at risk. The girl was unlucky, Walls agreed, and we should not go close to her or something bad might happen to us, too. Or was it too late? I moved right next to him on the motel bed.

'Can you ensure that nothing bad will happen me?' I asked, knowing how stupid and naïve I sounded, but we bonded most over other people's misfortune.

'Well no,' he said thoughtfully, stroking my hair. 'But I can assure you I'll always be there.' We drove on to Raleigh.

There is a catchy song that mentions dying in Raleigh, though I had never looked into what this might mean. Our holiday was nearly over. The heel of my right foot was sore. When I touched the bandage, I felt the stinging bulge of a small soft wound.

We found the restaurant I'd been aiming for. A blocky waiter with his shirt sleeves expertly rolled came to our table.

'It's nice to meet you both. What are your names? I'm Drew, and I'm going to be your server tonight, it's my third day, so you gotta go easy on me!'

'We're in heaven,' I said, and began to order up a storm: Creole gumbo; plantation salad; blue cheese and spiced pecans; fried-green tomatoes; Louisiana crawfish; boudin balls with pepper jelly and pickled okra.

'Good thing dinner's on the missus, eh Drew?' Walls said, and Drew said, 'SHEESH and isn't he the old romantic?' Everybody laughed. We ate with great appetite, licking the crumbs from our fingers and gulping back the day-expelling beer. Drew would come and say, 'All to your satisfaction, MA'AM?', and, 'WOULD YOU LIKE ANOTHER FROSTY BEER, SIR?' Food and drink kept on arriving and I took careful notes. North Carolina catfish, fries and slaw and remoulade. Hoop cheddar mac 'n' cheese. Shrimp 'n' grits, and cornbread stuffed with—

'What's wrong?' I asked because he had gone white again. I was doing it again. Writing in my notebook, smiling, it was my deathly flaw – vanity, delinquent self-regard. The space between us became tense, almost material, and I got up and sat at a separate table. Every so often I glanced up to see the pin-head pupils of his eyes across the room. And when Drew came with the long curling bill, I threw down some notes and left the place on my own.

This was unforgivable.

'No, I've had enough!' I stamped my foot, the good one, then cast around for the street the car was on.

We could have argued – could have really shouted. The idea stood suspended between two bright pairs of eyes. However, it wasn't a good time. It was just after ten o'clock. We were on holidays, and we both wanted the same things. An interesting night, young-person fun. We walked, shouting, then looked up and saw a tacky club doing drinks promotions. Still discussing loudly, but this time out of necessity because of the awful music, we exchanged a word about the drink-driving laws – he'd had too many beers and now he was ordering two cocktails for one. Driving under the influence was disgusting, was contemptible, obviously, but Walls was good company, out on the town, and I would have held on to anything good as compensation for all this. We got back in the car.

The roads were strangely empty as we kept an eye out for a place to stay. We talked, first quietly, about what had gone wrong at dinner. I said, 'You find a hotel then! If you know this world so well!' and I don't remember what else because he turned from the driver's seat and shouted, 'DAMN RIGHT I KNOW THIS WORLD

AND I KNOW HOW TO GET US OUT OF THIS WORLD
YEAH WATCH!'

He stretched his body long, and accelerated, and
the car sped up. He accelerated so hard the road shot
away – began to devour itself, the wheels lifting into
nothingness. I reached for a door handle, engulfed by
the gruesome night.

You understand, sometimes, that what is happening
is no nightmare or illusion. All precious things are out
of your hands. His face was elsewhere and the car was
now careening. I screamed at him to stop the car. Again
I screamed. 'STOP!' It is demeaning to have to be so hys-
terical when it comes to something as important as your
life. 'You're trying to scare me!' The words rang out.
There was the clear shape of a tree, then another tree.
Objects from the natural world moved past with their
integrity, then buildings, signs. Back at a reasonable
speed. We drove, saying nothing, only breathing, until a
box of light came up ahead. An enormous multi-storey
hotel, and we turned inside and parked.

Everywhere was white, with every screen and light
burning, one big mammoth fuse waiting to blow, but it
didn't. The world was impassive. What a comfort. We
were safe. He went to bed as he was so tired from all
the driving. I wandered the hotel, sat in the monstrous
lobby watching two or three TV screens play different
channels side by side, and drank sweet hot chocolate
from a sachet. I KNOW HOW TO GET US OUT OF THIS
WORLD; what a strange thing. What a troubling thing.
I wished that I could be more miserable than I was.

'Had another fight,' I wrote in my notebook.

We stopped in motels, in smoking rooms with fat,
winged bugs flying in the showers. We drove and drove

and drove and drove and drove and he made sudden clamorous protestations about having to drive all day every day and so I would tenderly dig my thumbs into the flesh of his neck, to release tension, as he shouted, 'Left! Yes! There! More!' We drove and drove. He had a compulsion, the odd time, to stop the car and run through a wooded area to let everything out, all the madness – 'Here, now!' and he'd pull into a verge in some bleak spot, the daylight fading, and get out and sprint while I leaned on the bonnet and wondered about, God only knows, lunch, dinner? He would come back glistening with sweat and say, 'Sorry about that. But we have a nice time, don't we, gorgeous?'

There was the odd exhilarating old song on the media player and I would sing along with an almost unbearable happiness. Or a Starbucks would glide by us and I'd say, 'Stop!' And nestle into the seat with a plastic cup of whipped-cream iced latte. At one point, we decided for no specific reason but with urgent inspiration to get to Charleston, South Carolina, by that evening, because life was so short, wasn't it. 'I mean how many lives are you planning on having, four or five is it, gorgeous? No, you get one. You get one life. This is our one life.'

We arrived at Charleston near midnight, and found a sports bar still serving food. My foot hurt, so I held it in my hand and hopped, then leaned on his shoulder. The barman carried two ice-cold pints on a round tray, and we tipped him. A great deal of food arrived. Hamburgers. Cheese nachos. Balls of potato like the McCain Potato Smiles I ate with disappointment as a child. We both came to life again with beer. I agreed to dig my pincers into his neck, look for knots along his cliff-side back and work them out. We were delirious, walking to the car.

He started up the engine. He was over the limit, but so was I, and he was bigger, and the Travelodge I had in mind was not far. I held tight the *Road Atlas* as he steered us up a wide, tree-lined avenue, and all of a sudden I saw our turn. 'Go left GO LEFT,' I said.

The impact came from my side. A giant thorn, an industrial wasp sting. An annihilating metal blow. Something wrong. Very wrong. We seemed to twist, and squeeze in the grip of this unhuman intrusion.

There was a car alarm piercing through the night. I wondered, drowsily, if we would be very badly injured. We were pulled out of the car through the driver's side, lifted into the arms of – a policeman? And I was standing at the boot beside Walls, who was looking in suitcases for a chocolate bar that would take the alcohol out of our breaths. I was stuffing a row of salt-caramel chocolate squares in my mouth as he said in my ear, 'If anyone asks, you were driving.'

In the middle of the junction was a bright-red sports car with the bonnet bashed in. The driver's seat was empty. I sat on the kerb, confused, while Walls walked around, taking witness statements using his voice-recording app. Two excitable women were telling him how the other car had been going very fast. The driver had run away, left his licence in the car. 'What a jackass!' someone said, and Walls said, 'Yeah!' They did not breathalyse us. I knew we shouldn't have drunk the beer. I knew it was possible I had been holding the map sideways. The policeman drove us to our Travelodge, which was not at all where I had thought it was.

In bed that night, my heart banged. *If anyone asks, you were driving.*

I was completely uninjured. Not even whiplash. I woke up, the next morning and the ones that followed, realising that I wished I had been physically injured. I'd wanted to be partially crushed.

The last stop was Washington, for the flights. Maybe we got there by bus. There was also a small airport. And there was another hired car, provided by the insurance company possibly, but the details are gone, forgotten. I was only vaguely conscious most of the time. We booked ourselves into an inn with carved bedposts and dainty curtains and pastoral pictures in little gilt frames. I stared for some time at the ceiling, then rolled sideways on the bed and took off my shoes and socks. I had been putting this off. Slowly, I unpeeled the dog-eared bandage and peeked under. The room quivered. The back of the foot was sick and red and swollen. The wound wept. I whimpered. Walls was gone running. I considered shutting my eyes and refusing to move until our flight. Instead I phoned reception.

There was a doctor on the hotel's emergency contacts list who was willing to see me, and he was just a couple of blocks away. No one else sat in the waiting room and I was brought in immediately. The doctor opened his surgery door and said in a lilting way, like in a Western, 'Take off your shoes, lie down, what is your name?' and I wanted to melt into the foam bed of his care. This doctor picked around with silver instruments, and I bit my fist and looked away. He bent his knees, turning his head this way and that. The doctor went very quiet. He called a second person in, another doctor or a nurse, and she ran steaming water from the sink into a basin. 'May I?'

The doctor plunged my foot in the basin of warm water. He picked around some more; I worried as usual that I was going to die.

'It's gangrenous, you have to chop it off!' I said, and then the doctor pulled from the hard mushroom flesh of my heel a fat shard of cocktail stick dyed with blood. Missing just its miniature American flag.

The doctor bandaged the hole in soft white gauze and neatly taped it, then wrote out a prescription for antibiotics and painkillers to which he added, in strong cursive, 'elevation and bed rest'. As we said goodbye I wanted to thank him from the bottom of my heart – I wanted to see him again, this medicine man, and even marry him.

I lay dazed in the quaintly furnished inn, another establishment still intent on drawing me back with promotional emails.

'Wound got infected,' I wrote in my notebook. I cleared my throat then. 'That wound got infected,' I said aloud. Walls sat up next to me on the pillows.

'Infected? Infected? Awful. Horrible. My poor sweetheart. You have suffered, you deserved none of this. I'm taking you out, I want us to have one good memory.'

We chose a high-end Italian delicatessen in Georgetown and it was spectacular, the hanging hams, everything, but he didn't like a cheese that I did, so we ended up sitting at different tables, exchanging dirty looks. We ate opposing Black Forest gateaux, and he sent the bill to my table.

My Success

The job was quickly organised by my father so I could repay the money I had borrowed for my travels and debaucheries. I had never done much photocopying or sat at a computer. I still hadn't thought of death or madness. I'd never felt the rabid terror of my obsolescence drawing nearer every day. I was willing to be helpful somewhere.

The hours were 8am to 4pm and I should wear black and white, they said. The bus number to the financial district was 122. I'd be on the seventh floor.

On day one, a man with papery skin and smiling eyes led me through the foyer to the elevator, saying, 'Good morning, now I'm George the catering manager and I'll bring you up to the girls.'

Maybe by now I had been told I was going to be making tea. You see the country was rich, and the firm was making so much money, the office was already magnificently overstaffed. But they had to find something for me to do.

The elevator doors split open, and we talked about university. George had a great love of books. 'Ah, I must have read every book under the sun, every book under the sun,' he said, shaking his head fondly. He carried a mop and bucket in one hand, a walkie-talkie in the other. We reached floor seven.

Five or six or eight women in stiff outfits were shuttling round with trays; one by one, they waved, and nodded, and disappeared, and reappeared.

'Bernie, Roz, Dolores, Mona, Geraldine.' Or was it Jacqueline. George was introducing me to people who weren't there. 'And Ray over there, that's Ray.' The chef wore a striped apron, and he stood against a wall, holding a telephone with a spiral cord, writing something in a book. He glared at me.

We passed a cleaning lady, though she had no name. Nobody told me her name. She wore a purple smock, and looked away.

'Testing, testing, coming in from Mars,' George said, and he handed me a walkie-talkie. 'Seven floors, eighteen meeting rooms, four-hundred-forty-six staff. We'll need to be able to reach each other. So that's you darlin'. Over and out!' He left with a wave. I stood in the corridor and the women darted around, stacking teacups onto rows and rows of saucers, pushing trollies away.

One of the neat woman was cutting the plastic coating off a Jacob's biscuit tin with a pair of scissors. 'What can I do to help?' I asked her. Maybe it was Bernie. She pulled off the lid, then reached underneath the trolley for another tin.

'Let me see now love,' she said, considering me a moment. 'I'll tell you what you could do is just leave us at it. Head off and have a break.'

She marched away, and I went down the corridor into the toilets, locked myself inside. But I could so easily be found, so I took the elevator to the fifth floor and locked myself into that cubicle. I shut my eyes. Half an hour passed.

The next day, at the same time, I went down to the toilets, as I was very tired from the night before. My head was a kaleidoscope of gorgeous carnal visions that I wanted to return to. I folded up tight on the cubicle floor and took out my diary, in case I might write some of them down. But they were too enjoyable. I thought of nice things until sleep overcame me.

Every day, the tea girls opened up the building and set up the breakfast meetings. They worked from 7am to 4pm then finished up and went home to their husbands, and their children and grandchildren in the cottages and council flats around the Docklands.

But in the middle of all this, when lunch was done, they sat and had a break together. Bernie's husband might have won some money on the dogs. They talked about the greyhound fixtures. Lotto numbers. Weight Watchers points. Fifteen points, twenty-five points. They spread low-point snacks around the table and as they ate each rice cracker or blueberry, they totted up the points.

September arrived, and the elevator down to the toilets got busy with the partners returning from their holidays. You had to look up and say hello more often. The numbers for the teas and coffees rose, and sometimes there was a trolley that you had to push.

They let me fill the boilers for the tea and coffee, and bring refills into the boardroom, where my father's slight frame was crumpling in a meeting lasting hours, a cold cup of coffee marbling at his elbow.

I planted the replenished flasks on the sidetable, smiled at my father across a row of dark suits – we twinkled for a moment at each other.

I still had so much to learn about helping people inconspicuously. It was in that blue-chip firm I was taught never to carry a glass into a lawyer with my bare hands – the glass must be placed first on a folded napkin, then on a plate, then on a tray, maybe lest it be finger-printed and besmirched with human touch.

The biscuits and refreshments were laid out, and I took the elevator down to five, retired to my cubicle, to curl up and think about the good times I'd endured the night before.

You couldn't just spend all your time in bathrooms, so once an hour or so had passed, I'd go back upstairs to continue to place saucers onto trays and coffee cups on saucers upside down in stackable rows. Then we would sit down at the small table along the corridor facing the kitchen, sky turning dusky through a window on the other side, and have a break.

Pink Lady apples, matchbox sized low-fat cheeses, packets of Lite Crackers. Fifteen points, thirty-five points. They talked quietly about Roz's son who had no intention of going back to school when term began, nor could he be forced. One time, Bernie told me her husband was laid off yesterday. 'Laid off?' I said.

Roz regarded me with exasperation. She explained. 'They let him go.'

I still wasn't sure I understood.

'He won't be going into work tomorrow,' Roz said, and Bernie nodded quickly, with a grim stare. She sliced an apple into halves, then quarters. Bernie and her husband had four children.

We finished tea, cleaned up the tea and then returned to the laying out of Bourbon Creams in a fan shape on a doily. The cleaning lady in the purple smock came in, and Roz led her around the kitchen with Ray standing with crossed arms, and showed her all the places she had not been cleaning properly – 'And we said it to you before,' Roz told the cleaning lady with no name. She pointed in behind the gadgets and equipment, into the back of cupboards, and the cleaning lady hunched her shoulders, looking straight ahead of her.

I was on the biscuits. The lids popped open, and I spread the biscuits out and left them on the plates to grow a little stale, or to be eaten, in handfuls, by the young bloods in the boardrooms having sugar lows, or tipped into industrial bins, that or something else.

And I went back down to lock myself into a cubicle and cover my face and wait for everything to go back to being great. And returned to the soft pornography of recent memory.

I blackened out the day, replaying ecstatic visions of the night before. Wild thoughts. Delicious feelings.

Nobody asked questions. George would have understood. A dreamy man, he was okay about the shirking of a duty that did not exist. I was tired and poisoned from the late nights and it was in the bathrooms getting well again that I best served the organisation. I closed my eyes. In came the surge of bliss, wild feeling.

Except for a strange sound, on the day I'm thinking about.

A muffled sound was trembling from my bag. I didn't, at first, believe it could be coming from my bag, but my bag was ringing. I looked in. The screen flashed with a number on the walkie-talkie.

The dread that it was me that someone wanted over-powered every febrile thought.

I pressed at hard round coloured buttons.

'Hello? Hello?'

'Howya Margaret.'

It was George. He was talking quickly, out of breath.

'Sorry for bothering you but I've a Mr O'Mahony down on the third floor. Are they all gone home, Bernie, Roz, Geraldine, Mona?'

I checked the time; after four o'clock.

'I don't know, I'll try and catch them.'

'OK. It's only that we have a man down there, a Mr O'Mahony, a client, he's come up from Cork and he hasn't eaten anything all day. Do we have a plate we could warm up?'

'A plate?'

'A plate of food like. Had they done a roast pork at lunch?'

'I don't know. I think so, yes.'

'Good because we're going to need to give him something for his lunch.'

'OK, we'll look after him.' Bernie and Roz, Geraldine, Mona, Dolores and myself, we would all look after him.

I unlocked the door and rearranged my shirt collar in the bathroom mirror. You had to look so smart in this environment.

On the seventh floor, I found them, putting on their coats to leave. Mona, Bernie, Roz, though not Dolores, they didn't really like Dolores – she was always leaving early. All the girls were setting off for home as I tried to articulate what George told me – a Mr O'Mahony was down there. He'd driven up from Cork. Hadn't eaten anything all day apparently. Had they done a roast pork at lunch, and could we warm some up for him?

They understood immediately. Geraldine bounced past. Mona unwrapped cling film from a tray she lifted out of the fridge, and found the meat – ducking underneath her, Roz found the balls of mash and vegetables in their sealed containers. Bernie switched back on the water for the tea, got the milk jug and the sugar out.

Mona was wrapping cutlery in a serviette. The microwave rang. Roz got to it first, and the sweet-smelling slices of roast pork, the mash and vegetables were ready, piping hot, the meal placed under a cloche, and onto a tray, and onto a trolley, with the water jug and on the bottom shelf of the trolley, the tea things, and just when I thought we must have everything, Bernie ran towards us with a strawberry trifle.

With Roz, or Bernie, whichever it was, I jangled it all down the corridor and pressed the elevator to the third floor. With every second, I knew, the plate was cooling underneath the cloche but the elevator flew straight down, it stopped for no one and delivered us to three. Bernie, Roz – it doesn't matter does it, who it was – she looked straight in front of her. I went behind Bernie, behind Roz, who had the trolley now and as she pushed it down the hallway, we didn't say a word because we knew we would make it, just in time, to Mr O'Mahony.

At the secretary's booth, my father passed me with his briefcase, and a rueful smile my way, both of us too busy to stop. I'd have to wait until another time to tell him all of this.

The secretary nodded, stood out, opened the board-room door – or she wasn't there at all, we were doing this alone – we pushed on through, and found him right there sitting with the window at his back and a spectacular view of the coursing river and the rooftops and steeples of the north city beyond – Mr O'Mahony.

He was large-chested, with a foggy head of grey, a timid glisten in his eyes. He smiled, revealing an uneven cluster of yellow teeth. Roz was right there serving him a glass of water. Bernie might have been there quietly placing cutlery on the table, or maybe it was Mona – it doesn't matter. More important is that Mr O'Mahony, he'd come all the way from Cork and he hadn't had a thing to eat all day.

I laid the tray in front of Mr O'Mahony, who took all of us in with the most shattered face of gratitude.

Did he have everything he needed, asked Bernie, or she didn't ask, she was already gone – she was on the bus home, with dread inside her stomach because her husband wasn't going to work tomorrow. Bernie, Roz, Geraldine, Mona, Dolores – let's forget about all them.

Most important, loud and pounding in its urgency was that Mr O'Mahony had driven up from Cork that morning and he hadn't had a thing to eat all day. That was what we had to deal with, without any warning.

Mr O'Mahony was a big man, an appreciative man. He tucked his napkin in his shirt collar, and he closed his hands together for a moment's grace. He lifted the steamy silver cloche, discarded it on a chair, and sliced quickly at his luncheon. Hadn't had a thing to eat all day.

Sparkle

Patch had to see me out of his apartment and back down to the street because the doors were locked from inside. He shut out the drippy music and went down the metal stairway, two steps at a time. He was in some kind of a rush, unlocking the front door, and I was forming my exact goodbye when he turned and took both my hands in his and kissed me against the stone wall. I dropped my housekeys in my pocket and yielded to his kiss. His lips were plump and mellow but it was a strong kiss, thick and powerful, tasting of wine and flesh, and his hands reached around my body, pressing me close to him, and my legs seemed to come loose. Only he existed now. The long way home, the next morning, no need for any of it anymore.

We moved along the wall behind a pillar by the row of cars and nothing that had come before could ever matter now. He was being a little fast, a little pushy. Much too fast and pushy.

'Steady on Patch,' – I untangled him.

'Whatever you say,' he sang, tossing his head with his eyes closed.

I wondered for a moment, but then he kissed me so firmly all over again. I thought what the hell – and put my arms around his neck, split his legs apart with my knee. He got at his belt; his jeans came down, jeans fell to the ground, Jesus. He was in boxer shorts. We were out here in the courtyard in the early morning him in boxer shorts and he was trying to get off my sports bra – 'There's no hook,' I said, 'it doesn't come off like that,' and then he grabbed his thigh, his own thigh, and he stroked it.

'God look at that,' – he raked his fingers down the hairs along his thigh muscles. 'Look at that gorgeous—'

'Patch, that's your thigh. You're feeling up your own thigh.'

His knee to the wall, head to my shoulder, and his head – his head was heavy as a cartoon bomb. I reached down, then paused.

'I should go,' I said.

'I have a car,' he said, and he pointed a key and a sound went – lights blinked, knobs jumped open. The car was parked right there at the door. It was a small basic car. He climbed in the back, pulling me with him. We were going to be reckless then were we. Apparently we were. I found something on the floor, a raincoat, or a tent, arranged it all beneath my head, and watched him rise above me. So this was happening with Patch. It was really happening. He was crazy for me, he was in a bad way. It was amazing. To have set out wanting something and then to have gotten so much more than you had asked for, everything at once, without even trying. There was something I was forgetting though. Something important you should not forget to do. I reached, straightened up his head and stared into the black pits of his pupils. What was I forgetting? He kissed me very closely again. His weight was pressing on my chest – I shoved him off and tried lying differently but could not get comfortable. I remembered then, what I'd been about to say, and I removed him once again. It was stupid but I needed to express this. I knew from past experience that you should get some promise from a person. Just some guarantee for the next day, like an insurance policy.

'Patch?'

He didn't hear me.

'Patch, Patchy.'

I slapped his face.

'Patrick?'

No answer.

'Patch, I wanted to ask you – I'm curious – does this mean anything to you?'

No answer.

'Patch, listen. You're not going to try and just ditch me tomorrow, are you?'

No answer. He tried to put his dick back in.

I laughed. 'Can you hear me?'

'Oh yeah,' – he was saying things. He was saying nonsense. 'Wouldn't you know, altogether impossible, altogether, not at all.' For a while it continued. 'Whatever you might say, when I was a young man, when I was a boy, yeah, altogether …' Insensible nonsense. I couldn't just listen to it.

'Can I check, how high are you?'

No answer.

'Patrick – what's my name?'

Patch slicked a tumbling lock back from his face; his monstrous eyes rolled in their sockets.

'Tell me my name!'

I couldn't hear what he was saying then.

'What are you saying?'

He was saying names.

'Emily. Emma?'

I laughed. 'Patch, who am I?'

Patch looked helpless.

'You don't know who I am.'

His weight buckled and he laid his big bomb head on my shoulder, and it slid, mashing in my torso. He did not know who I was.

When I told him I was going to leave now, be on my way, he knelt back against the window and made aim at me. A shocking aim, as if he was pissing down through a gutter. I pulled my knees up and shut my eyes – I thought of the road home. And I felt him, gouging into me again – but, oh. He was pretty good at it, considering. It didn't feel bad, it could work out fine. I relaxed back as he banged away. This had to be a good thing. I had always wanted to be with Patch. Finally, a tunnel of breath warmed the plastic raincoat musk around my face and he subsided onto the floor of the car, since there was no space for two to lie. This had taken place. Patch had had sex with me.

I've thought about it over and over. Written it all down too many times, wondering how I could explain it. That I had been to Paradise – to Ithaca – to Tír na nÓg. I had flown all the way to the heavenly place, only to find it was a backwater.

—

The plan had been to go straight home when I was leaving work at five. It was one of those irresistible hot days and I just couldn't sit there trying to work a moment longer.

When I say 'work', I'm not sure it's what you think I mean. I was renting a desk in a run-down building with its own charm. The building had no floors, and it was filled at every corner with stuff belonging to other people: stacked cardboard boxes, mildewed rucksacks, paint buckets. The walls were hung with unclaimed peeling art, posters of forgotten bands, forgotten festivals. A sink of cups, a fridge of gone-off food, a fire of ash. I thought, too often, this is no place for me. And I doubted my potential, when I sat late at night, scratching at my compositions – fragments of ideas for a story, profiles of commercial theatre stars, fashion notes. The summer had been drab and motionless. It had been intensely hot for weeks, and coming home each night along the quays you saw the junkies and the down-and-outs relaxing on the front steps of the Four Courts. The problem, always, seemed to be doing the thing you knew was best for you. Coming home I thought about the healthiest pursuits, of fruit and yoga. But it was a warm Friday night of unbearable potential and I wanted so much more than what was best for me.

I cycled on, committed to the greater plan, to my hardship posting, and I really was about to turn the corner when I saw him walking along Parliament Street.

The back of his unmistakable head, outline of a robust cheekbone. His shaggy garland, the swagger of his arms. He and his friends took up the whole pathway, swelling up the hazy summer throngs. I pulled on the breaks, called out, 'Hi!'

He turned slowly, and with a look of high summer, of reprehensible ease and low celebration his face broke into a smile.

'Oh, hello. Where are you off to?'

'I was just on my way home.'

'You were?'

'Yes, I think so. What about you?'

He smoked with his friends while I locked up the bike, my fingers sliding around the task, my heart like a jelly-fish. Then I walked through town with Patch – walked along, right next to Patch that Friday night in June. I smiled stupidly as we walked, with each step seemed to soar upwards to an ever-better place. I hadn't seen Patch in months, maybe a whole year, and meeting him now was such a hit of magic, such treasure, like finding a crushed-up fiver in an old pair of jeans, or twenty even.

It wasn't that I was in love with Patch, not that. We had a boyish friendship, laced with something else, some-thing offbeat, tender and flirtatious. I felt that he should really fall in love with me. Patch was a guitarist in a kind of Celtic rock band. They had a boisterous sound, a lot of big hair, and their concerts guaranteed everyone a good time. They weren't in it for the money or the fame. They were hard to predict, dependent on prodigious numbers of their friends for crowds. They'd made two albums and they threw them around free at gigs, with little whiskey bottles. Only one interview existed on the internet: Patch, sitting on his bed with his guitar strap around his neck, tells the camera he must have a clean bedroom before he sits to practise.

Once, after I took the train two hours just so I could watch him play, Patch drove me to the door of the weird little house where I was staying and we sat in the car and listened to the end of a song. The car went silent and the wind went oooh.

I said, 'It must be so difficult to write a song.'

'Not hugely. Songs have always come quickly to me. Though if I'm honest, I'm not sure it's me that writes the songs.'

'Really?'

'I kinda believe in the muse. You know Plato's muse? The muse enters, I genuinely leave my body. I'm hardly conscious, anyway, in the act of creating. And then I have to purge myself of this new song. It's a bit stressful. It's not a very nice experience.'

'How do you mean?'

'I suppose – I'd like to write better songs. Take my time more. Be more mindful.'

'Maybe you need a new muse? Could you put out a casting call?' I laughed at my joke.

'Maybe I just need more sleep,' he said, shifty, impatient, fiddling with the keys in the ignition. 'A healthier lifestyle maybe?'

He did seem debauched to me, with those crackly eyes – in need of protection. 'Would you like a cup of coffee?' I asked, glancing at the isolated little country cottage.

'Jesus, no I couldn't. I'm completely brain-dead. And I have guitars and everything in the boot.' He saw this had assaulted, utterly, the moment we were sharing. He said: 'But we could meet for a coffee maybe, back in Dublin?' He took my phone number.

Of all the people back then I would have most liked to have had coffee with, it was Patch. And it was presumed that we would meet, even when he disappeared, off to his festivals, off on his corporate tour, off with his whiskey sponsor, to play old favourites. Off with his wedding band. All his texts concerned his busy schedule. I tried to put him out of my mind. Those months, as I sat typing and deleting sentences at my paint-bespattered desk, he returned in fitful visits in my mind, and I wished to be with him, wished for this earth to throw up some surprise, some concession for the long and lifeless days.

Five or six friends were sitting at the coffee table, sipping a Rioja Reserva Patch didn't want us to drink.

When we first went in he had stood, awaiting our attention. He had spoken: 'In about ten minutes, I might say that you all have to go.' Slowly, he had uncorked the bottle, which was bound in a pretentious golden wire he felt he had to ceremonially remove – and he had measured out six glasses. Then he had unlocked the doorway to the balcony, and left us.

I sat on his sofa and sipped the expensive wine and wished I wasn't there. These weren't my friends or anybody's friends. The old photographer with the bulging stare. The chef with the pencil moustache, who kept playing records and mouthing with outlandish feeling the words of the songs, and he kept stacking the records on top of each other without their cases. This twitchy beautiful girl, sitting right beside me on the sofa.

She was shawled, with hair that shimmered, red and bushy, like a fox's tail. Sitting near enough that we could talk, but so many minutes passed, it soon felt much too late. Her eyes darted fearfully, which I couldn't understand, she was so beautiful. I wondered whether I could get to Patch before her. When, every so often, someone would get up and leave, Patch would come and seize a bunch of keys and walk them out. The gates were tall and needed codes; getting in involved a complicated security system, and getting back out involved the same system, and only Patch had keys and codes – and so, the only way to be alone with him within this arrangement was to leave.

The only way to him was the last way, was goodbye.

It got very late; I glanced around and wondered. Really only about him – I hated when I got fixated and obsessive like this, found it exhausting. I should go, I thought.

The woman touched my arm, surprising me.

'I just thought I'd ask – by any chance do you need to go?'

'Sorry?'

'I'm thinking about finding a taxi, if you wanted to share one?'

I looked around the ashen crowd, then checked the balcony. Patch was twisting, gesticulating, in the middle of some funny story or performance. 'I don't know,' I said, and she leaned close, with these wide open, gentle eyes. She said, her hand reaching to my sleeve, 'It's a real comfort that you're here.'

This, I couldn't forgive her for saying.

'I think I'll hang around for a while, actually,' I told her. 'But thanks.' She kept her eyes on me, and offered me a cigarette. She had this probing and insinuating air. 'Sorry – I know I don't know you,' she said. 'But you look a little sad. You're sure you don't want to get out of here? I mean, I think the party's over.' She started gathering her things, pulling on a sparkling rose-pink sequinned handbag that she must have got on some ethnic stall or vintage shop.

Patch was now leaning back into the railings of the balcony, with his elbow covering his eyes and his knees slightly buckled. The others were laughing and his arms and shoulders looked big and powerful and I was much too tired to leave.

'Yeah I think I'll hang around,' I told the girl, more assuredly this time because if there is one thing no one gets away with doing, it's telling you that you look sad.

'Safe home, then.'

'Bye.' I waved at her.

I saw Patch walk her out the door, then settled back with my decision, waiting for him. My throat was scorched with borrowed fags. I better head off now, I thought. I lit up another cigarette and thought to myself, better head off – rehearsed how I would say it, when he returned. I'm off home, thanks Patch. The people were becoming loud now. I better head now, I thought, go home now, in a moment, straight home. He seemed to be taking a long time coming back from seeing her out.

When I opened my eyes, the chef was dancing by himself, and there was Patch on the turntables. I didn't know how long I'd been asleep. I checked my bag, put on my jacket, and waved at Patch, who came out from his record collection and with the keys high in the air and eyes wide and blank he led me into the bright hallway. It was our turn now to say goodbye.

When we got out of the car, he tucked a stray shirt tail into his jeans, and he pointed the key, shut one eye like a sniper, and locked it.

'At least you remembered to lock your car,' I said, but Patch wasn't able for any kind of joke. He opened the apartment door and flung himself against it.

'But I'm going home,' I said.

'You can't leave,' said Patch, one foot planted in the building. 'It's too late.'

'Can't go home by yourself,' he was still muttering as we mounted the stairs.

The flat was empty. The empty wine glasses stood on the coffee table, with the can rings and plastic bags. I have been young for far too long, it's just gone on and on. No music played, and grooves scarred the sofas where the friends had all sat, the friends who must have passed us in the car.

'After you,' said Patch, and he elbowed open his bedroom door and punched the light. The bed moved, and the beady sparkles of a pink handbag slipped onto the ground. A rope of hair quivered like an animal on the pillow. The girl sat up and looked around.

How happy I was to see her.

Baked Alaska

Margaret didn't like Walls, so why had she agreed to go walking with him in the mountains, and afterwards for a drink in a remote hotel bar? She had no self-control, she broke all her promises, she was weak, gormless. Not all she thought about, unlacing her boots at the fireplace, just the fog through which she battled each day. A thick and bracing fog of personal contempt. But she functioned ably in the fog and had even started writing feature articles about young dance professionals; Walls ran the Shooting Star Dance Convention every year from his home study. It was one of the pies he'd got his hands in, after the magazines failed – and the pie in his hands was the type of phrase he used, standing over Margaret while she wrote her articles for the Shooting Star blog page.

'You should take off your socks too,' said Walls. 'So that your feet dry properly. Hang them from the mantle-piece, here.'

'Can we just do that?'

'Do you think we have to behave ourselves?' He shot an impish eye around. 'In this dump?'

Margaret smiled with a charmed disapproval. It was the end of December, and it was a strange, antique hotel – empty, save for some old people at the collapsing little bar. It wasn't what you'd call a dump, if you were new enough to the customs of taste and extravagance she had lately been treated to. But she liked that he wanted better for her. True, she'd grown picky with experience, but it felt nice; she felt a sense of belonging to a corrupt old world. An old, boozy world of velvet button-back armchairs and good-natured sleaze all cossetted by the once-splendid rugs and drapes of colonial voyages. She felt, in this world, herself, at last. Better than herself, glowing with insights, with new material to tuck away. She settled in her chair. The loose chair legs shook her in her seat. The evergreen branches strung along the man-tlepiece looked feeble, picked clean by time, and even the fish in the cases on the walls were dead.

'Evening.' A narrow-faced unsmiling man lowered a tray of hot ports to their table.

'Thank you, my good man,' said Walls, reaching for his glass handle. He blew, and sucked back the port. 'Hits the spot. We were out at Glendalough today, hill-walking with the best of them. Do you get many walkers this time of year?'

As the men found things to say Margaret cupped the port in her hands and dipped her nose to the bitter scent of liquor, lemon and cloves. She took a long drink, gazing affectionately around. Cloth-bound books, maybe of poetry, listed backwards on the little shelves. The empty floral armchairs sat facing each other, reclining, arms outstretched as if caught in a ghostly confab. A grandfather clock sounded. It was strict, censorious, like a clacking tongue.

'It's a nice place to come and disgrace yourself anyway, isn't it, gorgeous?' Walls picked up *The Shooting Gazette* and read aloud from a story about gundogs and winter grouse, making Margaret laugh. He propped his bare foot on his bulky knee and leaned back, testing all the strength of the chair. His legs were long and sturdy. How much were the rooms here anyway? She didn't have to decide on anything yet. Margaret gulped her port, sinking back, sinking further inside an evening she'd never imagined she'd agree to.

On Christmas Eve she'd sat on a kerbside on Dawson Street with her bags of presents spread around her, and into her phone typed: 'Not only do I not love you, I don't even like you.' She paused and her chest seized before she added: 'Now leave me alone forever.' And she sat in the sleety cold, reading back through all their texts: the block paragraphs of his voluble accusations alternating with her neatly edited retorts, her spicy prim dismay. It was minus two degrees and she did not feel safe. The shadows of ruthless passers-by bore over her and the corners of boxy shopping bags swung in her eyes as her ass cheeks froze on the cold stone.

Margaret pressed send, then put up her furry hood and fled the streets. Their love was over, and it had been only lies. On Christmas Day, she kept her phone switched off for discipline with the added benefit of torturing him. On St Stephen's Day, she turned back on her phone to see three new emails from him. One sad belated Groupon offer for ice-skating, now expired. A press release for the pantomime, subject headed 'Matinée with me?' Then a sonnet, typed into the body of his email and evidently authored by him in some dismal late-night rage: the couplet ended with the words 'dishonour!' and 'suicide?'

On the twenty-seventh of December, she replied, because no one should feel like throwing themselves out a window on Christmas. 'Hope you'd a good break,' she wrote. 'Awful,' he wrote. 'I'm sorry,' she wrote, not knowing exactly what for; it could be any number of things. On the twenty-eighth they texted, then he phoned her and they talked through everything. The whole nightmare. It all came out unstoppered. Very soon they were laughing and the season became a beautiful snow globe, trapping them in its plastic blizzard. Now we find the former soulmates on the twenty-ninth of December in this hotel with buffalo horns displayed in the creaking mahogany hallway – something about the Boer War, the concierge had told Walls – and sullen photographs of aristocrats in sporting gear.

Why had she come all this way? Because that morning she'd opened her curtains to a bright winter sky booming down on her. She did have a car, or shared a very old car, with her mother. Sometimes it broke down but normally it delivered you somewhere. 'Beautiful day,' she'd texted, and exactly an hour later she pulled into the traffic island opposite Donnybrook church, grinning and waving at Walls like a long-lost friend. He got into the car, bulky and ungainly as the wrong jigsaw piece. He looked so suspect, checking around him – always so guilty, stigmatised by some yet unclear wrongdoing. She liked the boyish glint, the boyish smile – he was terrible, incorrigible – he was her punished pupil. They got along so well. They both liked walking in the mountains, they liked wine, books, train journeys. He liked politics, men's worlds. Both liked the idea of causing trouble – of escalating something, shocking other people. He took the applications from the dancers in his spare time and she'd been his intern and his girlfriend the past year. His protégée, his unpaid apprentice, the weirdo in the corner of his study, eyeing him while he worked, blushing at his glances, bloodshot from their drinking, beckoning him – though she never undressed him there and then. Their fantasies remained just that, ethereal, abstract ideas transacting between them, through a shuffling clutter of newspapers, laptops, coffee cups and sandwich wrappers. All physical sex was had after dark and in the dark. Why was it, she wondered, that he insisted on referring to it as a round of sex. Round of sex? he'd ask, nudging her, with a wicked face. Or – do the act, he'd say, we're overdue the act. Why, she despaired, opening her legs, why.

The way he looked at her, she didn't feel it would ever be possible to be anywhere else. She gazed back at him like a sedated hawk. And when he got exercised about the world, she thought no person had ever been so funny. Then, about once a week, or twice a week, one of them would say something pointed and disruptive and they would argue. Arguing would last hours or days. Arguing became shouting, slamming – love was flammable, unhinged, something she couldn't account for. Once, on holidays, he'd driven her drunk late at night and told her he could get them both out of the world. He'd speeded up the car and scared the shit out of her. She never asked him about it afterwards, she told the story only to herself, she reasoned with its oddness; it was all bluster, wind-up.

At Glendalough, the surrounding hills were plush and velvety with deep colours, and snow lit up the mountain peaks. The cold air blanched her face as the soles of her boots gripped the railway-sleeper tracks along their path. They chatted happily, normally, like decent people, offering nods to ruddy-cheeked women and their big cheerful dogs. The sky grew dark and the hikers dispersed, leaving them alone in the mountain range. She felt shy and elated; she wondered would this lead to a kiss. When her ankle turned on a rock along the track, she almost tripped, but he grabbed her wrist and held her glove, looking at her with tender fright. After that she let him hold her ungloved hand.

The gaunt man came with two more hot ports, and some complimentary slices of Christmas cake, encased in white marzipan, with little mince pies in paper cases laid out on a doily, their star-cut pastry tops dusted with icing sugar. Margaret spooned whipped cream all over a mince pie and bit in.

'I adore whipped cream! I think whipped cream must be my greatest pleasure. If I had whipped cream every night I'd be happy for the rest of my life.' She licked her lips of cream and sugar powder.

'We could actually eat a dinner before we go,' he said.

'We could. But the ice. Would the ice be dangerous if we left it too late?' She had no interest in the answer to her question, just a formality in the resistance she would need to provide. Her limbs felt heavy, her skin baked in the heat of the flames.

'They have a table, if we want.'

'Oh, you already asked them?' She screwed up her eyes as if she was considering something. 'I am very hungry.'

The grandfather clock ticked, jaunty, like horses galloping. Tick-tick-tick-tick-tick-tick-TICK, it went. So percussive, so repetitive it couldn't possibly herald change, or progress.

'Leave your boots,' he said.

The dining room was a solemn rectangle with every table set and nobody dining. Serviettes were ironed into fans, candlesticks stood unlit. Margaret admired a very big fork, and touched the white tablecloth as if it were a sheet of gold. 'This is all so nice!' She gave a dramatic shudder and at this cue, Walls took off his jacket and tossed it on her shoulder. Corduroy, a flickering russet shade, well lined. The jacket buried her in his familiar warmth, and as the chill eased from her body a big bottle of red wine came.

The bottle did seem bigger, fatter than an average bottle, and she assumed it was expensive. The pungent blood-red wine toppled in their glasses. Getting home was going to be impossible, though they both had a history of reckless driving. Margaret needed to learn to take better care of things. Dishes arrived at the rapid pace of an establishment with very little to do: scrolls of ham with out-of-season melon cut in half-moons, thick slabs of game terrine. A blue fish with a crispy eye was placed in front of Walls and for Margaret, a piece of meat stewed in dark juices.

'How are we going to make it back? I'm so tired for driving,' Margaret said.

'Look, the rooms are fine, if you want.'

'You think ...' She let her voice trail off – she would not contribute any more opinion to this. He knew where she stood.

'Only a hundred euro a head, dinner included,' he said. 'And it's on me.'

'You don't have to.'

'I owe you anyway.'

'That's separate.'

'Sure.'

He must have been referring to the fee he'd promised her for the promotional interviews with those two stilted choreographers. She had invoiced him. He still hadn't paid her. She sliced a piece of meat in two and ate quickly the morsels on her plate. Next week, she'd have to send him the invoice again, for the third time. It took her days to write those stories. Walls sloshed more wine into her glass, and she filled her mouth.

'Let's order dessert,' he said.

'OK! Or did you see the cheese on the trolley earlier? I think I saw cheese.'

'Apple tart, sticky toffee pudding, blancmange, or – look at that. Baked Alaska. Now that takes me back.'

'Does it?' Margaret gazed up.

'Oh, seventies Dublin, that would have been the last word in culinary acumen. My mother would carry it high—'

He was talking, she was smiling, then staring, behind Walls, to the dining-room door that brushed over the carpet. In came the serving lady and behind her, a tall fair-haired couple in handsome coats. Margaret's head lifted as the man and the woman crossed the room. Her head turned. Her eyes were tugged, locked, as the man pulled off his hat to reveal a face that was as familiar to her as it was improbable, in its classic lines of beauty and clear, healthy skin. Anton. It was him. German-Irish entrepreneur. Millionaire, or more. He had once invited her to a show at Grand Canal Dock. He had a spare ticket, he said; Margaret got the impression he'd been dumped, and no other person in Dublin was free at such short notice. In the bar after: Walls, in a red smoking jacket, and he told Margaret she looked like an agèd ballerina. It's how they met.

Anton was with a smiling girl with two curtains of blonde hair ironed straight either side of her face. Her beauty only matched his in its icy credentials. Margaret didn't feel good. Ideally, she didn't care about wealth, but lately she'd been thinking. These people moved easily in the world, had such rich experiences. Margaret kept tabs online, she'd seen all his skiing photos, his clean-water project in Namibia, which must make him feel so good on top of the world becoming a better place. Anton had fulfilled more dreams than Margaret.

'It always seemed like magic that the ice cream would stay frozen under all that heat,' Walls might have said.

'Oh does it, that's so funny.' Margaret was dazed. 'Did you see who just came in?'

Anton and the woman were sitting at the farthest corner, leaving a barricade of empty tables between them and the now inferior, now scruffy Walls and Margaret. Margaret touched her mouse hair, damp and unbrushed, and seized a silver spoon to check her reflection to find the face of a bumpkin, nose, lips, eyes blown up. She tilted in her chair, trying to catch Anton's eye while also paying Walls extra attention.

'Did you see the waitress?'

'All I saw was you staring at the prat over there.'

As ever, it came in a single rough blow.

'I wasn't—'

'You were.'

'But—'

'You were staring at him like a little girl at a shop window.'

Margaret heard his voice and turned.

'Ah!' Anton stood from his seat. Walls pulled himself up too.

Anton kissed Margaret's cheek, and the other woman and Margaret shook hands, then changed their minds and kissed.

'Julia,' she said.

'Julia,' Margaret said, forgetting, for a moment, her own name. 'Margaret', she said then, pointing at herself.

The men faced each other, chests puffed. They talked about Christmas, and cleared their throats looking around them. Anton would have known about Walls' bust magazine group, but not necessarily about his involvement with Shooting Star. Julia and Margaret talked for a few minutes about their jobs.

'I'm hoping to specialise in equine law,' Julia finished.

Margaret dropped into her chair to see desserts and cheeses all laid out.

'This is really great,' said Walls. 'I'd have to say the food has really been first class, you wouldn't have thought it.' Hunched forwards, he cut open his meringue. 'Layers of sensation,' he said. 'Taste, here.' Margaret recoiled. Like a child she shut her lips to the advance of his laden fork.

'Oh, are you annoyed or something? Because I teased you? Come on, weren't you looking at him? Don't tell me you're not mesmerised. I don't blame you – he's a handsome guy, he's a seasoned guy. And who cares? Do we want coffee?'

'No.'

He continued talking. She continued watching him talk – watching him explain all over again the difference between equality of opportunity and equality of outcome, because they weren't the same, he said, waving hands, and her mind was aglaze. She was superglued and stitched into the furniture. Everything would run on, this way, facing Walls, answering to Walls. Excitedly he explained, and furtively she checked her phone – still no coverage. They were stuck out here. Later it would all be forgotten. *Round of sex*. Breakfast. Two newspapers, and outside, the gardens, terribly bleak this time of year, old ladies would say, and maybe a stroll in the woods. A petrol-station picnic table. Back to the office. Wretchedness had crept inside her, shut the doors.

Margaret was jolted. 'Sorry, what?'

'The prats are leaving,' he said. 'Don't you want to say goodbye?' She swallowed. She thought of them upstairs. The act. Breakfast, newspapers, dead garden. Her chest was tight. Seizing as if in a fever Margaret did something that seemed to lift her from her seat in its unlikeliness. She asked the serving lady for the bill for dinner – yes, just dinner.

When the bill came, she had her credit card out and ready. She paid the bill and zipped up her wallet.

'That was very generous,' said Walls. She laughed, looking at the floor. She had drunk too much and knew it but she kept laughing.

'What's funny?'

'I'm just very happy.'

'I can see that, gorgeous.'

'I'm so happy. Really, you have no idea how happy I am. Because I remembered something, just there. I'll never, ever have to do this again. I'll never have to sit with you again. You have nothing to do with me anymore. Remember, I broke up with you?' She tore a handful of grapes off a branch and popped the grapes between her laughing jaws. 'And you know maybe I was looking over there. Maybe I wasn't. I can actually look, ha ha, I can look at whoever I want, whenever.'

'I'm not stopping you from doing anything.'

She hacked out a wedge of yellow cheese and lined up three crackers. 'And you know I will think about all these other people, other men maybe. I might even try and kiss them too.' Margaret flashed her eyes at her defeated lover. 'I might even go to bed with them. And then, well, who knows what might happen? Once I'm alone with them.' She leaned over the debris of cheese rinds and blue crumbs and broken biscuits. 'I'll take my clothes off. Every piece of clothing, one by one. Down to my underwear, and then I'll sit on the bed, and they will look at me. And imagine what they will do to me! Oh! I am so young, and you are not. I am so young and free, and you are so irrelevant!'

She could keep going. Tell him all the things that she could do, with the imaginary men, or just carry on insulting him, get all the bile out on the table. But someone had to drive them home. Margaret was over the limit. And she knew enough not to disregard the fear that he could try and kill her, or at the very least, threaten to do so, which also chilled the blood. She drew in a series of deep, imperious breaths, then picked up the wine bottle and upturned it in her glass. She drank the rest and sat up.

'I've to go.'

'Go,' he repeated. 'Just go, just like that.'

'Yes, now.'

'And you probably want to go home without me, do you?'

'Oh God yes.'

'I booked a room. But you don't care.'

'Nope.'

'That isn't very nice – I thought we—'

'Nope. I want to go. And you should drive, because I'm too drunk. And I don't feel like driving.'

Margaret tossed the jacket onto Walls' shoulders, handed him her car key and went out in front of him. She couldn't bring herself to look back at the couple.

In the darkness of the courtyard, he turned the key in the ignition. The engine breathed, and omitted a lengthy energetic sigh, almost a death rattle, then cut out. He tried again. It cut out again.

'Could it be the cold?'

'Is it the engine?'

He tried switching on and off the engine then banged his foot heavy on the accelerator. She allowed a shiver to pass through her, and let her head loll against the windowpane.

'I think I'll need your jacket again.'

'You threw that jacket at me,' he said. 'Threw it, in front of people.'

'I'm sorry about that,' she said, slipping her arms through the sleeves. They sat, each hugging their own arms.

'Look,' he said. 'I know you think I was out of order earlier. Look, I just really like you.' He rubbed his hands together. It would be fast. He would blow out short aerobic gasps of air. Missionary. Pitch dark. 'How about this?' she had said once. 'I'll show you, here.' 'Really?' he'd said, after she had entrusted him with the secret of her pleasure. 'Not much in that for me, is there?' She had rolled out of his arms and curled into the wall, her eyes wide open, staring into the dark and mapping out her route home. 'Lots in that for YOU, not much fun for ME,' he had gone on, and she had stayed clenched to the wall, and tried to sleep. But he'd gotten her all excited, she couldn't help that. She'd had to climb downstairs to the bathroom. That thing she did with the electric tooth-brush, wrapped in one of those Ryanair bags for liquids.

'Get us out of here,' she said now.

'I was just going to say—'

'GET US OUT OF HERE.'

This time the sound of pumped gas wheezed, then thinned into the night air. Tree branches crouched behind them.

Under her duvet, fully clothed and lit up with adren-aline, Margaret's head raced. With outrage, disbelief. Revulsion. Joy. Her phone was off so she could sleep. But she was overtired, her feelings too rich and potent. She lay there, playing it all over.

The next day, and not until then, she would learn of something wonderful and unforgettable. Something impossible, yet so obvious and beautiful. How, after he'd dropped her home, parked her car and handed her the keys and said goodnight and walked up to the main road, he'd hailed down a taxi to get back home. He'd crossed the Liffey. At his front door he'd patted his jeans, and looked in his rucksack, but couldn't find his keys because they were inside the jacket she was wearing. He'd gone back out onto the street to find another taxi, and waited – they didn't have the apps yet. He'd travelled back to her house, all that distance, phoning her repeatedly, but she didn't answer. His calls didn't connect. He'd gone around the side of her building, and stood under the window he hoped was hers, pelting it with stones. She didn't wake. He'd walked the roads again, found another taxi and once ejected back onto his own street, he'd gone around the side of his house and begun, miserably, to climb the fire escape. He'd become afraid, felt so tired, he climbed back down. He'd slept the freezing night in the side passage, folded rigid in his raincoat, until morning when he could wake her.

Lying in her bed, she heard no pebbles hit the windowpane. It was over a brunch of coffee and eggs Florentine in town the following midday that he told her everything. He smelled of BO and faintly, sour breath, which made her spring back as he hit her with it, telling his tale. She was sincerely sorry for him, she laughed with him, shaking her head. Then she straightened up and told him to pay her for the stories she had written if he wanted his keys. She'd thought of saying that just there, and it might have been a joke, she wasn't sure. He said of course, he was going to. 'But now? Come on.' He'd slept rough last night, he only had a hundred with him anyway. He had to pay for all this food. 'Great,' she said, 'you get the bill and then we'll go to the bank.'

She walked him to the ATM on Dame Street, and she watched, nodding, as each banknote slotted out into his padded fingers. In a doorway, he counted out four hundred and eighty euro. She questioned this. It had been two stories, two hundred and fifty euro each was agreed. He owed her twenty euro. He handed her another flashing golden fifty euro, saying 'There, how about that,' fidgeting in his pockets. 'Don't be a stranger now, I'm not a leper.' Trembling, dehydrated, she stood back from him on the pavement. She smelled the notes, still warm, and filed them in her wallet. And she placed his jacket on his shoulder and said goodbye, leaving him on the street. Leaving him at last.

Trouble

Negative

In the morning, Margaret got a negative result on her pregnancy test. By afternoon she was with Sergio again, eating salad in a little café up near Camden Street. It was a Tuesday afternoon in springtime and their plates were piled, they were making conversation, when a face went by the window.

The car salesman.

She froze, then laid down her fork. Sergio gave a rough and spiteful laugh and slapped the table. He left the café, she followed after him. The exchange on the street was quick and horrible:

'Hey. How's things? Why don't we have a word right here then?'

'Seriously, get the fuck away from me! Back off, I'll call my lawyer.'

'Oh you'll call your lawyer will you?'

'Yeah, listen man, can I pass?'

What Margaret saw were two men caught up in a confrontation, and the reason was herself. Her eyes flashed, a juicy thrill racing through her as she watched this awful spectacle, this teenage fantasy come true. To be the cause of this. It was miserable. Already she was skidding towards her love, pulling at his shirt. When the waiter came outside all she could do was smile, walk back in, pay for the food they weren't even going to finish eating now. Waiting for her change, she thought, well at least. At least I'm not.

For a week or so, Margaret had been plagued by the idea that she was pregnant. Days, she lost, untold notes of money, on early detection pregnancy tests. But that morning the test was negative so she came into town. She'd bought a black quilted Isabel Marant jacket from a boutique, half price, and got a haircut, then thought they could have lunch. Unfortunately, she'd picked the same place where she'd had lunch with this same car salesman some months before. Unfortunately, she'd gone other places too with this car salesman – a used-car salesman.

Now she had to cross two streets and run down an alleyway where Sergio paced around and kicked the graffiti on a shuttered shop, saying, 'It's me who suffers!' while she regressed, all over again, to a heap of pulpish sentiment, dismay, woolly regret, pleading, 'But I'm so in love with you!'

Always, his despair circled around the justice problem. His being the victim of a crime not punishable by law. A crime that could only be remembered, repeatedly, its impact reinforced. Punishment was an intimate consequence kept between themselves. Its shape, its rules, not yet defined. But she had never stopped loving him. It had not occurred to her, even watching him snarl and shout, even reading back on his most putrid instant messages, to ever be other than in love.

The next morning she did the last test in the pack of three and it was also negative. She might have bought another pack, because she used to take a lot of pregnancy tests. There was just too much of the crystal ball about a pregnancy test, too much suspense pent-up in their minute plastic screens to resist an opportunity. It was 2016, and she was thirty-one, so old enough to have confronted some of her tremendous problems. She was working for a newspaper, writing short stories to send away to competitions, and that year she wrote some of her worst work. It made no impact on the world, only kept Margaret indoors, revisiting her past.

But reality itself hadn't caused any serious obstructions lately. She lived with her new friend Maeve on the top floor of a Victorian redbrick just up from the old asylum at Grangegorman. It had happened quickly, with Maeve, who wore a sheepskin coat, silk shirts, high-waisted pants. Maeve worked for a PR company that did much more than just PR; she had lunch with Cabinet ministers, with disgraced businessmen, and her job seemed to involve turning around a person's worst idea of who they were. Her boyfriend was Marko, who ran a pizza chain. The two women ate free pizza, went to plays and films, bought a twenty-class pass for the yoga centre nearby. On Friday mornings during one of these yoga fads Margaret would set an alarm for 6.45am, go down the street and gnarl her limbs into Eagle Pose, into Warrior 1, down to Plank with a feeling of almost dangerous happiness.

Her days were caught up with loose arrangements with friends, drinking sweet Vietnamese iced coffee, or gin and tonic; reading long newspaper articles, falling asleep like a dog underneath her desk. This was her bachelorhood, and few real fears could break through the pleasures it imposed upon her. Then there was Sergio with his two little girls across the city, in a house of teddies and dolls and shattered Lego kingdoms and *Star Wars* characters she had trouble appreciating. While an ignorance of *Star Wars* didn't matter, she wondered if it should matter; feared under her most covert layers it already had begun to matter.

Prehistory

About two years before this, she and Maeve were on their way home from Sinéad O'Connor in the National Concert Hall. Walking in the close air of a belated summer, Margaret was thinking to herself it was enough to be a person. She felt capable of floating on home in the soft cloud of her epiphany. She had wandered on a futile quest, been careless, grasping, mindless. Now, it was enough to simply be.

Margaret walked around then like a pair of open lips, she moved like a marshmallow, trusting and bumbling and sweet to people – she wanted to be bitten into. She was malleable, following Maeve, who suggested a nightcap at The Vaults.

The Vaults was a free club, and she had more than once been turned away for wearing rain gear. 'Not getting in here tonight, love. Not tonight,' the bouncer would tell her with a look of bland disgust, and it was humiliating to have to plead entry to a place you found so miserable.

Tonight, with Maeve who smiled at everybody, they let her in no problem.

That is where she first saw Sergio, resting an elbow on the bar. She glanced back at him. She forgot everything else. And when he turned to pick up his pint of Guinness, she was happy to note a bald patch, just in case he found himself too great-looking.

'No wedding ring,' Maeve shouted, and she told her to talk to him – go, now – and slid along the bar, moving her hips to the catchy song. 'Guinness in a nightclub?' she asked, and she sounded brash and vulgar. But she knew he must be from another place – 'Yes,' he said, his eyes smiling softly.

He was Italian, from a town called Casalgrande, near Modena, but he'd emigrated years back. He had a job in tech Margaret couldn't comprehend. 'We came here for work and we never left,' he said with a kind of deflation. 'My wife and I,' he added, gesturing at the dancefloor.

Two women in tight jeans were listlessly dancing, one with wet-looking curls tied in elaborate knots, and beads around her neck and wrists. 'Her?' Margaret asked. He nodded. They had two girls – the music blared, they stood close enough to hear each other. He was saying something heartfelt about his girls, and Margaret was looking for things wrong with his attractive wife. The woman turned, settled her gaze on Margaret. And looked away again.

As she was leaving, he came to her across the dancefloor and it was too late, she knew, to go back to the epiphany.

They arranged to meet in a coffee shop after work and he was waiting for her. His eyes were wistful, with deep smoky edges, his words were thickly accented. She looked far into his eyes, which were green on the outside with a fiery orange ring around each pupil. She thought of big cats. She thought of beaches, lemon trees. Sergio Fantasia. He sounded like a porn star. 'Fant*a*zia, really?' She laughed. 'Fanta-*see*-a,' he corrected. 'It's an ordinary name in the north.' Margaret could not believe he was real, and that he'd been here all along without her knowing it. His father went to the same school as Pavarotti. And did Margaret know Sergio was a corporal? Conscripted for two years before he joined the Artillery Regiment. Sure, he'd fired guns, missiles and canons. 'The surprise drills, you'd have loved those,' he said. 'But I need you to understand that I hated that idle and aggressive culture.' Leaving, he put on a golden-brown check tweed cap and gathered her into him, and she was certain she had met him before. She had known him in some other century, and now, he had come back to her.

The second time they met, he produced from his work satchel a magnetic chess set. Laughing, they took each other's pawns. He brought his knight forward, and she snatched up his queen with her bishop. What a reckless player he was – she felt she had to apologise. He took her queen, then moved his castle to her king. 'Checkmate,' he said. 'I'm sorry too.'

The third time, they were in a taxi going past Trinity when he told her about the labour camps and Nazi prisons. His grandfather was a partisan in the Italian Resistance who had been shot by German occupiers in 1944. The taxi driver was talkative too, and he said, 'Are you giving the poor woman a history lesson there?' Sergio sat upright and his face locked still. He said:

'They starved him and made him freeze behind barbed wire for one year and a half before they lined him up and shot him in the back of the head.' They didn't talk at all then for a while.

'You try to save your country from the fascists, you get murdered,' he was telling Margaret, going up Constitution Hill. As they reached her street, she nestled back, looked out the blurry window and forgot about the way he had been with the taxi driver.

That night he kneeled beside her on the mattress. He asked her to be patient while he left a marriage that was already over. He took her clothes off and kissed her.

After he had done that Margaret faced him, eyes blasted open. He didn't seem like someone who had spent four years in barracks and immediately after that met his wife and settled down with children and a job.

He used to visit her with laden arms. Balsamic vinegar, apricot jam, Pan di Stelle biscuits; wine with no label from the Fragolino grape that tasted of strawberries in the little glasses he poured out. He painted her fingernails and she lay on her stomach, admiring him. He brought two types of massage oil, as his back ached from sleeping in the box room, and he knew Margaret wanted to put her life at his feet.

He brought her a photograph of himself in uniform the day he took office, wearing his cap, and an oddly fitting blazer with bright-gold buttons and epaulettes. She kept it under her pillow so no one would laugh at her but she took it out at any time of day and looked into his youthful and ambitious face, his fluid greenish gaze.

The more times they met, the more he became who she wanted him to be. She'd been hit over the head, taken out, stolen by the fairies.

He was a Chief Technology Officer – a CTO. She didn't know any other CTOs. She didn't know that she approved, since she had no interest in new-fangled things, but he was the Chief. One time he held a conference call with her right there in his car, her feet on his dashboard, and she could tell that the people on the call wanted to impress him. His car was very clean, with a first-aid kit in the seat pocket. A tiny gold crucifix hung on a string from the rear-view mirror – Sergio prayed to God. You didn't have to believe, he said, to pray to God each day and ask for his help.

On the backs of the front seats were two Velcro plastic protectors called Kick Mats – 'They are two wild little girls,' he said. 'They fight, jump in puddles, climb trees. You'll see.'

She was in love, beloved. She knew everyone would think she'd made him up so she paraded him around town, broadcast his achievements. She wore him wrapped around her like a big fur coat and he protected her from everything that had been bad. People looked at him, and looked at her with a new and jealous approval, and she just gave her dazzled smile. She pitied anyone who wasn't her. Sergio and his wife were 'separating amicably', she told friends, his phrase. She brought him home to meet her parents, and he brought more extra virgin olive oil and more biscuits and more wine with no label from the Fragolino grape. He talked about the partisans, the labour camps, the massacres. Dante, Marcus Aurelius, the moon and constellations.

Margaret's eldest sister Lisa said, 'When John goes to Belfast, I like to think he's not messing around with some young one,' and Margaret hated Lisa.

Her next sister Caroline, a tax consultant who would not tolerate the kind of wilful stupidity that Margaret still thought lovable, warned her little sister she was digging a nice grave for herself. 'Talks a good talk. But a guy like that will never leave his wife. And she's not going to leave the father of her kids, is she?'

Margaret's father took her for a drink one evening in The Long Hall. He said: 'He's very *charming*, isn't he?' Just as he italicised the word, his eyes darted.

The night Sergio phoned her to confirm that they had drafted their separation agreement, her heart squeezed and made her weak with happiness.

Two nights later, he phoned to say he wouldn't be coming over. 'Something happened,' he said, and the line went quiet. He was unable to explain it. His wife had a sore arm. 'Listen, I have to go,' he said.

Days later, something else happened. His wife was walking the girls back from school when she had a strange fall, just tripped sideways on the pathway, into a hedge.

Some months passed, and he and his wife saw a number of specialists in different hospitals. All of the conditions they investigated spelled appalling news, so it was important to rule them out one by one. His wife would stay home in bed while Sergio met Margaret on Baggot Street, took her to a new exposed-brick restaurant. They grasped each other's hands across a distressed table, he said he'd never felt like this before. He wanted to run away with her to Rome, Milan – she wanted this too. 'Be patient, my love,' he told her.

A November evening, he drove up to her gate and sat, crying, in his parked car. One of the doctors had phoned him to tell him what it was.

'No,' Margaret said. Inside she folded over, shrank.

'Yes,' said Sergio.

It was worse than bad. The situation would be worse if the specialist wasn't top in his field, if Sergio's wife wasn't as young as—

'He's the top guy,' Margaret said. 'If anyone can—'

'There is nothing on this earth he can do for her. She has six to eighteen months.' He threw his head into his open palms and howled and shook with tears.

Margaret searched online and saw that the son of a US Democrat was living bravely with this illness. A few days after she read about him the politician's son died.

Sometimes, Sergio would bring nightmarish news of his wife's deterioration. How she bought all new clothes from TK Maxx to fit her new slim figure. She bought a flamboyant red wig, and it frightened her girls. She had a crowdfund page, a blog, and the *Sunday World* journalist who interviewed her misspelled both her girls' names. Though she had been told she would die soon, she would still send her husband to Little Italy for ingredients. She would still dance with her daughters. Margaret watched a video taken in their living room. His wife carefully places one foot over the next, and hops lightly, then hops again, singing softly, guiding each child in a hand, her fusilli locks bouncing around her shoulders. Margaret couldn't understand why she wasn't spitting at the walls and thumping fists in this video, how could she dance? She thought that if it was her, she'd put a pistol to her head and disappear.

Within a few months, Sergio's wife went home to her family in the village near Verona, and then to Rome where there would be new doctors and she hoped, a miracle. It was agreed on a piece of paper rushed and quickly signed that the girls would follow her. They were four and six then. She was thirty-nine.

Positive

That Friday, Margaret got a late period in the toilets of the Light House Cinema.

She was intrigued by pregnancy as a physical state. She thought she'd love to slip into such a story, with its drama already written, its threat of savage pain – a story constrained within a set time period. On the whole she loved the look of pregnancy. Though whenever she imagined it happening to her, she became terrified. Terrified at the idea of the baby that would be born at the end of the pregnancy, a baby you would be required to take care of, who would grow up into a child – a story unconstrained by any set time period.

Still, she was almost wistful the next day as she swallowed her painkiller. Wistful, relieved, resigned, and then over the following days, confused.

For weeks she'd been convinced something was amiss in her body. She went to her GP, who tested her for pregnancy and then, to her disappointment, chlamydia. She cursed her luck; how had she failed to see this coming, how had she concealed it from herself?

The results had come, and it wasn't chlamydia, but it wasn't a period either. It was nothing. Blank. Then on the Tuesday morning she walked to her parents' house and went straight up to the bathroom, peed on a stick, then lay on a spiky bathmat. After three minutes passed, she turned over the stick to see a faint pink line appear. That made two pink lines.

She climbed into her mother's bed and lay out stiff beside her. Her mother was reading a hardback biography of Evelyn Waugh, and her mouth smiled in one straight line at Margaret. 'I'm so tired,' Margaret complained, hoping her mother would ask why, though her mother hadn't noticed that her youngest daughter had become a different person.

Sergio, on the other hand, burst into tears on the phone then drove over with a box of multivitamins and some ginger sweets, plus a digital test to confirm the unsettling news.

That week, appointments were booked, mirrors studied and Margaret went farther and farther into her imagination, her own distorted world. Pregnant, she thought, standing on the tram. Pregnant, walking along. 'I'm pregnant,' she told women she didn't know, women on reception desks and phones, the actors she'd to interview for the magazine. Did she look different? Did the air taste different? It was something like going to sleep and waking up a queen or goddess. Not everyone would have seen it like that. But she believed they did, she believed they were about to stand in awe and envy at her good fortune. They would all hold their breath, reposition their gaze, step aside for godlike Margaret.

She found it hard to focus. The only thing she could do was to spend any money she had in Brown Thomas. A loose t-shirt dress. A billowing shirt. Black patent brogues because she had to make her name as a writer and she only had nine months.

Six Weeks

Less than nine months, because of that obstetrical quirk whereby the beginning of a pregnancy is dated back two weeks pre-conception. So at four weeks pregnant you have completed six, and time now will be packaged into weeks and days, not months or years. 'Six weeks' conferred a certain confidence, and smug fatigue, that St Patrick's Day as she walked on Dollymount Strand with some old friends. I will later, Margaret thought, retire to my writing desk and write in full the short story that will win. The sun shone across the glittering tide but her phone buzzed and buzzed because there was Sergio, across the city with his girls, entering a state of resentment.

Their names were Giorgia and Angelica. He always talked about them, incanting their names: 'Giorgia and Angelica, Giorgia and Angelica,' as if she wouldn't know who he was talking about. He was more often than not alone with Giorgia and Angelica, wrapping them up in waterproofs and driving them to parks, or to the aquarium or Eddie Rocket's. He drove them to birthday parties with their hair unbrushed; Margaret tensed when she saw Angelica's face of chocolate after a party. She imagined one day she might sit the girls on her knee and do French plaits, or press flowers or something. Their mother was gone just two months. Hospital leaflets were stashed around their house, new childminders had to be found and entrusted with delicate responsibilities, meetings with 'services' scheduled. The girls seemed to need to be fed constantly. They weren't like how Margaret had imagined girls, dressing their dolls, reading books in their bedroom. Their bedroom was a mess – they slept in sailor dresses and wore them the next day into school. On the weekends Sergio, a tall robust man, would lie on the floor in a pile of crushed laundry, matching Disney princess socks; he would be in a car park, buying good-quality leggings and tracksuits from an Adverts dealer.

'Paddy's Day is a family day!' he wrote now.

'You don't say!!!' she replied, and her phone sparked and raged until nightfall. It wasn't the first big fight, and it's never the last. Going home that evening she got off her bike to search 'abortion England', but her screen was getting rained upon and it wasn't at all what she wanted. He arrived later with another box of vitamins and the fourth edition of *What to Expect When You're Expecting*. He knelt at her feet with these shining gifts, the night went silent and time hurled everyone along.

Five Weeks, Two Days

One evening Margaret sat at her writing desk looking up mummy forums and other garbage sites until darkness swallowed up her bedroom. All day, on and off, she had been bleeding. Death was all she thought about as she walked in wafts of fear through town into the hospital.

The waiting room was full of pregnant women, that brave and withering look in their faces, like they'd seen it all by now. She took them in with awe: the blonde, pink-cheeked woman eating apples with her friendly faced husband; the grinning woman in tight jeans, on her fourth baby, his first.

A screen on the wall informed everyone shark meat was forbidden in pregnancy, also liver, and any kind of pâté. On and off, Margaret forgot herself, but the same shrivelling unease always returned. She picked up *Good Housekeeping*, an old *Vogue*, and *Cheltenham 2016*, with a forty-page festival preview, and a jockey on the cover with two long smile lines that looked like Fallopian tubes. Bad thoughts flowed through her like toxins. Fear was in her lungs, fear and self-reproach, to think how easily all this could have been avoided. A group of women came in wearing leather jackets over their pyjamas and talking excitedly. Sergio came in, darting to her; he held her hand in one hand and played a game of chess on his phone with the other. A thin girl came out of Early Pregnancy Assessment, crying, a man's arm around her. 'Fantasia,' the woman called, and it was Margaret's turn.

The doctor wore Prada tortoiseshell glasses, and this in some way comforted her. As the doctor put a gel on her stomach she had a sense that she was just watching herself in some budget drama. The doctor told Margaret bleeding can happen, and she gave her a small smile. Everything else was consistent with pregnancy, the thickening of the womb, that was good. She referred her for another scan, and that night Margaret lay awake next to Sergio with her hand across her stomach. What struck her was how endangering it all was. That you could overnight forfeit all possession of who you were to another being of uncertain shape, a thing and not a person, and it could screw up all your insides and throw your life in question; the pains had not gone away.

The next day a second doctor put a wand inside Margaret, and on the screen they found a pregnancy sack with a dot on it. 'Five weeks, two days, that's nothing!' this doctor said and she booked the patient back in for nine days' time. During that nine days, Margaret bled, she passed clots. She walked outside and into town, and pregnant women filled the streets. Harsh pains crawled up her legs. She sat up in bed, typing out an interview with an actress. 'Disquietingly gorgeous at fifty-two, she tells me in a whispery voice she lacks confidence on the stage,' wrote Margaret, and sordid pains multiplied and played up and down her side, spread around both hips, stomach, back, thighs. She lay there listening to New

Age music on Spotify, and couldn't eat. She couldn't talk to anybody. It was the very worst thing that had ever happened to her, this letting out of her body. She was still not comfortable with any kind of injury you couldn't shout about, that didn't give you some distinction. Now she felt the most obscure kind of sadness, curled on her bed while her sister Caroline tipped her thirty-five-week pregnancy between them and ate oatcakes.

Zero

She stayed in bed taking painkillers, coming out once a day to go for a mournful walk by the river, or stare at the television. She felt so sorry for herself. From time to time she took out the ultrasound picture and found it pathetic. A mysterious grey morass. Like the ghost of a life, or a fake picture of a UFO. How idiotic to get upset over a bunch of cells that would have caused full mayhem if allowed to advance, how insignificant her first tragedy, how malfunctioning – she caught herself, hurling self-hate.

The day came to go back into the hospital. She nodded past a very tired woman in a dressing gown smoking at the hospital gates, a woman pacing the corridor holding a pregnancy ready to drop. It was April Fool's Day, and nature had already played her prank, Margaret thought winsomely. Once lying down she asked the nurse if she could turn the screen away—hot tip from the internet. Sergio held her socked foot while the nurse fixed her eyes and moved the nozzle around. 'This is the heartbeat,' she said and turned the screen back to Margaret.

Six Weeks, Twelve Weeks

It was unexplained – a minor uterine rupture, small bleed, nothing dangerous. The worst thing that had ever happened to Margaret had been entirely imagined. That day they rushed out of the hospital grinning and arms swinging, because they both desperately wanted what they had thought they'd lost. And on the day they came out of the hospital with a picture of the baby's crown and pursed lips in profile it took all her stamina not to brandish it at everyone she met.

Sixteen Weeks

On her birthday Margaret went around Smithfield complaining to her sisters in separate phone calls about having to carry so many tomatoes in order to make the gazpacho from scratch. And you just couldn't get commitment when it came to numbers for food. She was so frustrated with everybody. She was turning thirty-two, she knew it didn't matter. Entertaining people was frivolous and indulgent, yes it was. But this birthday was her send-off. 'I never want to forget who I am!' she told Caroline before hanging up at the cash register at Lidl. She smiled at the lady, wondering did the lady know her secret.

Her palms were welted with the plastic handles when she arrived home and set to work. She cooked all day. She cooked with the kind of deadening regret she felt each time she had friends in. She skinned and cored tomatoes and blended them with bread and cucumber and peppers and onions and sherry vinegar. She rolled out pastry for a cheese pie, then boiled potatoes on the small hob and made mayonnaise with a whisk. She crushed hazelnuts. She hacked at parsley then at coriander with a knife she had no idea how to sharpen. The voices in her head rose in pitch, blaming her for being so idle as to have the time to do this; as she sliced hot baby potatoes in half, she thought of her mother and her foremothers, doing just this in their kitchens but because they had to. Margaret, on the other hand, chose her own depletion.

Her kitchen was filthy and cluttered as she mixed the batter for a 'Chocolate Surprise' birthday cake for herself. She made ganache, she cut strawberries and arranged them in a ring on top. By 6pm the dishes were all laid out, glasses ready on a tray and beer and wine chilling in the overfilled fridge. She squeezed into a miniskirt for what could be the last time in her life.

The buzzer went, and she ran downstairs with the same skittishness she felt at the start of every party, only this one was significant, fin de siècle. She opened the door, and Giorgia and Angelica skipped past her into the building and up the stairs, limbs seeming barely attached to their stick frames. Sergio stood exasperated. 'Where have they gone?' he said. In her hand they'd left two limp handmade cards. She read the one with writing on it.

HAPE BIRTHDAY MY BIRTHDAY IS NEXT YER
DADDY IS GETING ME
A LEGO FRENDS THANK YOU FOR THE
PARTEE WHAT ARE WE
GOING TO EAT.

She knew that they had gone into her room to rifle through her things again. She smiled at Sergio, shutting her eyes to receive his kiss.

Five of Margaret's friends turned up at different times and picked at plates of food. Everyone looked overgrown in her small living space, and Sergio would not sit down. Giorgia and Angelica, hiding in her wardrobe, were told to come in and eat, but Angelica said the food was disgusting. She pushed away her plate of bread and cheese in disgust. Giorgia was delighted with the occasion, and she jumped up and down. 'Do you have smoothies?' she said, on the balls of her feet. 'No,' Margaret said, and shuddered.

Someone played a song on their phone to entertain the girls. The score from a Disney film that she couldn't place. There was sudden dancing. Then a game. Oh, musical chairs, Margaret thought. This is going well. A glass smashed all over the kitchen tiles. Once she'd cleaned it up, Margaret stood boiling macaroni for Angelica, and Giorgia came to her again, smiling. Two adult teeth were erupting from the front of her gum to join a wonky set. 'Will we get party bags?' she asked. 'No,' Margaret said. 'I understand,' the girl said. 'Children are so wasteful.' Then she laughed and jumped at her sister but another wine glass clattered down on the kitchen tiles, smashed, and silenced the room. 'Oops,' someone said. 'Bravo!' someone else said, and he and Sergio both laughed. Two men, getting along fine. A friend was over with the brush and pan. Margaret sat on the edge of the sofa. A shard had entered her sandal, instantly pricking her heel. She found the particle, held it to the light, and threw it behind the sofa for the next tenant. Is this one of those days, she wondered, that becomes a memory you don't want.

After her birthday, she shopped in the maternity boutique on Wicklow Street. Giant pyjamas with a rosebud pattern and unflattering waistband. Then to Arnotts, to have her triple-the-size breasts measured for two quality maternity bras with nursing straps. She bought some maternity hosiery. 'Sixteen weeks, you wouldn't know,' the bra ladies said, and 'You're very neat!' She smiled and shrugged. It was all about her, wasn't it.

Twenty Weeks

In the early summer, when Sergio brought the girls to see their mother, Margaret stayed at home and organised her fiction binders. All this time she'd been working up some pretty voluminous drafts of fiction: hatchet jobs, dramatised mild trauma, partially veiled character studies. She had filled three clear plastic folders with passionate unfinished manuscripts, having binned all the rest as she produced it, like a reverse production line – filling the page, scrunching it in a ball, throwing it in the bin, missing the bin, or getting it in and hissing, 'Yes!' Then doing this again, and again, every Saturday and Sunday. She had big hopes though, menacing ambitions. People had wronged her because she was a woman, had taken advantage of her, and this could be her special niche, her feminist redress. Livid, sexy wrongedness.

She arranged to meet a celebrated writer who had once, in unspoken exchange for a flattering interview conducted on the phone, offered to look at her work. He was waiting at a table tucked into the back of his local pub, and she was late, wearing a diaphanous pink dress, gold hoop earrings and her hair in a ponytail. She squirmed into a chair and clutched the table end. She thanked him for meeting her and produced from her knapsack three folders, bulging with flopped manuscripts. 'I have about sixty stories here,' she told the writer. 'None of them are finished, and they are all the same story.'

She'd never been this close to an author of his level, such a quintessential author, with a Princeton lectureship and eleven books to his name. She was relieved he was unshaven, slightly overweight, with stale coffee on his breath. Though she had anticipated some tired kind of piquancy between them, he didn't seem to see the need for it. What he did was give Margaret clear advice. His words were blunt, sensible, lacking mystique. Workaday, almost. He told her that you couldn't just write when you felt like doing it, you had to make a schedule. That producing anything was something to be proud of. He wished he had a folder of beginnings. 'What is it exactly you want to write?' he asked.

She explained that she would simply like to write a story set in a city. 'But I have to move soon, to the suburbs, There's so little time, and now' – he followed her gaze down – 'it's too late. I'm expecting a baby and I can't make field notes. It's all finished now.'

The celebrated Irish writer said absolutely not. 'It's already in you,' he said. 'Everyone knows what such-and-such a city looks like and sounds like. What they don't know is how it feels. The emotions you had at that time in that city. No one else knows how it was for you.' They sipped their coffee dregs, nodding about this.

'So, what are you working on at the moment?' she asked him. He was making tentative notes for his next novel but he couldn't yet begin it. 'Because I don't know the ending yet. I never begin something without knowing how it ends.'

The Same Week

On the Saturday Sergio returned, it appeared again in their newspaper. Margaret realised it too late, having already dumped it on his kitchen table by the milk and berries. The ad for the Ford Fiesta. 'ANYWHERE.

ANYTIME,' read the back cover. Before she could conceal it he'd picked up the page and crushed it underneath his rubbery hand.

All the Weeks and Through the Years

She and Sergio seemed to disagree about many things and their evenings grew dire. Strolls and dates were a garbled wasteland of you you you, blablabla. They had no understanding of how to fight other than bitterly and to the end, no known control over what might happen at a given moment. But they believed in one another, believed they loved one another sufficiently to invest. Their first counselling session was set inside in a grey housing estate strung with Dublin football bunting and flags; a sideways doll pram and a rain-filled Fisher-Price cart met them on the pavement. Antoinette was a large, breathless woman with static plum hair and a mouth she kept carefully screwed up, lest she might smile inopportunely, maybe. Once they had filled out the paperwork in the stuffy reception, she led the couple up a squeaking stairway to an untidy room with ass-grooves in the sofa cushions and half-drunk tea mugs and pieces of paper half Blu-tacked to the walls, saying: 'Quiet the mind, the soul will speak – Buddha', and 'The only journey is the one within – Rilke'.

'Blatantly meaningless,' Margaret said into Sergio's collar, and, 'I could have written that.' He, pointedly, did not laugh.

After Antoinette had cleaned up, they began.

Sergio explained: 'My wife, my ex-wife, is terminally ill. My girlfriend had an affair. She is pregnant.' The therapist's face dried up with worry.

'Pregnant? By?'

'By him, by him!' Margaret pointed at Sergio, over-joyed that this much was true. 'And it wasn't an affair it was—' Here, she explained why she believed that what had happened was nothing like your typical affair.

'That is an affair,' Antoinette confirmed.

That first session was placid, introductory. In time, Margaret would say things like, 'You both have it in for me! Why did you drag me out here?' but normally it was just fraught and unpleasant. They mounted those musty stairs every Tuesday at 6pm and there was always that sense of being led by a stick and penalised, made suffer for the sins of their immoderate passions. Margaret liked Antoinette, the way she used to like schoolteachers who were afraid of their pupils. She felt Antoinette didn't hate them, that she honoured the contract. Though when she and Sergio started to fight she looked overwhelmed, and flapped her hands. 'Now, now, it's all very emotional!' Antoinette would say, and Margaret would say, 'Yeah!'

'She betrayed me,' Sergio would remind them, and Margaret would glare into nothing and chew the flesh inside her cheeks.

Antoinette became just another source of disagree-ment, a fresh bone to encircle and growl over. 'I'm never going back to Antoinette!' one of them would say, or, 'Antoinette says don't do that!' 'I've suffered enough!' 'You've put me through hell!' 'I'm pregnant!' She'd type abortion services on her phone, then cry again and tell him how much she loved him. We're awful people, she'd think, a waste of everyone's time.

Then one day, Antoinette closed the door behind them and the house receded into the mists and folds, never again to be driven by without a shudder. It was impossible for Margaret to determine what she might have taken from her time with Antoinette other than the knowledge that most counselling sessions are fifty minutes long, not an hour, and most services charge about eighty euro for couples and seventy euro for individuals, although couples' counselling is infinitely more distressing.

There was one day, however, when she sat on the backside-indented sofa doing the individual session you are awarded if you stay the course – your chance to tell your own side, get the truth out – when she suddenly started laughing.

'Sorry,' she said. 'This baby is kicking me. It hasn't done that before. Oh God, that's feisty.'

'Aha, must be a boy,' Antoinette quipped.

What if it is a boy, she thought then, and every day that followed. *What if it is a boy?*

Later, she told Sergio about the baby that had kicked her. 'Oh really?' he said. He looked at Margaret in the unusual way he sometimes did. As if she was a stranger demanding something of him. He looked at her like this, and then he told Margaret about the baby that had visited his dream. 'I dreamed of the baby last night,' he told her. 'The baby came out, and I roared in anguish. The baby had sideburns—' and he said it. He said the name of the Salesman. Margaret put her head in her hands.

Those Weeks

It had happened almost a year before, but the thing was fresh and prickling as a covered wound, lately exposed.

She'd been selling her mum's car and a cut of the proceeds was guaranteed by Margaret's father. Maeve's boyfriend Marko had a friend who sold cars. When she phoned the Salesman, he seemed very friendly, and gave her some advice for DoneDeal – 'Don't tell them you're a woman or they'll think you don't know what you're talking about.' That moment, she just said, 'Really?' and laughed. She drove to his garage, and he came out from under a car engine in a navy-blue boiler suit, with oil streaked along his forehead. He had dark sideburns. His eyes smiled, probing her, but he was businesslike. He knew about Toyotas and helped her write the ad, provided the model and mileage. The car was bought in less than a week, and Margaret earned three hundred euro, money in the hand.

Running into him outside a sports bar she disliked, she told him she'd found his comment insulting – 'the one about women and cars' – but she laughed as she said this. He offered her a cigarette, and she smoked and fixed her hair. He apologised and said she should embrace being a woman, just accept a lower offer. 'Listen, I'm winding you up,' he said, rubbing the back of his neck, looking in her eyes.

He wanted to know what she did, where she grew up, and she loved answering his questions. When he wrote asking her to lunch, Margaret said no thank you. They continued messaging and she sat, jittery and confused, the day she realised she'd agreed.

She wasn't sure how she had become friendly with such an overconfident prick. She questioned it with Maeve, who cheered her along. Sergio was married, this made him unsuitable and what was wrong with having lunch? The Salesman was a cultured guy, interested in classic cars, restaurants, vinyl, film, theatre.

She wasn't sure why she'd ever gone to lunch, and later on tapas, then later still a pint in O'Connell's on

Camden Street, making that two pints; why, days after this protracted regret, she rushed to see the Abbey's Christmas show with him. She'd messed his sideburn hairs in the back row of the scarlet seats while he dug her with his elbow, whispering. She didn't know why they liked each other. Their friendship was unnatural, so Margaret told Sergio all about the guy who'd helped her sell her mum's car. She told him he was a real character. Sergio looked strangely at her but left it at that; he was preoccupied by other things. When they went out these days, they talked only of his family problems, not of history, literature, the moon.

In late December of that year, he took the girls to Italy, and snow fell in his region. Margaret missed him; she lasted four days, then on St Stephen's Day, she wandered along the river Dodder in the frisking cold, a text message waiting unattended on her phone. By the end of her walk she had replied to the Salesman.

The pub was just up the road, and full of rosy-faced people, evergreen-and-gold Christmas bows along the wall panels. She liked all of it, the frothy afternoon pints, the horseracing, the cheers, the fried calamari that looked like dead handshakes on the table. The dissolution of cares in their greedy libations. She was touched by the Paul Simon record he'd picked out for her, just a little present. Christmas could be lonely, to be honest – he just wanted to buy her something, he said. The record was *One-Trick Pony*, and featured the artist in a leather jacket with a forlorn expression. 'Throw it away if you don't want it,' he said, shy, pleading and probing. He drove her home and when they reached her gate a force undeterred brought her to him. She followed its direction and her lips and teeth clattered onto his.

She climbed upon him, soaked in feeling, certain of the importance of doing what they would now do. Certain of the rightness of this feeling in the scheme of all misplaced desire. They drove to a quiet spot down by the river.

'We need to get this over with and never speak of it again,' she declared with arcane passion.

He took her wrists in one firm hand and with a jolt of the other, reclined the passenger seat. She panted in surprise.

Not again, she thought, in the fumbling. Not another car.

'I want you now,' he said.

'I want you too,' she said. 'Put on a condom will you.'

'I don't have any,' he said.

'None?' It only made her admire him more.

'We need to go to the shop,' she breathed exaltedly. They drove to a Texaco, parked, and strolled in together. Margaret went into the toilet, locked the door and squatted down. As the flood of urine splashed out, the beats of her heart slowed down. When she stood, her body had recovered something. Some rectitude, decorum. She looked in her own wide cautious eyes in the mirror above the sink. All the wildness had exited her gaze, calm had crept in. She looked frankly at herself. The girls were drawing pictures, the girls were coming to her with big brown eyes, and empty cups for her to fill. Sergio and his girls had been running through her mind since morning and now his face, his open-hearted face loomed in the reel of images. She would not go through with it. She got back into the car and said she needed to go home. 'Sorry,' she added, glancing over. The Salesman said he was sorry too.

They reached for each other, and she really did think only of Sergio.

She was glad when he dropped her home. Glad it was over. Because now, the matter was resolved. She deleted his number. And everything was fine, after Sergio returned. Everything was loving and romantic, until the evening he asked about the guy in the Ford Fiesta. 'I don't know – I don't know what type of car he drives,' she said. 'What do you know about him then?' he asked, and she began to stammer. He asked to see her phone. She handed it to him. Suddenly she wanted all this out in the open, freed from her bad conscience. He read through her messages, then turned to her.

'What was it like?'

'We didn't,' she said in a shrill voice.

'You must have,' he said.

'No,' she insisted.

'What did you do then?'

'You don't want me to outline every—? Oh Jesus.'

But she described something of the crashing around that had gone on in the Ford Fiesta.

'I don't believe you,' he said – and they were shouting again, she was blocking the doorway and the dismal vista was jumping out from behind her eyes. She stared at him.

'Handjob,' she said.

He laughed grimly. 'Nobody gives handjobs these days.'

'Well I did.'

'And did that give you pleasure?'

'Yes.'

He put his fist through the bedroom wall.

'Beg forgiveness,' he said, shaking plaster dust off his knuckles. Margaret tried to pull him back as he left the apartment. She cursed, and screamed, holding her face, peering out through her fingers like the woman in the horror film who sees it all before her, the destruction of her home.

In the following days, as his messages came in, she pressed buttons, begging forgiveness. She calmly understood two things. The Salesman, he should no longer exist in the world for her. And she should no longer live under one roof with the person who had caused all this. She knocked on Maeve's bedroom door, her insides tightly knitted.

'I'm sorry but I think one of us is going to have to leave.'

'You know I can hear everything. You shouldn't take that.' Maeve walked across to her. 'And I agree. I'm moving out.'

'What?'

'Yes. And I'm pregnant.'

'Congratulations.'

For the next week, through the walls, she could hear her friend pack up. Marko loaded cases in his van, gave a swift wave at Margaret, started the engine. The two friends said goodbye on the street. The ad for the new tenant was up and within two weeks, a nice botany student was ready to move in. She was quiet and studious. Alone, in the cold February sunshine, Margaret brought *One-Trick Pony* to the Liffey, snapped it in two and watched the colours flicker down into the glossy swell. She bent the sleeve in half and binned it on Manor Street.

She had been brought now to a point of wild envy. It was a loud, insistent crisis she had reached. Biological, insensible. She wanted exactly what Maeve had immediately. And when, on a Wednesday evening, Margaret got the pain, the same pain she always got, every month, she invited Sergio for dinner. Could it be that she was tempering all this unhappiness to her own irrepressible maternity? He arrived with a hamper full of good things to eat and drink assembled on a bed of crepe, and after the gnocchi with pumpkin sauce and the wine was all finished, he laid out a plate of Cantucci biscuits, poured two glasses of Vin Santo.

'I want a baby,' she said, sipping the sweet nectar.

'I want to give you one.'

How great that their love had survived the strain of such malignant forces. They forgave each other all their assaults. She would tell nobody anything and nothing, ever, would be the same again.

It took two months.

Any Given Week

By that summer, Margaret expanding, they were unable, or unwilling, to pass an evening without a fight. Because the bottom line here was she was pregnant. She just wasn't going to let him treat her in the way that she would comfortably allow herself to treat him. She wouldn't have it. Pregnant, you were basically already a mother. A gentle, loving person. Mothers didn't lie and try to fool everyone. Mothers were the source of love, the custodians of love, they delivered love and nursed it in their arms.

Late for work under her own employment, she lingered in the kitchen listening to two male relationship experts being interviewed by the male broadcaster on the national morning radio show. One expert said that a couple will rarely survive a woman's infidelity because for a woman there will be an emotional connection. Emotional connection being, she guessed he meant, the most egregious betrayal. Meaning a woman has the greater power to destroy what is good.

She laughed at these experts, but later, crunching on the silvery shells on Sandymount Strand with the tide way out and a foul stink rising from the matted seaweed, they both worked themselves up into tears. She would not afterwards remember everything they used to fight about, only that it always returned down that same spiral. It followed them around town, until she used to see him in the backs of people's heads. The Salesman. They would go into a café or a pub and have to run back out – she saw, once, the Salesman in the flesh. 'Too full in there,' she told Sergio, taking his hand. Now, there were whole streets they couldn't go to anymore, pubs banned, whole neighbourhoods, a whole chain of pizza joints, and the streets of Dublin filled with Ford Fiestas.

The night came that she lay in a dismal hotel room looking at the dismal sea in the dismal holiday town, and she cried: 'He finished it off himself, you know!' and he cried back, 'Well then it wasn't a very *good job*.' And she moved to the twin bed in the dismal room. She wondered who was left to blame for the conditions that had made her, for the complacency, neglect – was it all her parents' fault, teachers, classmates, the tennis club, neighbours, the bitches in the locker rooms, sisters, cousins, aunts, that man, his fault, her grades, dyslexia, or attention deficit, asthma, her mother, all her fault, and her own personal fault too.

Exhausted from crying, she thought, it's terrible when things happen that you're not able to tell anyone, only maybe one friend, a person you have not yet decided upon. Terrible when there are things you've forgotten because you can't even tell them to yourself. In the dark, her phone propped on a tear-stained pillow, she bought a gold lamé maternity dress.

That Week

One warm summer evening, she and Sergio were walking down the road from her flat eating Classic Magnums. They were just at the part of a combustion when the heat and pressure rise up to the front of the brain and it feels the only option is to release, and attack. She was saying, 'Act your age!' while he retreated into superior silence.

They passed Grangegorman Clock Tower, the former penitentiary, which at one time served as a transportation depot for women required to find themselves a better life in the colonies. Sergio took out his phone, then came to a halt. He stood in the middle of the path, and started mumbling in his dialect.

'Come on,' she said. 'Walk and talk.'

'I'm sorry,' he said. 'I don't know what Facebook is saying.'

'What do you mean, what's it saying?'

'It's saying that she died.'

That night they sat on the floor of his TV room surrounded by suitcases, folding dresses, and little shorts and t-shirts, bunching up goggles and Crocs and filling straw hats with knickers and vests. They were going on the 7am flight to Verona and the girls jumped around the room, shrieking, 'We're going on the plane, we're going on the plane!'

Their mother was buried in the churchyard in her mountain village. While Sergio and the children were throwing handfuls of earth into her grave Margaret was in town trying to pass the time. She went into Clarendon Street church and lit a candle.

Three or four people knelt in prayer. Margaret mouthed a name, the shape of a word, but still, could not fill it with her voice. It was the name of his wife. His wife turns to her in the basement, her curls spring up. In her eyes puzzlement, minor irritation – Margaret might be a buzzing fly in the heat – indifference. A blessing of indifference. And does Margaret see a glow of derision in the woman's eyes?

She left the church and walked to Mothercare. Three summer maxi dresses, two long camisoles, a maternity denim miniskirt, a vast denim shirt, all of which would join the bags of his wife's old clothes in the master bedroom.

Thirty Weeks

With him gone, she went back to telling everybody her astounding news. By text, she told estranged colleagues, old friends. She told Maeve, who wrote back: 'With Sergio?'

Margaret didn't tell Sergio who she was going to meet. She couldn't even think about how much it would inflame him to see Maeve, while he was away, and there she was, sitting at a wooden table with a flute of Prosecco, her bump weighing her at a backwards angle. She wore an ample denim shirt over her perfect round-ness. Her brown hair was big and wavy, her lips were red and plump and Margaret felt so soothed on seeing her she wished for just a second she could share her chair. She wished they could share another apartment, start again. 'It's not alcohol, I just asked them to put it in this glass for the ritual,' said Maeve, smiling, with her nose scrunched, and they hugged in a great rush of love; Margaret had missed her smile.

And before she knew it she was talking and explaining. What a big sordid mess. She was sorry about everything. She was sorry that she hadn't been in touch. Her speech trailed and her eyes grew as she realised there were things she couldn't explain, there were lapses, holes. Did she and Marko ever fight? Lately Margaret really wanted for people to tell her shocking, grisly things about their lives. She wanted people not to get along. 'We do,' Maeve said. 'But are you sure that's fighting, what you're talking about?' Margaret told her all about the girls. How the older one had been fleeing her classroom and the younger one kept stealing sweet things and trinkets from shops and houses. 'I'm worried I won't be able to handle them. What if I become their stepmother? Or what if we break up, and they get left without any kind of mother?'

'That's the kind of thing you should think about before you have a baby with someone,' said Maeve. The two women sat in baffled silence. 'Sorry,' Maeve said. She sighed. 'I just hope you know you don't always have to be nice to people.'

They parted with a deferential hug. That night Margaret lay in bed and filled her basket up on the maternity website. Halter-neck, polka-dot swimming togs, Kate Middleton turtleneck dress, workwear – a ruffled blouse, pinstripe pregnancy pencil skirt. Items she would pair with her pregnancy fishnets, maternity parka and Repeal the 8th badge.

Thirty-Four Weeks

In mid-August, they flew to Modena and descended from the aircraft in a thick and stagnant heat. It hardly seemed like air you could breathe. His mother welcomed

Margaret with dishes all laid out on a tablecloth, she hovered with a tea towel as Margaret ate sliced melon and pizzette and boiled meat and pasticcio. She sent her off to bed to rest. During the long dragging week in the apartment they walked in and out of rooms, trying to understand one another. His mother ironed Margaret's underwear and sewed buttons on her clothes. His brother complimented Margaret's *figura*, laughed, 'Don't end up like Gloria,' and mimed the exaggerated shape of his wife; Margaret said nothing, just smiled, then lay back underneath the air conditioner watching a fluorescent quiz show. On the last day his mother held Margaret in voracious hugs, returned to the kitchen, assembled the packed lunch. '*Basta Mamma!*' Sergio said, holding open the wicker bag for her to fill with food. They drove to the Amalfi Coast, stopping in hot, dusty towns. From Sorrento, they took a ferry boat to Capri, mosquito bites protruding from Margaret's ghostly flesh. In an old villa facing the sea, they read their books, and ate sliced figs and white cheese for breakfast, and the local women wished Margaret every happiness with her bambino.

They drove around rocky cliffs and swam in clear water, and ate Caprese looking at the superyachts. The children, with their grandparents outside Verona, each spent nights in A&E for different reasons. Sergio, enraged over a plot of land in the north of the country set aside for the girls, argued on the phone. He got out of the car to argue, walked along the rock clusters and even when Margaret turned up the glitzy voices of the radio presenters, she could hear his pitch rising in a language she would never understand.

She bought beach dresses from shoreline boutiques, a straw hat, animal-print espadrilles. Towards sunset on the last evening, he asked her to go and drink a naked negroni on the Piazzetta while he did some exploring. Margaret sat alone with an Aperol spritz and a bowl of peanuts, watching the sun dangle down into the clouds, luminous like a pinball. The next day, they sunbathed, and ate mussels with little glasses of beer in a cove, then ascended the rocky cliffs. The idea was to watch the sunset once again, but it was too hot and she couldn't walk, because of the baby and a yoga incident in the second trimester, which I thought best to spare the reader. It should be enough to say she was in pain most of the time.

Sergio was silent, looking at Mount Vesuvius turn a deep-grey shade with the clouds falling behind.

They walked until they were both irritable, then found a collapsing hill that led to a flashy little bar clustered with families eating ice cream, bearing selfie sticks.

She got on a public bench against some antique tiled cherubim, and slid down, tipped her body to one side until she was recumbent, spilling over the bench.

'You hate it here, don't you?' Sergio said, and she looked up. 'Yes, it's truly awful.'

The next day, after eating Sicilian tarts for breakfast, she ran to the bathroom and vomited. It was interesting to feel so terrible, nearly eight months along. They took a motor boat around the island, and he pointed out the stacked rocks and the inlets and she closed her eyes, seasick. She hadn't fallen in love with Capri. And their hotel room was cramped, considering the price. She thought of the two girls. She never missed them, never joined their echoing video calls, but she never stopped thinking about them either. She lay across a wooden plank, nauseated, and the girls ran in and out of her mind. They spent the day on a quiet beach, Margaret ailing on a towel and Sergio silent under an umbrella with his phone. But he wasn't playing a game of chess. He was just looking at the sea.

She thrust herself onto the bed back in the hotel. She wanted to lie there and complain, but he wanted to watch the sunset so he said, 'Come now, quick,' and what she always admired in him was a restless spirit that found better things to do anywhere they were not.

They walked past the little port, up a rugged track, and as they rounded the island, with the ocean glimmering beneath and the sun falling into the mists, he pulled her aside. His face glowed white and serious. 'The light is failing,' he said. 'I am extremely nervous but I wanted to tell you that I think the life we could have together could be brilliant.'

'No,' she said.

She saw he had a little velvet box in his hand, so she said, 'OK, but get on one knee.' He bent down on one knee and put the ring on her finger.

'That's my right hand,' she said. 'It goes on my left hand.' He pulled off the ring and squeezed it past the knuckle of her ring finger. A woman in white trousers with a little dog stopped to clap and cheer them and Margaret waved frantically at her, waving her away. She stood breathing heavily, a red oval stone on her finger.

'Is it a dummy?' she asked him. 'It's not real?' she put the ring between her teeth and bit down on it.

'It's a ruby from the old jewellery shop on Capri.'

'And this?' She felt along the band.

'It's gold. Nine carat, yellow gold.'

'How much did you pay for it?'

'Margarita,' he said.

'Tell me! How much?'

She hated the things she was saying just as they flew out. But she had not seen this happening. She had never imagined it like this, on this corrupted little island, browbeaten with morning sickness. She had never pictured a ring, hadn't known just how much good stuff it was possible to have – her greed flared and she knew it. But she couldn't let it go.

'Please, tell me how much.'

'I can't tell you how much!'

But he told her, in rough terms, not without pride. She asked him to get down on one knee and do it all again.

They sat together on a bench with fingers interlinked, admiring the ring. The evening sun had left behind the mountains, the light was gone and she knew that something significant had happened and just as quickly passed. It was in the past now, the life event.

Champagne, or knock-off, was ordered in the most glamorous restaurant on the island. Margaret had to tell him just how bad her lower back felt; Sergio requested cushions to prop her up, and they made a wincing toast and took some pictures, video called her parents, then his mother. Grotesque plates of food arrived; her stomach was upset. She twisted the ring around, stared into its charming angles.

'Do you like it, really?' he said, and she smiled at him. He held the ambivalence in her unblinking eyes. She knew she needed to tell him now that she did like it. But she didn't say she liked it. She took it off and placed it next to him. The simplest mistakes and breaches can cause the most lasting damage – she already knew that.

There was silence. The box was still in his pocket, and he took it out now and placed it beside the ring. He said, 'Are you giving your ring back to me?'

She still smiled, her eyes bright circles.

'Go on, put the ring in the box,' he said. 'Go on, I can sell it on Adverts.'

She put the ring in the box and immediately regretted it.

'I think I just want to go home now,' he said, standing, calling for the waitress.

'No!' she said. He paid the bill and left the restaurant.

She was aware of the waitress who'd taken their picture and the people at the nearby tables, watching with a quiet thrill. 'He's sick,' she said. 'Mal. Arrivederci!'

She took the half-drunk bottle of sparkling wine and ran out the door, fast as she could go, back into the past where this hadn't happened.

The little streets were lined with gift shops, ice-cream bars and families at tables, drinking beer, children playing, women in big spotty dresses. She found him at a small cove near the port and sat next to him by the lapping tide, where he said, 'Go back to Maeve, go back to your car salesman and your Ford Fiesta!' As he walked away, he turned and added, 'Just tell me how much you want per month for the baby.'

She sat on a rock by the stones and seaweed and dead crabs and bottle tops and glass shards. The day before, she'd bought a silk paisley dress from a beach stall, and the colours shone and quivered in the moonlight on the rocks from which her stomach ballooned out in relief. The waves rolled and trickled towards her fleshly form as she lay back whimpering and swollen, a starfish, a beached mermaid, a whale.

She sent emotional texts, and looked up flights home. She wrote home, fearing her mother had already spread the word all over. She sipped from the bottle, and admired her ring with a new poignancy. 'I love it,' she wrote to him. 'I love you!' She imagined a future alone, she thought about his innocent girls; and as she wept the baby kicked and punched her with affectionate reproof. She walked, unevenly, in flip-flops, back along the coast to their hotel room. Anyone who noticed her might have thought she was a woman in some serious and very private trouble. Nobody noticed and she was grateful for that.

Back in the hotel room, he had drunk every one of the bottles in the minibar: fernet, Cointreau, Limoncello, mastic, Bailey's Irish Cream, and had scattered the empties on the mattress which he'd separated off from hers. She said, 'Please!' but he raised both his arms in the air. He began to move his body with a sort of grace – he was dancing, mumbling Italian words. 'The song of the partisan soldier the moment he is captured by the fascists,' he said, silencing her with a hand as he moved his arms. '*Mi seppellire lassù in montagna. O bella ciao, bella ciao, bella ciao ciao ciao.*'

'If I die here, in the Resistance, you have to bury me up in the mountain' – later, he translated the dirge.

She wept, she retreated, back into her image reel, her phantasmagoria. She tossed around, squinted at her phone, looking up articles about foetal alcohol syndrome, the lifelong effects. She undertook a tragic image search, certain she had ruined her baby's life. She saw the future jeer back at them, inflicting hard hits, bad injuries, devastation they might not recover from. Her head hurt; the Aer Lingus website was incomprehensible. For hours she said blablabla to wounded Sergio – then fell asleep whispering to her child she would never neglect it. She would take care of it.

The next morning, she found him in the breakfast room. A young girl brought heart-shaped waffles with honey and walnuts, and as coffee was served, the night wore off. Something in the elements of the day began to collude. Their boat was booked. Days after their boat, their flight, with the girls, returning to live with their father in the country of their birth, in Ireland. She twirled the ruby around her finger, found pleasure in the touch of its smooth, flat surface on a finger already worn and lined. She took a picture of him, in sunglasses, with his golden suntan, about to bite into the round edge of his heart waffle. Only later it occurred to her he might have ordered these novelties in advance, only forgotten to cancel them.

In the picture, he half-smiles, reflecting the love he seems to see bursting before him. He is the one she adores most. This is the happiest she could feel. The happiness in the picture when she looks at it years later is real and true, not minding everything that went before, everything that came after. There it is captured, a moment of pure love held prisoner to an idea.

They left the hotel to take a boat home, returning first to the same bench overlooking the sea. Wearing his ring, she texted her mother to say it was back on with Sergio Fantasia.

The day was overcast and they embarked for the mainland on a boat thrashed by a vicious storm. Gifts followed, on return to Dublin: a bottle of real champagne (lost or stolen in the later house move), a six-cup silver Bialetti (burned apart mid-percolation the morning she forgot to put in water). The ring was small for her finger and became, in time, another subject they could not discuss.

Thirty-Five Weeks

It was the end of October and the baby was due in a month. She wrote a list of pregnancy symptoms that looked something like:

Thing 1
Thing 2
Thing 3
Thing 4

It went on until offending Thing 31, and the ink ran before her eyes until it was a black stream of Things.

When weekends came, Sergio met with Adverts dealers, picked out car seats, a Moses basket, bundle offers of muslin cloths and snowy babygros, a changing table and other systems and accessories she couldn't understand the need for. He went to a parking lot to pick up the second-hand buggy and its obfuscating component pieces. There was talk of a car seat, special car-seat fixers. Then he wept on the phone: 'Margarita you do not seem to be taking an interest in this new arrival. You know what, the other day, I had to put the clothes for the baby into the baby's drawer on my own!'

Thirty-Seven Weeks

The baby was due in three weeks, and it was time to move in with the widower and his children. In her flat, she emptied cupboards and filled boxes of her things to vacate her room for the new tenant. As she packed up her wardrobe, Margaret's father arrived with a selection of his tools and spent the afternoon patching up the hole in the wall made by Sergio's fist on the night that he'd found out about the thing with the Salesman.

'It was so strange,' she told her father as he worked. 'The corner of a table I was carrying just crashed into the wall. It was so heavy, the plastering chipped off. Strange.'

Margaret's father made no comment; he hadn't asked in the first place.

'Not perfect,' he said, packing up his tools, 'another coat of paint might do it, or they could hang a mirror there.'

Sergio loaded all the boxes in his car where Giorgia and Angelica sat bored and restless, with new Furbys. The last of her possessions were stuffed into the basket of her bike, and bangers went off and bonfire smoke cooked up the air as she pushed down Rathdown Road into Grangegorman, and back up the hill, through Stoneybatter, over the James Joyce Bridge and up through the old Viking city that she loved. She arrived, breathless, to her lover and his daughters sitting around the table, next to welcome pictures and a square confection made from a Betty Crocker brownie mix, decorated with jellies, or holes where the jellies had been picked off.

Thirty-Eight Weeks

The day Margaret fell on top of herself going past Stephen's Green, ripping her Italian tights, cutting her knees and being helped up by strangers, was the same day a memorial for the girls' mother was held in the local parish hall. She was upset, hooked up to a trace monitor in Holles Street, that she couldn't possibly make it to the memorial. What never occurred to her was that she might not be wanted there. If it had occurred to her that a congregation of their late mothers' friends might feel uncomfortable meeting a new woman at the church, a woman who was heavily pregnant – or worse, that they might be a little titillated by the scandal of her presence

– it was only a distant rustle of sense that she didn't hear, not then. It didn't figure that a new woman, new baby, a twinkling ruby, could cause intrigue. That she and Sergio might be eating those very funeral baked meats that furnished forth the wedding table, as Hamlet put it in her English Leaving Certificate textbook. It didn't occur to her that she might not be welcome generally, at this occasion or in that wider community, ever again, nor he, nor their children. That their new life was a transgression, and they would have to make it on their own from now on.

Sergio rearranged his house, cleared out half his wardrobe, his wife's clothes and boots and French cosmetics. In the mornings, he delivered coffee to Margaret's bedside. He did her laundry and made salads. He gave her a special padded gadget for controlling backache, and the application form for her health-insurance policy, she just had to add her PPS number.

Wedding pictures were all taken down. Boxes of his wife's things were brought to the church hall to divide among her friends, the rest carried out to charity shops. Her bronze and orange costume jewellery, which hung by the door the first time Margaret slept in their bedroom, was moved elsewhere. Three recipe books were kept, all in Italian, and some gadgets: Magimix, Nutribullet. So was the subscription to the Irish fashion magazine that came through their letter box every month. Did Margaret want to keep the subscription? She did, she decided, so over her morning coffee up in bed while he went off to work she read about feasting ideas and inspirational Irish women in business, and finding happiness post-divorce. In the afternoons she hid from the children, and she could not look inside the tiny room intended for the baby.

At thirty-nine weeks, she found she was wandering Arnotts department store. She'd been told your feet get cold when giving birth so she bought three pairs of luxury purple knitted socks, and a few months' supply of tights, Wolford and Falke. On the way out, she passed the kids' and babywear and paused. She fondled a miniature velour babygro, then bought three, in white, blue and lemon yellow, thirty-eight euro each. She thought, if I get four more babygros that's one for each day of the week and we'll be set to go.

Thirty-Nine Weeks
The fridge was stacked with supermarket produce. Birth contraptions loomed inside a special box. She reread her hospital bag list, which went something like:

> Item 1
> Item 2
> Item 3

Right up to unnecessary Item 18.

She stopped, dismayed, at one item she'd been recommended to pack. Size 0 nappies. She could hardly stand without backpain, or eat an apple without her gums bleeding. There were nappies of different sizes? More to the point, she was expected to know about this today? How would she fit everything into her new season StorkSak? At that moment, she didn't find it fair she had to pack for someone other than herself. She read the list again. Size 0 nappies, barrier cream and WaterWipes. It was all a source of disquiet.

Time edged forwards and then seemingly backwards and got stuck. One night Sergio asked would she mind taking the children to Cheeky Monkey's Jungle

Castle in Tallaght for a birthday party in the morning. They talked in raised voices until eventually the words projectiled from her mouth: 'You think I'm a free child-care package?' 'I wouldn't trust you with it!' he returned.

That night she packed a different kind of bag and said that she was going to live with her parents. She got as far as the car door then came back and went to bed.

Forty Weeks

On her due date, there was no baby, just some lightning sensations that made her feel she would give birth on the side of the street. On Dame Street, outside Gino's Gelato parlour, she doubled herself into a wall. The moment passed. She went to the theatre to review an Oscar Wilde play and also to show off her bountiful new figure. With this watermelon up her dress, she felt rare and extravagant, as if she had rented out some wildly overpriced couture ballgown, and would never be this special and majestic again. The gumption of having something that enormous stowed inside her body, the blazing fertility and voluptuousness of the whole picture, was almost too exciting to contemplate.

As she found her way to seat E15, the artistic director of the theatre boomed across the auditorium, 'Christ almighty, nothing to do with me, is it?' His row of grey-haired friends looked up, laughing nervously. Margaret laughed, and anyone who noticed her there on display would have picked up only her sweet agreeable nature.

That week she wrote her last column, then walked around department stores. She bought bad Christmas gifts and weird self-gifts – two repulsive faux-fur blankets that slid around the house for years afterwards. She used to stuff them behind doors, thinking who let these beastly things in here? Where was I when I consented to buy these?

Forty-One Weeks Plus Two

Another Sunday. She was splayed out on a bench in the playground while Sergio went off to get coffee and scones. The two girls ran around on stalky legs, pony-tails flying, and back to Margaret for handfuls of nuts and raisins. Margaret took out her notebook.

They weren't like the girls in playgrounds who sat on swings or went down the slides beaming at their parents. They hid in bushes, they disappeared up trees. Here, at least, they let it all fly out. Playgrounds, Margaret thought, wrapping her maternity parka around her vastness. They really are the answer to everything. She thought about how much she admired Sergio for having got her this warm coat, second-hand. He was so ethical. She worried, huddled there. The baby was a week overdue and each morning she would wake and ask herself, will I die today? She worried, looking at the other babies with their mothers in the park, because she didn't find the babies at all cute. What lack of human feeling did this point to? She had no love for what she was expecting.

A shout came, interrupting her important reverie, and both girls ran towards her, one holding out her arm. Giorgia with a cut. Drops of blood fell on the tarmac. And they were standing at the boot of the car while the girl said, 'No Papa!' and her father barked orders for first aid, then stuffed his family in their seats, one girl's arm bound in toilet roll.

'What happened? What happened?' Angelica kept repeating, while the car jumped. Sergio drove in the bus lanes and broke red lights. He sped through town, through Merrion Square and Margaret glimpsed the imposing redbrick facade of the National Maternity Hospital. Her hospital flashed by and they carried on and crossed the river to the children's hospital.

They spent the rest of the day in A&E, filling forms and visiting the vending machine. Befriending other children, trying not to look at the open cuts of a boy in football shorts. Trying not to stare at the swaddled baby whose face was blue.

A short film called *Frozen Fever* played above the seats and the sound was tinny. When the film ended, it started again. Kids watched *Frozen Fever* or other things on phones, or cried, and the baby kicked and pushed its weight. She thought: it's just today, right? Spending all your time with kids. Some part of her was well aware this was their destiny. Accidents, and blood, and pens attached with string, crisps and sweets, stitches, dressings, and no dinner waiting back at home. And little girls pulling at her, and women in scrubs, asking, 'How did it happen?'

What happened was the girl had scaled the branches of a hundred-year-old tree. Something gave, a bough had snapped, a piece of broken bark drove a gash into her wrist. What happened was unsupervised.

That night, alone again, she returned to the short story she was working on, the one about the dissipated hopes, and she finished the whole thing, then sent it off in wakeful exhaustion. She didn't know anything about anything. Who her friends were, or her family, how to take care of a baby. She didn't know her story would meet with a kind rejection, the first of seven from that magazine alone, and she fell very deep asleep.

Maternity Benefit

The rocking chair he brought down from the attic was a cream colour, with fabric ribbed upholstery and matching footrest. I wouldn't have picked it out myself. Its function was for feeding babies, with a label that read 'Easy Dream', and I used to sit there with my novel, reading, or more likely thinking about someone I could text, or send a picture to. Then back to the book. The intention was completion, was improvement, so that the book – one of the great works of Russian literature everyone should read – might join the bookshelf I was working on creating in the living room belonging to another family, now my own.

The girls would slide into the living room holding up their leggy dolls, chant, 'Hi!' and rush on through the glass-paned door into the kitchen where their minder would be cleaning up, earphones in. The younger girl would stand, and she would stare at me, just waiting to be asked a question; the older girl would pull her away, saying, 'Stop disturbing her!' They were boisterous and affectionate. They weren't to understand what had just happened, they couldn't object to such an imposition as this woman parked here in their living room, drinking raspberry-leaf tea, reading literature and *Dr Spock* the tenth edition.

One time, playing with pink Lego at the fireside, Giorgia asked me if I'd like to be their new mother, since they didn't have a mother now.

The time I told her I was pregnant she ran, crying, from the room.

—

The house was in the suburbs, and I had no friends out there and hadn't yet discovered any coffee shops. The only thing to do in this alarming situation was to make sure to leave the house before the girls were due in from school. It was my primary objective on languid winter mornings when I sat by the window with my stack of books and my hand upon my stomach counting baby's kicks. To unlock the front door and get out of there – and on Tuesdays, when my maternity benefit came in and fattened up the digits in my bank account, I would be straight onto the tram to do my messages in town. I got the state payment, a respectable wage, if someone other than you paid for everything, and there was nothing that fulfilled me quite so much as going into town to do my messages.

I would wrap up warm and stagger to the tram stop, thinking about shops and cafés and the big department stores that engorged their lonely denizens from lipstick counters up to deep corridors of fragranced bathrooms. Everybody says we should take care of ourselves. The tram would shoot off into town and always, sitting, with my stomach like a basketball perched on my lap, and my book open on the basketball, half-watching as the houses and the trees swept past the carriage window, I could feel peace and freedom returning to my bones.

—

It was getting close to Christmas and the baby was ten days overdue. At Charlemont a fresh gust of freezing air blew in and a woman grabbed a seat rail, reversed her pram, and parked it between us. She wore a thin black jacket over jeans, black boots, and on her jeans I noticed a tiny reddish stain.

'Bitter. Isn't it?' She squinted at me. 'How many months? Nine?'

'More like ten months actually.'

'First baby? Yeah. Hell isn't it. Weight of it. My joints are smashed around the pelvis. Destroyed. Weight of it. Where are you having yours?'

I had hoped to finish all *The Idiot* before the birth and you could do twenty pages on a journey, but now I marked my page and shut the book. 'Holles Street. How old is your baby?'

Her baby boy was fast asleep, clamped with a soother, face watery under his plastic transparent rain cover.

'Eight months – should only be six months. The two boys were premature.'

'You have twins?'

'Two months early, four weeks in intensive care.' I put my book back in my bag and sat right up to try to understand her; she was talking about organs. Lungs, the baby. Kidneys. 'Waters broke,' she said. 'And I went into labour on the kitchen floor.' She continued – fire brigade. Hospital. 'Five litres of blood,' – my hand went to my stomach. 'The labour. Six midwives. Theatre. Four obstetricians, four of them, gloving up.' I wasn't following. Organs again – kidneys, lungs. Some condition – medical terminology. How she'd tried to tell the doctors all along, but none of them – not one of them – and then. Infection.

'Here,' – she drew a line along her concave stomach. 'The baby,' she said, and raised three fingers. 'Three infections.'

Prince Myshkin had only just arrived in St Petersburg and I was getting confused between Natasha and Anastasia, but then again. Maybe it did no one any harm that she should talk, and I should nod and seem to listen, if it helped her to unpack it all. We only had three stops to go.

'Got the tubes tied now. No more heartbreak,' she said, shaking her head. 'No more heartbreak.' I nodded, thinking that I understood her.

'He seems to be doing great though?' I didn't really think this, looking at the sleeping boy consumed by his blue soother.

'Better than me,' the woman said, and I laughed, but she wasn't being funny. She had a distracted air, as if what she was saying didn't really matter all that much. Her eyes fluttered around, half-open, and she kept rooting around in her bag and zips. She tied up her long brown hair, looked out, scribbled with her finger in the window fog. A tiny tattoo on her wrist, a red love heart, speared with an arrow. She rummaged again, pulled out a teddy with a rattle through the stomach, and an empty bottle of Coke.

'We're in accommodation on the Rathmines Road,' she said. 'It's calm enough, it's not degrading anyway.' She was talking then about her family. Father, granny, auntie. Older children, twelve and fourteen, they live with their father – he lives in Wexford. I said, 'Oh!' because to live apart from your own baby's father sounded like a tragedy to me then.

'I wish you every bit of luck,' she said. 'But you have to expect things to go wrong for you in this filthy world. It's worse than ever now. No one cares. If you don't take care of yourself then no one else will in this filthy world.'

I couldn't tell her with any certainty that there were people who cared so I thought to change the subject.

'How is your other twin getting on?'

'He's dead.'

Of course.

'I'm sorry – I didn't understand.'

She nodded. 'The way I see it, at least one of them was spared this filthy world we're in. This is ours. Good luck, now. I hope it all goes well for you in the hospital.'

We were at O'Connell–GPO. The woman swung around and she was gone, one baby boy still fast asleep under the plastic, jostling up and down. The doors closed and the tram moved away.

—

It had been going on about a day when I was sent home to endure the violence in the comfort of my home. 'You're not in labour,' a midwife had said, and back home I crawled under the duvet. Pain is such a dark and private thing. At first I thought I should describe it – thought that I deserved that honour, somehow. But then, has anybody asked? They haven't asked.

The night went by, twisting up the covers. I was aware of some few things – the baby's father texting on his phone, the winter rain that flung itself against the glass. Most things didn't matter. The Dublin Mountains behind the house, the fullness of the moon. The filthy world – none of that came near my thoughts. Only an obscene ritual pain. I wore, I know for sure, an out-sized green embroidered nightdress given to me by the baby's *nonna*, and I lay writhing in this costume until I could bear no more. I barged into the bathroom, held the cool enamel of the sink against my burning cheek and wailed – caught sight of myself. A savage creature in the mirror. Hysteria patient. Electrocuted cat.

I ran a bath and poured in all the Epsom Salts, upturned the bucket and lurched in. The waves of anguish got a good bit worse immersed in all this luxury. And as I sank down clutching this catastrophe inside my stomach I thought, if only somebody had told me.

—

Some weeks before, when the basketball had got so big that I'd become a little bit unnerved, and very puzzled, about how it would get back out, I sat my mother down to interview her about the subject of her births. Jen, the redheaded businesswoman who put on the two-day Empowering Birth workshop in the Radisson, had encouraged all of us to talk 'or even interview!' our mothers on the subject – 'Because it's the most incredible experience! We need to learn from family and compare notes more, to normalise this.'

She won't like that, I thought. But the interview went ahead, at the little kitchen table in my flat. My mother glanced around her, dug the spoon into the sugar in the sugar bowl, played with her rings. I don't know that she liked being detained in such a sudden intimacy. When I said, 'So, could you tell me how it was for you?' she looked dejected, said: 'Oh, I don't really want to get into it right now.'

'But,' I said, 'it is kind of the whole reason for this interview.' She said there were other things that she could talk about, her life was much more interesting than just being a mother.

'What could you talk about?' I asked.

'I like literature,' she said. 'I love going to the library, finding new authors.'

'What else?'

'I like finding new recipes.'

'You never cook,' I said.

'True,' she said. 'I don't really cook anymore.'

'It's too much trouble, isn't it?'

'It's a lot of trouble, but you still have to put a meal together sometimes, otherwise you spend so much money—' We chatted informally for a few minutes, and I folded up the piece of paper I'd intended to have filled with my research.

'Oh, look, I thought all my babies were just gorgeous,' she said suddenly.

—

In a café at the very end, Basketball monumental, a lady in a furry parka came over to my table to wish me well. A lock of hair above her forehead was pulled back with a Hello Kitty hair clip – I guess she couldn't find another hair clip before she left her house. She came over and she said, her eyes all screwy: 'You know, it's going to really hurt. I'm only telling you that now, so that you know. Because like, no one told me.' She was the only one who said a thing, and I thought she was a madwoman.

Strange, not to know what you are in for – but I can't imagine you would want to go ahead with it then, would you? On such a lonely expedition. Even afterwards, when the job was done, I said to a midwife, 'AND WHAT THE HELL WAS THAT?' and she grinned and said: 'It's kind of like the best-kept secret, isn't it?' 'Never doing that again anyway!' I told her, and she said, 'Famous last words.' We chuckled, shook our heads, and in some realm I sealed my lips. I understood the pact, and meant to keep to it – they had my word.

—

Out of the bath, on the side of the bed, shivering took hold. We put maternity leggings on, leg by leg, under the minty-coloured nightdress, which blew around and flapped, and the turquoise ribbons criss-crossed at the neckline kept getting twisted in my fingers.

Then the winter coat. Then a warm fleece blanket around my winter coat. The stairs, then the front door, blasts of cold. I clutched onto the wing mirror while the baby's father scalded ice from off the car window and then, my teeth began to chatter. The teeth lost all control and chattered grittily. It was not nice, this, not at all nice – to be bound in blankets in the back seat of his car, clutching my hospital file, the road bumping Basketball around and around – then so much more unpleasant, more fundamentally unfair that I had to get out, and walk down the road, because I had to stop on the street corner, double over, and there was a man with a tabloid, and a lady walking home from work or something – was it Friday, Saturday? – in high-heeled boots. Everything continuing as normal.

—

At the hospital, a slight grey-haired security guard looked in my eyes, gauging my fitness for admission to his nightclub.

'How are you my dear?' the security guard asked.

'Not so good,' I said.

'Doesn't look like it,' he said. 'We'll get you sorted now.'

He glanced behind my shoulder.

'Sorry buddy – you'll have to wait until she calls you.'

He handed each of us a paper mask and I took a clipboard with a pen attached, and filled out the form, didn't miss a single letter or misspell a name, with the bottom half of my body slowly unhinging from the rest as the wall supported me.

'Are you OK?' the smiley woman at reception asked.

'Yes,' I said, handing her my hospital file with all the information. The receptionist nodded. Good, I thought, she's going to leave me alone now, but she came out from behind the desk and placed a sign there saying 'CLOSED'. She offered me an arm. I said, 'Thank you very much, I'm good from here,' but she remained beside me. We strolled down the corridor together, then stood outside the elevator waiting to go up.

'So do you know what you're having?' the nice woman asked.

'No idea.'

'The surprise is the best though, isn't it?'

'I wouldn't have it any other way.'

We got into the tiny wood-floored lift.

'Do you have children yourself?' I asked.

'Oh yes, but they're nearly grown now.'

'Oh! Boys or girls?'

'One of each!' Look how capable of conversation I was – I asked her about each of them – the son was studying accountancy and the daughter was in digital marketing; she had her first job interview on Monday, over there with LinkedIn.

'LinkedIn, that would be a very good job.'

'It would, it would, so fingers crossed now. She's very nervous. And of course, she can't find anything to wear. And of course, it's all my fault!'

'Oho!' Another death grip came around me, and I felt that I should hide. That I had done something embarrassing and should hide from the respectable people now.

'It's true. Boys will wreck your house, girls will wreck your head!' she said.

'HaHA!'

The lift opened and the woman pointed to a chair on which I buckled, folded and disintegrated, clutching Basketball.

—

My mum phoned me up, a few nights after our attempted interview. She was breathless and excitable and I knew she had been building towards this phone call. She often processed her concerns at night time. She said: 'I am sorry I wasn't helpful when you asked about childbirth but all you need to know is do your exercises and don't listen to scary stories. And do you think that you could try to just take each moment at a time? And enjoy it. Just enjoy it. Babies are gorgeous creatures. Having a baby is a very enlightening experience, women are very lucky when they get to do it.'

—

A narrow corridor unfurled, grey and hazardous in scale. 'Try walk up and down that corridor,' a midwife said. 'Go on, keep it moving.' I took one step. A Christmas tree sprang out from the walls, about halfway down, drunk with coloured lights and decorations. I was very feeble now but all I had to do was reach the tree. I focused on the tree, thinking, go on, keep going, it's not so far. My feet, I noticed, were bound in purple knitted slippers I had never seen before; who had bound my feet in purple knitted slippers? The corridor swam. Lights and baubles shone. I reached out, and touched the spiky ferns, then turned around. I slid down a wall. The pieces of mosaic on the floor blew up and scattered as the darkness overtook me.

—

A cellophane-wrapped sandwich selection came and a pot of tea, gone cold before I got to touch it. I'd seen cholera wards before, in war films, seen military hospitals in epic films. So I had some idea how to contemplate our situation, listening to the women thudding through the night. Sometimes a woman moaned, or vomited. Sometimes she wept.

The curtain opened, and a stolid midwife with a drifting eye came forth. She had an accent, German, and her hands were soft and caring. She was here to give me some injection – she was here to tell me it was time. It's not what she suggested.

'Why don't you go to the toilet again,' she suggested.

'I don't want to.'

Her head moved and her mouth moved.

It was a long walk towards the toilet, an old toilet, much overused. When it came the pain was dazzling, and to have brought it on myself. This was so unwise. So typical of me really. First to get myself in all the trouble. Now to be unable to cope with it, to end up beached here, writhing in a toilet. And the haemorrhoids, the blistering piles – 'I can't,' I told this midwife, poking out my head again – 'I can't go into that toilet anymore.' I would, I felt, burst every haemorrhoid vessel like a bunch of grapes becoming wine.

—

But when it was quiet, and sometimes, a stillness and a quiet came, you could hear the hearts of all the other babies on the ward, beating on the monitors. Tick, tick, tick, beat the hearts of all the little babies waiting to be born into this world.

—

After a day or two I became aware of quiet mumbling from the next compartment. It was a woman on the phone, describing her kidney infection. She had three weeks to go but the way it was, she might as well stay in. She was saying goodnight to her children, wishing them a good weekend, telling them she loved them – but she needed rest now, she was staying in the hospital, until the baby came.

A midwife or a nurse or doctor came in.

'So you're all good from our side,' the voice said.

'No I don't think so,' the woman said. She didn't feel at all well here – or here.

'I think the rest would do me good,' she said. A little time passed. The midwife or the doctor came again, pulled back the curtain and examined the woman again.

'Your urine's clear, and that blood pressure is back down, so I don't see any reason why you can't get home today.'

'I've only three weeks left.'

'But sure you're ready to go home.'

'Wouldn't it be just as well if I stayed here though, I can't walk, I can't move.'

There was silence. 'We're going to get you home now.'

'But I've ordered shepherd's pie. I've only three weeks left.'

—

Hearts were beating through the ward and I was curled up on the spongey mattress with a pair of headphones, listening to woodland sounds; sounds of crickets, rustling, the lulling hoots of owls. The opioid injection had taken effect. Now I became aware of texting on the chair beside the bed – rapid texting – 'Who are you texting? You've been on that phone all night.' I took the phone from him and scrolled back through the chat, to read a long block paragraph – 'How much longer do you think you are going to be? The girls are very badly behaved here. They won't stop hiding. Giorgia bit my finger. They have already broken a lamp and two glasses. They are out of control.'

Their minder. I read the next message.

'We will need to discuss please how much you will pay me – I am working around the clock – ' the letters froze, the screen webbed, picture shattered, and I began to die again.

Then another tray came – green apple, diet yoghurt, and an iced bun with a glacé cherry on the top.

—

After all of it was over, I wrote a letter of complaint to Jen, facilitator of the Empowering Birth workshop. During the workshop we equipped ourselves with knowledge, we studied diagrams of the baby in the womb, we learned about breathing exercises, meditation, mantras and the hypnobirthing way. We watched footage of a woman in the 1970s with her vagina slowly peeling open. The camera pans away as the baby's crown emerges in one bulging line and the woman, who is whimpering, then breathes her baby into being. None of us could hold back tears. And Jen held a medical baby doll while we each birthed our own invisible baby from between our legs.

'Dear Jen,' I wrote, from the sheet drenched with turning milk on which the baby woke each morning. 'I may be too late to send feedback on the workshop but

I wanted to be as honest as possible. I for one found the labour and birth a violent and miserable experience. I'm not saying I wasn't happy in the end but felt we could have been forewarned and therefore better prepared for what lay out there, which was basically a violent and miserable—' I put a lot of thought into the letter. She never replied.

—

'The chaplain's here,' a midwife said, beyond the curtain. 'If anyone would like a blessing. Ladies, girls, the chaplain.' I pulled back the curtain and climbed out of bed. 'I would,' I said, and I stood before a kindly faced emissary in a dog collar, saying nothing, just opening my heart to him. With melting features I made every effort to convey all my distress.

'I ask God to protect you, and lalala, and lalala—' he said. He had a chiding look of empathy, delivering his blessing. 'That your pain will be over and your baby will be well and healthy lalala—' I bowed, self-conscious, in my frothy nightdress, as this boyish priest criss-crossed my forehead. Wishing he would free me from this deathbed, or boarding-school dormitory, wherever it was we'd ended up.

—

In the reaches of the night I must have undergone a further cervical exam because this time there was a top result. 'Congratulations, come with me,' said a midwife, tall, willowy and seasoned – no. I will not sit here and describe a single other midwife.

The delivery room was big and airy with a swaying tropical dimension. There was a great big bathtub lit with neon pink, and a photographic mural of sunlit waves swishing, horizon and puffy-clouded bright blue sky. Once lifted to the bed, and hooked up to new monitors, a tube was brought to my lips, attached to a cylinder. 'Now suck, that's right,' said the glowering midwife, watching me. I held the tube and drank back its contents. My head was bathed in lightness. Definitely what the doctor ordered and much more. I giggled. Looked at my accomplice. 'Have you ever tried it? It's not so bad, it's just like Prosecco at a wedding, on an empty stomach? Maybe you should try some? Wow, what a fabulous room!' I gazed around the flashing discotheque. Music poured out from a speaker, dry ice – who could tell. 'So, what made you interested in midwifery?' Here we were, conversing away. All of this was marvellous, the bed, the water and the waves, the feeling. Midwives, my fast friends. Though maybe not all that good. It was too much, I'd overdosed. The baby lurched within, descending horribly. I grabbed the air and gobbled up some more, it raced to my head, but I didn't like it anymore. The whole hallucination. At least no one could see me now.

—

I know not everyone gets out of here alive. The midwives walked the corridor, a baby screamed, a woman faintly moaned, and I remembered the story of the woman sometime in the 1950s, in this hospital. Maybe on this corridor. Her baby girl didn't survive. Stillborn. Heartbreak. The mother lay in her bed crying. The midwife, intending to console her, went out of the room and came back with a live and screaming baby, someone else's baby, and put it in the grieving mother's arms. Minutes later, she took away that baby too.

—

'Are you ready?' the midwife asked.

'I don't know what you mean.'

'I mean, do you want to have the baby now, or not?' she asked.

I was on the bed again, nightdress around my hips.

'I don't think I can get it out.'

She leaned over my face. 'You can. But you have to do what I say. So do you want to go ahead?'

I thought about it.

'If you think you can get it out then I do.'

She rolled up her sleeves, if she had sleeves. 'Right, I'll tell you what to do and you'll have the baby.'

'OK.'

'Now pass me this leg.'

I pointed my toe at her. She bent my knee and held the calf into her stomach.

'Now pass me the other leg,' she said. 'And put your chin into your chest!'

—

The problem was, with every one of these, I gave up some of the way through. Got bored, moved onto something else. The problem with the stories, letters home, or vanity projects – the problem was the loss of interest in the task at hand. The loss of spark. The light of momentary cleverness would go out, and everything went drab.

Late-afternoon haze, apathy, weakness, laziness, often dread. Occasional weeping. Just a few times, thoughts of jumping out the window. The thing was, no one ever asked me to say any of this. This was uncalled for. Often sleep overcame me as I sat clacking at the keys, and silence, deep grey dissolving thoughts. Why inflict more stuff upon the world, more pages full of words? Sleep lulled me, sleep knocked me out – Morpheus flew in and punched me in the head, I fell unconscious. It was bliss – and when I awoke I moved onto other things and quit those too. Years passed like this, babies were born and people died before their time, ice caps melted at alarming rates, and I turned away.

—

'Do you want to have this baby?' The midwife was trying not to show her profound annoyance.

'I can't. I just feel like I don't want to. I'm fighting the urge.'

'You are fighting the urge, I can see that.'

'It's too difficult.'

She eyed me, from the end of the bed, as if she had never come upon such laziness and lack of will. As if I was the first woman she had ever met that was so impudent as to refuse to do this.

'Right, come on, let's go.'

'I'm sorry but I'm just too tired now.'

—

It always seemed so strange how everything went on as normal afterwards. After we brought the baby home, it was left unmentioned, everything. I gazed into the walls of kitchens, coffee shops, gazed cross-eyed in a trance, into the rich deep ripples of my big adventure story, waiting for the moment I could bring it into conversation, impress friends and family with my heroic deeds. But I couldn't find a way. What a baffling and exciting thing. That one day you can be one, the next day two. The opposite of death, when one day you are one and then you are none. I thought so anyway. I lay in bed, while the baby slept, with my abandoned novels on the nightstand, and the girls running up the stairs, the girls crying about different things, and I tried my best to recollect it all. I'd been shaken up, destroyed. I'd been flattened by a bus and then returned to shape, but it was too much. Too much to accommodate, in the everyday. It had to be set aside. Forgotten, not exactly. But left aside and tactfully preserved.

—

The midwife was ordering me around, clutching at a couple of my limbs. I squeezed my body. We all waited, clenched. And something. Something hard and round came bruising down and this here was possibly the moment we had all been waiting for – stand back, brace yourself. We waited. But whatever living thing had made its way up to the surface just went back inside. The moment passed. What a relief not having to complete the awful task. But she still held a leg – he held another leg, the baby's father. All this time he never left my side, and yet I had no idea who he was.

It came gripping me again and squeezing at my contents, and this time a scream accompanied the effort.

It was too loud, but the scream came, very hard, until all the life expired from my lungs. Something had got out so far it didn't want to go back in. It had to be that it was over. I had to scream again. Out came something. Out it came in one vile force of will, then somehow, its own powerful will, helping me at last.

The midwife brandished the baby at me.

'Did you see what you got! Did you see!'

But it couldn't be the end. I should suffer more. Now I had come this far, imagine what I would be able for.

The baby was in my arms. The baby shivered, with tiny hot red palms waving in the air, its eyes creased shut.

'Is it a?' I said. 'Is it?' I couldn't say words.

'Boy, yes!' She cheered.

The baby softly cried. The baby shivered, crying, its miniscule palms waving in the air, its eyes creased shut. I cradled the baby. One black eye opened, and then slowly, glued by its first long sleep, the other. We gazed into one another's eyes like strangers, reunited.

—

Happiness was a problem. Happiness was uncontrolled. It's unseemly to be this happy in the world – I knew I should tone it down, but how. Standing up was transformational – to be so light again. Surely I should not disclose how happy I now was – it was so excessive.

'You go off and take a hot shower now,' the midwife said.

I charged into the shower and pulled off my bloodied rags, and here we have a person who has entirely relinquished all control of how she carries on. I washed until the water ran from red to crystal clear down the plughole and I would have stood there in the spray but I couldn't wait to get my hands on it again, the baby. I burst back in. Midwives were coming in and out to take a look at what we had. A midwife, busying with paperwork, asking my permission for this thing or that. Everything was good and everyone was legendary. The baby had black hair, a rosebud mouth, a lifetime had just passed.

'That baby's a little genius,' the midwife said, watching how he latched.

'Isn't she just gorgeous,' another midwife said.

'She?' I said. 'Didn't you say it was a boy?'

'Yes, and this one's a girl. This is fiction.'

'Can you just do that?' It was all so strange.

'She's just gorgeous,' the midwife said again.

'Oh, aren't they all,' I said, wanting to be modest.

She gave me a confiding look and leaned in.

'Well you do get the odd ugly one.' She chuckled. 'But you can't say it. No, you can't say it.'

—

The first night, a Friday, Saturday or a Sunday night, the baby lay swaddled in a blanket, behind the glass rocker, sleeping soundly as if nothing in particular had happened earlier. I lay looking at the baby on the narrow bed, taking pictures, looking at the pictures, sending pictures. I tried to sleep, amazed, absorbed, thrumming with a happiness too great to suppress. Billowing, vacant thoughts passed in and out of me. I pressed my nose up to the glass, and I laughed aloud and sat up and counted on my fingers. I was thirty-two years of age. I could have at least six more before I even got to forty, and what if there were twins?

For an hour, I slept. And in the early dawn the trolley woke me, jangling down the hall, with a woman calling, 'Tea or coffee, boiled egg, porridge, or toast!'

—

In the afternoon a voice called from behind the curtain, and I sat up. The midwife said that it was almost time to go.

'It's what?'

'It's time for you to go now,' she repeated. 'We are going to discharge you.'

I said: 'My tea is coming. I need an hour. Two hours – it will take that long to get the baby's dad in here.'

'He's here already,' she told me smiling.

'But, I ordered lunch,' I said.

'You're going home now shortly.' The blue curtain drew back all the way and there he was, pressing clothes into the suitcase, readying the car seat.

He was packing them all wrong, the miniature vests and starry babygros and giant underpants, sprays, creams and sachets, and out thudded to the floor *The Idiot* by Fyodor Dostoevsky, the way I remember it.

—

He pushed the pram, I ran behind him down the corridor with the midwife; she held my file, the pages flapping in the breeze. Every few seconds, she stopped, threw her head back with a devious look.

'This guy too?' she said. 'Sheesh, you know how to pick 'em don't you.'

'Oh no, I've said too much,' I said, running to keep up. 'No one asked me and I said it anyway.'

'But have you caused offence?' she asked. 'Have you offended anybody?'

'Only possibly in what I didn't think to say. But it's too late for all of that now. I've answered all the questions I was able. Because what is fiction, what are words and paragraphs but an avalanche of answers to the questions no one asked?'

We got the baby safely in the car; the midwife did my seatbelt and blew me a kiss goodbye.

—

Pretty soon the rocking chair had coffee stains, and butter stains and pen scratches on the pristine cover. I sat and fed the baby, trying not to be bothered by the two girls, prancing in and out of rooms, or crying over something. Their father intervened – the girls would have to knock. They were kept out of rooms, given iPads, ice lollies, Christmas presents. The older girl, she still cried, and I couldn't shut away the sound. A lazy, wandering, high-pitched wail poured through the walls. They would be sent up to their beds if they wanted to behave like that. This arrangement suited me, because I could read my book and stare at the baby – and because there was another story, one I didn't hear until too late – the story about the girls, tripping into rooms, looking for their mother. They couldn't find her anywhere. They found another mother in the Easy Dream cream rocking chair where their own mother had once sat nursing each of them. Heartbreak. Another soft and bleary mother and her baby got the chair.

My Mistake

A few years ago my husband recommended me for a job in his company, and I thought it would be fun, so on certain mornings a woman named Rosaleen would ring me for a chat.

'Hello,' Rosaleen would say quietly. 'Free for the chat?'

'Yes, hi, hello.'

Rosaleen was a senior director in the firm, and these were scheduled chats, but I was always unprepared, running from a room, looking for a pen, or out in the rain, pushing the baby in the pram. Rosaleen had a terse and serious manner that unwound with listless expectation when my turn came to speak. I would say something, and she would wait for me to say something better. Rosaleen savoured a pause. The line burned with a shared misgiving even as she made me an astounding offer of employment.

'That's the job. So you'll want to fix your rate with me,' she said. 'You will be paid weekly. You will accrue annual leave. You will be entitled to holiday pay. You can have your own desk here, or you can work from home, it's whatever you want. Some weeks you will work thirty hours. Other weeks you'll do nothing at all, it's whatever you want.'

Whatever I wanted – anything at all. I'd never really worked before, never had a boss. For years, sitting at some rented salvaged desks in run-down buildings, I'd wanted a real office and colleagues. I wanted work trips, meetings over sandwich platters, late-night deadlines, I wanted to drink a lot of coffee. To spend the day in a heated room, and go to a bathroom that was clean.

It was a big branch of a big consultancy firm – say no more. Big enough to get lost inside, and go unnoticed, I presumed. My salary was fixed with a flat and awkward bravado.

Rosaleen said: 'Your rate, then,' and a figure dropped from my mouth.

'Hmmm. I'm gonna need to bring that down.'

Another figure wilted on the line between us.

'Fine by me. Welcome on board.'

I was due to begin on the first of October.

On the first of September, Rosaleen phoned.

'Where are you? When are you coming in?'

'I'm due to start on the first of October.'

'It's supposed to be today.'

'Oh, really. Let me check my calendar.' I moved the baby off my knee and stared into confusion on a screen.

Neither of us claimed responsibility for the mistake, but I reassured Rosaleen. I would see her on the first of

October and, in the meantime, I would review all the documents and make my comments. 'I look forward to that, you know we really *need* you,' she said, before she hung up. What I could not forget was the way she said that word need. Longingly she said it.

The night before the first day, I tidied the children's bedrooms by way of preparation for my new life. I dug out the iron and ironing board, and pressed my favourite shirt and my best skirt into neat envelopes, then placed this raiment on a chair before lying down to sleep. My sister Lisa who stopped work to raise her kids had said something like: 'If ever you start getting down about having to do work just think to yourself, *Cha-ching*.'

That first day, my husband drove us into work in rush-hour traffic. I was queasy with excitement as we walked from the car park, through the office plaza and spinning doors, into the shining, toffee-coloured foyer that seemed so remote and out of the way.

In the lift, I brushed my hair one last time and checked my reflection. I thought I looked pristine. If my tights did have one ladder, it was up the back of my leg and nobody would be able to tell. It was ten minutes to nine – we were almost too punctual. My husband let us through with his key card, walked me down rows and rows of matte-white desks to a window where a woman in black sat curled into a screen: Rosaleen.

Rosaleen stood and tilted her head with a slight smile and said: 'Oh.' She said oh in syllables. We shook hands, her head twisted, taking me in with an interest that was circumspect, but open-minded, while my husband plugged my new company laptop to the desk beside hers, then took his briefcase to the far end of the office. It was open-plan, and he worked along a row of desks with the other technical people. 'Will we have a chat then?' said Rosaleen.

'That would be great.' We looked at each other.

'Can you book a room,' she said.

I understood that to book a room I would need to have some idea how to use the computer, with its pass-words and its different programmes. I sat at the screen and moved the mouse around, seizing on the obvious icons until I gave up and went to my husband's desk.

It's not true that I had never worked before. After college, I'd completed a year-long internship in the Dublin office of an international think tank. For the first month or so, there was nothing for me to do inside the think tank. I asked around, and nobody could think of anything, so I just read *The Brothers Karamazov*, propped against my keyboard for all to see. I made coffee and emailed friends, and read about the gross betrayals of the sons of Fyodor Pavlovich Karamazov while my new colleagues all clacked on their keys and went to and from the filing cabinet. One day one of the bosses (we'll call him John Murphy) was walking past my desk. John Murphy had his own department, his own office and nameplate, the only man in the building who sported a full suit – navy pinstripe or, in summer, cream linen that smelled when it rained. 'You're bored, aren't you?' John Murphy said, with a glance from my Hotmail, to my Russian novel. The following day he invited me to his apartment for a glass of wine. I was still living with my parents and when I came downstairs, dressed in jeans and a sequined gilet, my mother asked where I was going.

'To a party in my boss's apartment.'

'Oh well I hope you're not the only one invited,' said my mother and she gave me her particular smile, with both eyebrows arched in mischievous delight.

The situation with John Murphy lasted eight months and ended in desperate texts and emails full of blame. I wasn't offered the job that might have followed the internship in the bustling, respected think tank, not because John Murphy came in the way of my employment but because I had no interest in applying for it, no motivation. I just slipped out the door and went to work on my own, in rented box rooms, scratching away at interviews and other puff pieces, before settling down with my husband and his family, and giving birth.

Now I'd been offered a good job, and I wanted to rise to its demands and to excel. I wanted to produce, in a white heat of cleverness, to disappear into some difficult task: I think oblivion is what we all seek at work.

I booked a room for Rosaleen, though not properly, in that my husband did it. Or he got a secretary to do it. Either way, the room was booked for us. The room was very white and it faced the sea. October sunlight beamed onto the sparkling ocean ripples, and seagulls soared up and then back down the sky as a ferry slowed into the harbour. But this gorgeous vista held all the comfort of a screensaver. The sea might have been a wistful memory in the room, it was so remote from our present anxiety. Rosaleen entered and banged her materials on the table, and I said, 'Hi Rose,' to silence.

'People do call you Rose?'

'They don't, actually,' Rosaleen said.

She explained the business to me, talking in perfect sentences while message boxes jumped around a screen above our heads. She talked in a language hard to fathom. The business seemed to be concerned with awesome, far-fetched things, like the shape of the scaffolding beneath everything, like creating a smooth passage from one world to the next.

'You can do Criterion B Question 6,' she said, and got up.

Back at the desk, I typed in my newly chosen password, then clicked on the emails that had started coming through, with attached documents. The documents were forty pages or so in length. My chest started to tighten and I felt warm. I looked around for help.

'Rosaleen?'

'Yes.'

We swivelled our chairs at each other.

'Could you remind me, which am I to do?'

'Criterion B Question 6. Two-thirds of a page.'

'OK. So will I do Criterion B Question 6.'

Rosaleen nodded.

Questions, I thought, showed great interest in the subject and a readiness to learn; questions showed curiosity.

'And just, how long should it be?'

'Two-thirds of a page, that's what I just told you.'

'OK.' A few minutes went by in front of documents.

'Rosaleen I'm sorry but I'm just not entirely sure what I'm to do.'

'B6, right in front of you.' She sighed. 'This is why we needed you a month ago.'

The hallway seemed a quiet place. I stood in the hallway, then backed down the stairs, and very soon my husband came, and led me down the next flight of stairs, holding me with his apologetic eyes. I began to cry. 'It's a mistake! I shouldn't be here.'

Criterion B6 was left undone. Someone else did it – as they well should have, I felt, going home. Why should I do something that would take me hours to figure out, and five minutes for them? Something I had no interest in ever learning how to do? The key thing would be to make friends and identify who I could work best with.

At six o'clock my husband and I let ourselves in the front door and the two girls hopped up and down, saying, 'Papa! Look!' They flapped pictures. The baby called out my name from the top of the stairs then pitched himself forwards, turning upside down. He thumped all the way down the hard, wooden stairs until the last ghastly somersault and his forehead hit the parquet tiles. He bawled crying in my arms and his tears soaked through my shirt.

I hadn't married my Italian husband, not yet, but I wore a ruby ring he'd given me, and we fought plenty. We really needed the salary from the big firm. Mushrooms were growing in the bathroom from a gap between the tiles and wall, right in behind the toilet. Every few days one of us picked away these flimsy toadstools and then we got back to doing nothing about it. Leaks were liable to come in through the ceilings. The kitchen cupboards were falling off their hinges, the fireplace was dark. If we lit a fire, gusts of smoke ploughed through all the rooms, because of a nest in the chimney and a problem with the flue no one had the wits or the interest for solving.

In the evenings, underneath the fridge, a family of mice made scratching sounds. We'd bought this house soon after the baby came along, and for all its faded charm it was very expensive. The bank had just permitted us the mortgage break that became, over the years, more a way of life than a break. But we didn't talk about our money problems.

For the rest of my time working in the office I was ten or fifteen minutes late every morning. My husband drove in early because his job was important to the running of the place, and I waited for our minder to come, then got on my bike. Sometimes the baby cried and wrapped his arms around my leg. I put him back inside the house, and shut the front door on his tiny streaming face.

Bicycle was the only way to travel, the bus service being unreliable to a degree that could ruin a whole day. The distance to the office was seventeen kilometres each way and I would arrive weather-beaten at the desk by ten fifteen or so, feeling guilty and ashamed. I vowed to subtract the missed ten/fifteen-plus minutes from lunch hour, which by the end of my employment shrank to five minutes, then well into the minuses until I entered a moral twilight of strange hours, diddled timesheets, private debts to my employer.

In the mornings it was difficult to sit down and begin the work that I was here to do. There were several things you needed to have in your possession. The key card, you needed strung around your neck at all times, but the baby might have wanted to play with the key card the night before, and might have hidden it, so that I couldn't get through any one of the doors and instead of having to ask the secretaries for a replacement card I would stand at each wall of glass for minutes on end, waiting for someone who had remembered their key card to let me through the door.

But I might not have even got that far. There was a problem with my bike lock – rust had got into the keyhole and on a cold day the key would get stuck in the lock and the bike couldn't be parked. You could be standing five minutes in the wet and cold, swearing at the bike. Lockers were a problem. All work equipment was kept in lockers with tiny keys, but the baby in our house was fascinated with tiny keys and he used to do away with them. One of the secretaries would need to come up with a spare key before the moment came when my laptop was recovered and I could, at last, sit at my own, spacious desk, and get down to work.

Sometimes the computer stayed black after I'd switched it on. It wouldn't work. If my husband wasn't at his desk, I would go and find a secretary, or a friendly colleague, and this brilliant person would resolve the problem, and head off with a smile. Then it wouldn't work again. Another quarter of an hour might go by. I'd move desk, then move again, each time conscious of the clatter of laptop, the clunk of cables, my haphazard shape hovering over straight rows of colleagues who had no problem studying intricate designs and richly detailed spreadsheets first thing in the day. These colleagues all seemed committed to their work in the company. No one secretly watched the news or wrote emails to their friends; nobody seemed to be hiding anything. They all sipped their keep cups of coffee and got down to it. I found it strange.

The job itself was quite mysterious. The job was 'writer', a role that was new to the company, they had created it for me. Other companies in their field were doing this, and the recruiters had furnished them with a list of exciting examples from the international market. I figured there was no option but to blaze a trail and do exactly what they wanted: be indispensable, be everywhere. Be the fount from which everyone could draw answers, a trove of human capital this office would be able to brag about to other outposts and companies, and then make lots of money, all because of me.

The words I wrote needed to be clear, precise, truthful but persuasive. Fact and evidence based. The problem was that everything was written already. All I needed to do was put a comma here, a phrase like 'armed with expertise' there. 'That's a cut-and-paste job,' I'd be told of anything that needed doing, or, cheerily, 'No one reads it anyway!' I really wasn't sure why I was there. I had no answers, only questions it became too late to ask.

Mornings, I would behold the documents, sectioned into grades, levels, stages, phases, categories, or 'cats', criterions, schedules A, B and C, and quadrants too – sometimes 'waves', with appendices. And lots, and multi-lots. I would sit at the desk, and touch the keys, and click the soft, clean mouse that had been polished, the night before, by the tired smiling man from the cleaning company. I'd vow to focus all my mind on just one document. I wanted to nail this one, fast, to have all the answers and work non-stop. I'd print out the document in the industrial printer that required a key card to operate. I would have to go and find a key card, and I would run into a problem. I would solve this printing problem, and at last I would staple up my document and sit down to read.

After the first two lines I was gone – confused, my heart beating faster, blood boiling. I'd rifle through folders on the computer, open all I could, seeing stages, waves, cats, quadrants piling up until the queasy boredom spread through my whole consciousness and physical being; my back and shoulders turning knotty, face getting damp, my armpits slippery, and warm tears would surge up through my vision. My husband was busy sometimes and I phoned my father from the corridors. 'Quadrants,' I said. 'I mean what are cats and quadrants! This job is not for me.' 'It will make a man of you,' he said, and I would force myself back to the desk, pull out my chair, and click. I was afraid that I would fail spectacularly. That I might make some kind of public mess and leave in disgrace, and have to go back home and look after the children.

'IT'S A MISTAKE!' I'd tell my husband.

'It's going to be OK,' he'd say. 'Let's get Martha.'

I first met Martha, a senior secretary, in the office kitchen while stuffing handfuls of lemon drizzle cake into my mouth.

'Sorry, I didn't have lunch,' I told her, washing my hands and drying them. We talked for a minute or two, and her warmth and authority poured through me like a smooth glass of brandy. Martha had worked here for years and understood exactly the job I was required to do – in fact, she was already doing it perfectly well, they just didn't call her 'writer'. I really didn't know why I was here, but now, I had Martha. I visited Martha's desk every day.

'Can you tell me,' I'd ask Martha, 'what is meant by this?' And so I sent the documents to Martha, and she sent them back to me completed and I smuggled them into my files.

Every Thursday, I submitted my hours to accounts with Rosaleen cc'd for approval. And every Thursday without fail, a one-word email came back saying 'approved', its unpunctuated lower case hinting at the greatest disapproval. On a Friday, the money would roll in, an incredible sum all for me. *Cha-ching, cha-ching, cha-ching*. I'd never seen my bank account like this. I felt a need to spend a good portion of it, to turn the metaphysical into something tangible, and I'd stop off at the fancy delicatessen and fill the basket and weigh the handlebars of my bike with fresh quality produce.

After I started working with Martha, I'd think, why not persevere with something so completely odious? I couldn't believe my luck, the scandal of just being there. 'It's a big job,' I told my dad. 'I'm getting overtime, and holiday pay on top of this.'

'Your mother arranged it for you,' he told me.

We often commented on my mother's interventions, because she had died just a few months before. In July. Friday the thirteenth. She died without so much as mentioning what was happening, and the life she lived became a greater mystery than before. My mother didn't talk much about herself and she didn't like to dwell on anything too difficult. She once told me that after my brother was born, her second of four children, she drank gin and tonic at a wedding and came home in tears. Soon afterwards, she took a job as a typist in a law firm. She told me about how, on the first morning, she faxed all the work to my father's secretary to type up for her. This was in about 1976. The secretary sent the work back to her completed. My mother must have felt she couldn't do any of it herself – maybe her typing wasn't quick enough or she didn't understand the instructions. She lasted two mornings, and never worked another day outside the home.

Now here I was, nepotised into another fold, sending documents to my husband's secretary. Martha shared a row of desks at front of house with three other members of the senior administrative staff – they weren't called secretaries. One day, walking away from their desks, I turned around suddenly having realised I'd forgotten my pen. Martha was making a face behind my back, a grimace of exaggerated torment and despair, with her mouth hung open and eyes set in a pantomime glare, and the two others sitting next to her were making similar faces. I picked up my pen and walked away as if I'd seen nothing.

In December, a plastic Christmas tree appeared in the foyer. A tree with frosted branches hung with glassy blue baubles. We made hampers for homeless children, saved e-invites to lunches and enjoyed a Christmas Confectionary Competition every Friday. The Christmas party took place in the infernal basement of a flashy sports bar. We were given three drinks coupons each. Platters of wedges, onion rings, spring rolls and battered prawns sat around ignored. As the night wore on, we exceeded our three coupons and tables of directors, associates and hirelings rose to the occasion, tanking pints and nipping to the bathroom. At some point I wandered to the table-tennis tables and took up a bat. My opponent was a wiry, brainy company director named John – John O'Shea.

I threw for serve, won the serve and aced the table. Over a breathless half-hour in which a very small crowd gathered, I beat John O'Shea three games to nil.

'Another set!' I commanded, trying to make light of my glory by exaggerating it.

'I think I've had enough,' John O'Shea laughed.

'Last game then,' I said.

I served, John O'Shea returned, and I smashed the ball, rousing a cheer from one drunken colleague. We rallied for a few minutes. Then he served, and I smashed it again. He was consistent, but he couldn't return a top spin I hadn't even known I could do. This was incredible. Weeks before, I had spent the whole evening resizing the fonts on John O'Shea's CV, and inserted advanced symbols. I'd lost an hour over the file type of his headshot. Now it was my serve and I heard my name being called – my husband at my arm.

'It's nearly midnight, we have to get home.'

'Just let me finish this game.'

'Come on, we promised your dad.'

Outside, we saw a taxi. I suggested we keep going, stretch our legs and take the Luas. We walked, in time to see the last tram leave the station.

It was a chaotic December night and there were no other free taxis. We walked for the next hour and forty-five minutes in an icy rain through a town ransacked by people having fun. My husband was silent for much of it, and when I asked why, he said we could have just got that taxi and he was so sick of everything being so unplanned. Why should he have to walk home in the rain? We arrived home two hours late for my dad, who was sitting by the cold grate of the fireplace with a box from Fanagan's Funeral Directors, writing and enveloping sympathy thank-you cards. As he was leaving, the baby appeared at the doorway and raised his arms to me.

The baby stayed up for two more hours, until about five-thirty.

'Down,' he said, having climbed from his cot again.

'No,' I said, 'You have to sleep.'

We were on the floor of the landing, where I was blocking the stairs in a drooping heap.

'Down,' he said, and then he punched me in the face. I told him this wasn't kind. He punched me in the face again and glared back at me.

The younger girl woke as usual around six and was ready for action, parking herself at the TV and asking, 'What are we going to do today?'

There must have been a point when I started to make friends and go for lunch in groups. On quiet days the office was a kind of rehabilitation centre, it was so clean and set apart from family life. Like waiting in an airport for a slightly delayed flight, or going to the doctor for some trivial complaint. On these days the whole atmosphere was calming. The white surfaces free of anything. The temperature and moisture levels just right, the chairs perfectly comfortable, the height of the computers optimal. In the sterile kitchenette, a tap shot boiling water in a mug for tea in moments: no standing, waiting, daydreaming required. Machines spewed coffee all day long into the cups of pleasantly chatting colleagues. I signed up for the mindfulness workshop that was considered billable hours, I put my name down for the women's football team.

Some afternoons I would sit listening to people talk quietly into mouthpieces at web meetings, their mouse buttons clicking, computer keys thumping, a muffled male voice saying stern and crucial things into a conference call, and I would surrender to the great bliss. *Cha-ching*. For this I was paid. It felt like being in a large protective shell, buried underwater. No one talked of any virus or dystopia. No one could have known that within a couple of years the place would be wiped clean of humans, these busy corridors would be empty, deserted, lonely bastions of a better time. We worked in this office in a Golden Age, little did we know it.

One of these afternoons I was clicking through image files when my eye fell on the room in which my mother died. I froze. I hadn't realised this was what I had been hoping to find, when I clicked on the words 'Our Lady's Hospice'. But here was the exact place of her death – or at least a room on the exact corridor, built to the same specifications. It had the same overbearing languid beigeness. I forgot where I was as I enlarged the picture, stared into the mechanical bed, wheels, metal bars, medical devices; the peach armchair we took turns to sit on. The light coming from the patio that had been stalked, in the days before her death, by a lone magpie. There were her plumped pillows, her turned sheets. The caption read: 'Contract included the preliminary design of a new Palliative Care Unit. 36 single room beds, 31 square metre dimension, each with an en suite. Each has access to an outdoor courtyard, giving superb views into landscaped gardens. Completion: third quarter 2018.'

I added a hyphen between 'square' and 'metre', and copied and pasted the information into my documents. Before the word 'views', I deleted 'superb'.

—

Weekends, when the baby woke me, I could already hear the TV squeak from the room downstairs, where the younger girl would usually be sunken into the sofa, surrounded by food wrappers. One January morning, I left the kitchen for a minute and returned to see the baby had got his own breakfast. His independence always impressed me but this time he was standing on a chair at the table surrounded by milk. The baby had gone to make himself a bowl of cereal and milk and apparently continued pouring the milk, and it had spread across the table and trickled over the edge and through the cracks onto the floor. The baby stood in this lake of milk, eating a bowl of cereal, wearing, for some reason, wellies. Outside the sun shone from a clear winter sky.

'Let's go on an adventure,' I proposed, having cleaned up. The three children piled into the car and I backed us out the driveway and onto the street. Winter sunlight beamed down on the window condensation and I remember saying, as the car moved forwards, 'I can't see anything.' The parked car was right where you'd least expect it. There was a clang, a jerk of the wheels. The pavement was scattered with smashed lights and the door of the parked car was bent out of shape.

At the car park by the forest, the baby could not be removed from the car. The zip of his jacket had jammed shut in such a way that it overlapped with the straps of his car seat, trapping him in a complex arrangement of fabric. Not one passing dog walker could figure it out either. I used my picnic knife to cut his quality winter jacket off him down the middle.

That night the car owner called, since I had left a note with my phone number under his windscreen wiper.

The insurance company dealt with the crash, putting me at ease and charging me the damage through subtle means that would be revealed in bills to come. The repairs to my own car (lights, bonnet) came to about two weeks' net salary.

Rosaleen presented me with fresh documents and asked would I run through Schedules B, C and D in Cats 1 and 2 for the presentation I was to give when the big one arrived – the most important document. 'D – you could show that with a pie chart or something,' she said and slipped away.

Rosaleen was normally low-key, but given to sudden frightening movements. In meetings, she used a sarcastic tone and made diminishing remarks ('It seems to me you weren't listening,'), and got away with it. I was interested in expanding my rapport with Rosaleen. I liked skidding off to fetch her a coffee, or answering a hurried call from her late in the evening. She was overworked and I wanted her to know that I was there for her personally, any time of day or night. I wanted to be her shining assistant, her right arm, her star. I couldn't hope to understand her work, I knew I couldn't be of much practical help. But what I could offer was something like emotional support. I liked walking corridors with Rosaleen – which we did on occasion, in tapered skirts and polished shoes with a low heel, laptops and folders propped high in our arms. People would look up at us and in their dreamy stares a curiosity could be picked up.

But Rosaleen was busy and she didn't like being approached. If I surprised her at her desk with some query, she would lift her head in slow motion and shrink me with the pupils of her eyes. She would look at me like I was a floor and she was searching my corners for dirt. 'Would you have a moment?' I'd ask. 'I don't think this is a good use of my time,' she'd say. Or simply, 'No. I don't.' 'Just one second then,' I'd plead. Only now that I have home-schooled three children do I appreciate how irritating this must have been for Rosaleen.

But drawing up a pie chart, that was easy. I took out a pad of paper and drew a circle. Inside the circle, I drew two lines, two cuts of pie. I wrote 'project' inside this triangle. For a while I sat. Then I went outside for some fresh air. Later, I sat back down with a coffee, and looked for something else to do. I could feel the minutes pass unfilled, and I could fret about it, but remain still and outwardly unhurried. Colleagues passed, we said hello. I looked at the screen, into the glaze of my wandering mind, that lost, unpeopled place you go to when you aren't being where you are, seeing what's in front of you. Johns sat around me. John Ryan and John McCarthy and John McDermott and Yannis Papadopoulos walked past. I caught the eyes of John McCarthy, then looked away. I thought about different things – different scenarios. Bike shed. Hotel. Storage room. Things I shouldn't have been thinking about, and should not ever write about.

I fidgeted around with the files, opened some other document. I would not draw a pie chart, though the temptation to excel and deliver work had not left me. I got someone else to do it.

On the more solipsistic cycles, wearing earphones, or late at night slouching over documents on the company laptop, I became fixated by the idea that I was living the wrong life. Wrong, mistaken, miscast. Living in a strange house, with a family I didn't really know, going to and from a place I never wanted to belong to; writing, copying, pasting, in a language of acronyms and other dry abominations so that I could buy buffalo mozzarella and book holidays.

It had a chilling, damning effect on my intelligence, I believed, to have to write words like 'deliverable', 'buy-in', or 'sweet spot', with my own fingers. I felt so superior to my lived existence. How had I ended up out in this colony? Did I need to find a means of escape, or would I somehow get used to it all, make a home of it – is that what growing up and earning money all amounts to?

Shrill tears met me at the door to home, complaints, unmeetable demands from hungry children. Three of them seated at the kitchen table, knives and forks pronged in the air, and nothing ready for their supper. At night, once the children were asleep, my husband and I sat in different rooms, sending each other excoriating texts.

We didn't agree on which movies or series we should watch. Once, he suggested we play a Richard Burton movie called *Massacre in Rome*. I told him I had just become addicted to *Mad Men* – what about we watch an episode of *Mad Men*, then watch *Massacre in Rome*? And he turned to me. The room became so still and dark – that room was poorly lit, with a bulb missing in the main reading lamp. He asked me if I remembered that his grandfather had been massacred. He asked, straight-faced: 'What do you know of the heroes of the Italian Resistance? What do you know of Italy? What do you know of Roman civilisation?' We both raised our voices until I couldn't listen to us anymore. I went to bed. Afterwards, we didn't talk about it.

Cycling up the hills in gusty rain, my self-pity was fulsome and consuming. I would wonder, why had all of this befallen me? Why did no one seem to share these problems but instead led lives that were real and competent and not beset with peril? I would wonder again, who were my family and friends? Also why was I forever talking about my life in the past tense? None of this had ended.

One morning on a day off I was sitting on my bed, plucking my eyebrows in a pocket mirror, when I got a horrible fright. All my bottom teeth had turned brown. I clenched my jaws for a better look: every tooth in my head had been stained golden brown, the colour of strong milky coffee.

On a bright wintry Sunday I drove the three children to the beach. I loved taking them out and making them tired, to escape from indoors and feel the elements around us. I stood under the great blue sky in the cold sun, feeling grateful for what we had, while the girls found shells and stones for their little brother's knapsack. To see them being nice to one another blasted heat into my insides. I remembered that it's always possible to transform your mood by going to the beach, to see things differently. Nature is a powerful cure, I felt, taking in the expanse of sea, the cry of seabirds, salt in the healthy air. I drove them home in the rosy dusk and surrendered to a belief in something other than this, something unseen taking us under her protective wing. My mother. Mother Earth. God Almighty. Or just the mysteries of the universe. Delivering peace in surprising forms. Through the rear-view mirror I could see three pairs of eyes drifting closed. I hadn't felt this relaxed and full of hope for so long, and drawing near our road, noticing too late the lights turn red, I crashed into the back of another car.

The baby swung forward in his seat and burst into tears; a girl said, 'He-ey?!'

Nobody was hurt. The German tourists driving the car were understanding. Though for such a minor accident the damage to both cars was immense, as not only those subtle adjustments were made to my bills and insurance reputation, but three weeks' pay went to the mechanic to repair the wreckage I had made of my bonnet and lights again.

In the late spring, it arrived – the big document, the most important document and my whole reason for being there. It arrived in hard and soft copy running some eighty pages in length, and I was to read this and other eighty-page documents and present my findings before an assembled board. The directors had all been invited, Danish pastries had been ordered. In the days leading up to the big show I learned PowerPoint and gave my presentation to the empty kitchen table. It took several nights, and I won the boardroom with my slides and insights and sparkling wit each time.

I was first at the big meeting and remained in the background while five or six men and two women shook hands. I used to quail before these men and women and fawn all over them. I made myself ill with envy for their positions, though at the same time had a great urge to support them.

A jug of water had been left for us beside the pastries. I poured out seven small ridged white plastic cups and placed them around the table. Everyone sat, fitted their laptops into the plug sockets, and as we murmured our preparatory small talk a plastic cup turned on its side. Water flooded the table and got into the electrics. Laptops were grabbed, everyone jumped to their feet. I mopped the table with paper napkins, and the door swung open – Martha, with the blue roll.

I had been working in the office for six months and become so attached to the income and sound routine I had decided to stay on a bit. It was for the good of the family. One wet and dismal afternoon I was playing with the fonts on an infographic when I felt a presence darken over me.

'Free to have a chat with myself and John Fitzgerald?' Rosaleen asked.

Not John Fitzgerald. John Fitzgerald was a heavy-set, suntanned director at the very top. When someone like John Fitzgerald wanted a chat like this it meant there was a folder of work, an urgent deadline, a crisis I could help resolve. I pressed save and rose to my feet, picked up my pen to show my readiness for whatever assignment needed cranking. Rosaleen and I walked together up the corridor to the meeting room, heads bowed, as people looked up from their desks at us. It was rough and stormy out, and the sound of slashing rain was clamorous against the glass walls.

'You're not cycling home in that, are you?' Rosaleen asked.

'Yep, I am.'

'How long does it take you?' she frowned.

'About forty-five minutes.'

'And it's uphill all the way, isn't it?'

'Yes.'

I could never think of anything good to say to her. Nothing seemed adequate, I simply feared Rosaleen as a woman who had made herself important in a world of men.

In the meeting room, John Fitzgerald stood facing the window, looking out onto murky grey sea and clouds. We took a long time pulling out chairs, and once seated John Fitzgerald told me that my contract had come to an end. I didn't know what he was talking about. 'You've been very helpful,' John Fitzgerald said, as Rosaleen nodded.

What upset me was how kind and compassionate their faces looked. Their kindness wrecked my instinct to take issue, deprived me of true outrage. I put away my pen and notebook and said it had been a fantastic opportunity. They'd done no wrong, and this was such a shame. I walked back down that corridor alone, and everything it could have been, with Rosaleen, John Fitzgerald, my husband and my colleagues in the firm collapsed around me. I was small; I was verminous with insignificance. It was about ten past four and I had to sit there until six before I was allowed to cycle home in the rain. Then I had four weeks to get my things. To clear my tracks, erase what I had done, and disappear.

From the chaos of my bicycle, I phoned my father: 'I think I've just been fired.' He listened to my story and tried to console me, acknowledging the humiliation all the same. 'That was a hard day,' he said. 'But what you have to remember darling is that you are brilliant.' I cried harder and felt stupider.

—

To wrap things up, Rosaleen invited me to lunch. We met in a smart Italian restaurant near the office. 'Will you have a glass of wine?' she said. 'Only if you're having one,' I said. 'Not for me,' she said, explaining they were hosting a group of European directors later on. She ordered spaghetti and ate it in relaxed, twisted forkfuls, and she gave me a goodbye card, with a fifty-euro voucher enclosed, and the same well-wishing note from everyone on the team, multiplied all over the card in biro. Walking back, I asked her did she have any nice plans for the summer, and we talked about the south of Italy, of which I had so much knowledge.

'Pompeii, Herculaneum, definitely worth a visit,' I said.

'Actually, I just can't wait to sit by a fountain and read my novel,' she said. She laughed, embarrassed.

'Your novel.' I was stunned.

'Oh, that's all I dream of doing. Reading novels in the sun. Anyway.'

For some reason, I'd become speechless, but we'd reached the office plaza.

'Well, goodbye,' I said, and Rosaleen crossed the street with her plume of dark hair bobbing, her heels hitting off the concrete. I knew she was among the most interesting l people I would ever meet, and also that we'd never have any reason to speak to each other again. I know it shouldn't matter when a person walks away forever but it does. All of it matters. This was my mistake – mine, and no one else's.

Two Nice People

I was burying my little boy in sand when the policeman came right up to us. He cut out the sea and sky and I thought, what have I done now?

'Hello there,' he said, bending to our level. He was a shiny, compact kind of man, got up in hi-vis, shell tracksuit bottoms, sporty trainers; his summer uniform, I guessed. He didn't wear the hat, but I knew from the badges on his arms and chest.

'How are things here now don't worry – because these days with everything people might see a policeman and think, Oh, I'm in trouble or something.'

'Heh – no.' I sat up straight and folded up my legs in such a way that he would not see any pubic hair. My swimming togs were very old and didn't fit me properly. How many of them were here this time? I looked around but it was just this one policeman. 'I'm Sergeant

Pat Hourican,' he was saying. Or Houlihan? O'Halloran? I didn't really want to know his name.

'I'm on duty up at the station on the main drag. And – hello there? This is your little fella?'

We both looked at the boy, buried to the waist. He was patting, imperiously, the sand around his body. Sand had got in everywhere, into his hair, his ears, eyebrows, nostrils. Once he noticed we were watching him he broke away and walked up to the dune to pick up stones and things. His only piece of clothing was a UV tank top with clouds and rainbows on it, and his little ass was coated in wet sand.

'We're obviously contented anyway, ha,' the policeman said. He looked at me again. 'Now, it's a hot day, and very crowded out here.' His eyes were bright like candle flames; his nose and cheeks were sunburned, as if they'd seen too many beaches.

'Are ye visitors to the area, or …?'

'Yes. I come here all the time, I grew up here. We're not just on holidays.' I wanted to convey my separateness out here, and the policeman nodded; he understood.

'I hear you, not exactly blow-ins.' He edged closer on a taut calf muscle. 'So. I just had a call there at the station, and I came to check if you were alright.'

'Oh!' Somebody came, I thought.

'A call from a gentleman you may have met on the beach today.'

A gentleman. I couldn't think of any gentleman.

'A man who was a little bit concerned.'

'Oh dear.'

The policeman nodded regretfully. 'About the two of ye here, yes.'

'Oh.'

The policeman looked inside me now, and I felt very peculiar, very bad, like I was being poisoned by my own friends. The boy was busy, collecting shells, seaweed, bits of rope and other debris. I saw the sleepy crowds, the tide, white horses, shimmering sea. Our patch of things. Mangled towels, opened suncream, sand-coated flask. Lunchbox, no lid; Wagon Wheels wrappers, one filled with a sand pie. In the game, you had to eat the sand pie and be sick. But I hadn't played the game this time. Why had I not played the game this time? My book, a classic love story I was keen to finish and have read, was discarded, face down on its pages.

'I'm sorry to have disturbed you, but I'm just responding to the call,' the policeman went on. 'So I hope it's OK if I have a word with you here, ask a few questions. Just to find out what the story is.'

He took a pad of paper from a pocket in his jacket and he gave me a gallant little nod.

It was a half-truth, that I grew up here. We used to come here on our holidays, to a farm along an avenue where sheepdogs leapt, blackberries clustered in the briars, and bright-green cow-dotted fields, hiding flat white mushrooms, led right down to the rocky shore, and to the sea; and on hazy afternoons straw bales were tossed by the farmer onto trailers and the air was thick with pollen and wild perfumes.

The previous winter, I'd ended up very suddenly alone with my small son. Now it was time for freedom, time to be seen – maybe to be given some reward for tough endurance. Always I felt owed some happy time, some crock of gold, had no doubt but that it awaited us.

The Airbnb, a bedroom and kitchenette, was clean and tasteful, and the farm just up the road looked much the same as I'd remembered it. They let us pick eggs and give a carrot to the horse. The weather was incredible, in fact it was a dangerous heatwave, with red warnings on the news. Every day we dragged ourselves into the car, and to the beach to cool off in the sea.

Today was the hottest day. In Europe, people died. Here, people went around in a daze.

Up on the cliffs, the cars were sprawling from the car park onto the road and grass and golf links. The bins were overflowing, and long drooping queues of colourfully dressed families trailed from the Mr Whippy and chip vans. CAUTION, BEWARE OF BEING CUT OFF BY INCOMING TIDES, the sign read. We parked into a ditch and, holding hands, climbed the steep path down the cliffside to the beach. A sign said: DANGER, SUDDEN DROP BELOW.

On trips alone with my small son, to a beach or park, on planes or train journeys, I used to go up close to other families or friendly looking people. I had a beady eye for friendship on these traipses, for that gleam of openness and understanding that just might lead to company. At this beach, I pulled the boy around, checking faces under hats until we found a spot. It was a whole extended family. Mums, dads, aunts, uncles and kids, passing around crisp packets and soft drinks. The women stretched out on towels, the dads having conversations looking straight ahead of them, out to sea, the boys throwing a ball or digging a moat. They had castle moulds, pirate ships, sticky rackets, balls, snorkels – and we hadn't thought of bringing any beach toys. I placed our bags in their periphery.

DANGER, COLLAPSING SAND DUNES. CAUTION, INCOMING TIDES. I unrolled our towels, shook the sand away. I set out the boy's lunchbox: a peanut-butter sandwich sliced in triangles; four apple quarters turning brown; two Wagon Wheels, both already melted in their packets. And his turquoise water flask, decorated with pink octopi. The flask was stainless steel and the lunchbox bamboo, so – doing everything the right way here.

We had absolutely everything we needed. I looked around for something missing, something to be anxious over, nothing came to mind. I got hold of him, coated him with Factor 50, put his cap on, stretched his limbs into his swimming trunks and rainbow top. He took his swimming trunks back off again, and sat down to play. He took his cap off, threw it away. Sun lit up his golden hair, and the shadows of his long eyelashes swept his face in lavish streaks.

I took out my paperback, and looked for my page. I had forgotten water. His flask was full, but none for me. I looked up at the cliff, and the distance made my mouth feel dry. I lay back under the burning sun. You can't have everything. I reached for his flask, but he got to it first.

Carefully, the boy unscrewed the flask, looked inside it, then tipped it upside down into the sand. He shook it hard to empty out the last few drops, then buried all the water, squatting right into his ankles. I unstuck my tongue from the roof of my mouth, and pulled myself to standing.

'Come on.' I took his hand. The tide was so far out it took forever, pebbles pushing at our heels, before we reached the water. We waded out and farther out. The sea was shallow, murky, strewn with seaweed and dead crabs. We went a little deeper, then with his arms around my neck and his legs around my body we plunged in. The waves surged and tossed him up and down and he broke away, gasping, flapping his arms and kicking his legs until he was completely separate from me, gulping and spitting seawater, laughing, showing every tooth inside his gums. I've never had the strength to test it, but it seems there is no limit to the fun this boy is capable of having. He snips up cables, opens teddies. Sometimes he bursts out laughing in his sleep.

There is not much to report about the day now that I've sat down to try. The sun shone, birds called; I worried about the sun, about sunburn, I worried that I didn't worry half as much as someone should. I worried about all the wrong things. The group beside us, they knew how to live – their bored and diligently playing children, a woman drinking Diet Coke, reading from her phone, on her back a tattoo of a bat with its wings spread.

He was running up and down, playing in the water of a little stream that trickled from the cliffs into the sea. It occurred to me that I should put his cap back on, and his swimming trunks. The sun shone down, and I turned from right to left to let it cook me on both sides. I felt its hot rays cutting through the parting on my scalp. Fizzy drink, I thought. Iced lemonade. Cold beer. Ice cubes. Cold glass of water.

The men, arms draped around knees, had their conversations. Talked of these extremes in temperature. Of boats at sea – or county councils. Planning applications, objections to the plans. They talked about the schools, they talked about the coaching – the hoops you had to go through. Most likely all of that. One had dark hair. I moved along the towel to get a closer look. He had a beard. He had a beard and yet – the face. Easygoing – small, hooked nose, cheeks stretched now, dark impressive beard – eyes that seemed sad, or just afraid. He was heavier now, but distinguished, by the beard, kind of – time had passed, but he'd remember me as well. I'd already pulled myself to sitting and was clambering forwards on the sand.

'Excuse me? Hi?'

They turned to look at me.

'Hi. Did you study Arts in UCD? Ten years ago – no, fifteen.'

The bearded man leaned back. His friend or brother glanced from me to him, the bearded man pointed at himself but I knew already. His face, up close, distorted into someone else's.

'Sorry,' he said, looking at his friend or brother. 'We're from—!' The name of a town. I hadn't heard of it. His friendly Northern accent forgave everything. They laughed it away. I laughed back, and they turned back to face the sea. The boy at his marsh of sand, pouring in the seawater, mixing up his elements. Running to and fro in an ecstatic hurry.

I held up the book to block the sun, checking on him with one eye. My novel was insufferably long and heavy in my hand. I'd been reading this one for about four years, even though it was a classic and a bestseller. The book jacket, its technicolour drawing of a frightened woman running from a burning house, had come apart from being carried around. I'd seen the Netflix adaptation, so the story held no mystery anymore, I knew who murdered who and why they did it, knew there was a shipwreck coming, two shipwrecks, that in the end a human skeleton would be fished out of the bottom of the sea.

I read a paragraph from start to finish, and the effort could have killed me. Half the words were cast in shadow, and the tiny print felt harmful to my eyes. The boy was lining up some rocks along the stream now, rushing, in great hurry.

DANGER, GOLFBALLS FLYING. I thought to take a little break from looking, so that I could be right here, just sink into this time. One eye was still open; now it drooped and rested closed and everything was calm. This way I could employ my hearing at its most acute. I could appreciate the heat, and air, the sound of waves, for what they were. DANGER, or CAUTION, BEWARE OF BEING CUT OFF BY INCOMING TIDES. You can really open all your senses, absorb the moment, take time, when you're allowed to close your eyes. I stretched an arm, found the book, and placed the pages on my face.

'DO YOU HAVE A SMALL BOY, THREE, BLOND??? A SMALL BOY, THREE, BLOND???'

Loud like torchlight or a speeding car. I sat up.

He was on his hunkers, talking in a phone.

'SHE'S HERE, I'VE FOUND HER.'

Pink man, yellow thinning hair. Short, doughy build. He had a job at hand. He didn't have a whistle round his neck but it seemed that in some other situation he would have had a whistle, and a first-aid pack, and ID.

'HE'S WITH US, HE'S OVER BY THE WATER!'

The beach had emptied. I reached around for things, then threw myself to standing. My legs were stilts. My legs weren't working properly. Half-words fell out – not what I'd have said if I'd had time to collect all my thoughts. But I understood the urgency, and I would not begrudge these people their distress. One foot found the sand, and then another, and I ran, with difficulty, on stilts.

My little boy was standing, seeming very little and confused, at the shore, beside a woman in a sarong. She was talking in a high-pitched voice about the water, staring in my eyes, with her hair all nice and with her hand on the shoulder of my little boy. I pulled him in and picked him up.

The policeman wasn't particularly enjoying any of this either, I was to understand.

'And do ye mind me asking, are ye alone together on your holidays?'

'Oh yes. But lots of help around. Lots of family.'

'Oh yes surely, good to hear, it takes a village doesn't it.' He made some scribbles in his notepad.

'A village.'

'Well to rear a child, doesn't it.'

'Oh, sorry, yes. You're telling me!'

'And how did ye get down here, was it in the car today?'

'We parked illegally, Garda.'

'Well I think now you wouldn't be the first, heh heh.'

'No, heh.'

'The car park is choc-a-bloc, alright.' He seemed to look inside me, with a tilt, and the most inveigling compassion.

'Are you alright?' He looked in my pupils.

'Garda,' I said. 'What do you want?'

'Right. Well, this afternoon I received a phone call. What happened was you, ehm, your child, came to the attention of a gentleman on the beach here, and a lady, two nice people. They said to me that you were there with a book, that you had your face inside the book. Physically, inside the book. Not just looking at the book, but unconscious, underneath the book.'

'I was reading, Garda.'

'OK, listen, when you got up off the ground, you seemed disoriented. They said you weren't making any sense, they said – look. OK – I'll tell you. They said you looked a bit dishevelled.'

'Dishevelled.' We both looked down at my appearance, which was of course dishevelled, a worry almost. All our stuff. Scattered everywhere. I shut my knees together and hugged them to my chest.

'But look sure, you seem very well. And he's a great lad.'

'I am very well. I'm – I've just been burying my kid in sand here.'

I reached out for my beach bag, and opened it, and found my sunglasses. Tears ran down behind the frames while he told me about his kids.

'They are a handful, boys. I've two myself at home, I have your sympathy, I'm sure.'

'They'd send you to an early grave,' I wept, laughing. Tears burst from my face. He wasn't to know.

'Oh, you're preaching to the converted you are,' he said, and shut his notepad.

'You've been very helpful,' the policeman said.

Before he left, I asked him where the two nice people were. I would like to thank them one more time for coming to our rescue. He pointed at the cliffs, where the rocks were clustered in a jagged ring, where the man and woman had been watching. I shook out our towels.

—

On the way home, we stopped and bought the last remaining can of 7up and two Cornettos from the petrol station. The moment we arrived back in the Airbnb, it filled with sand. I stood at the shower, rinsing down the boy, who twirled and laughed under the warm spray. I scrubbed him clean, washed the sand into the plughole, dried him off, then unwrapped his ice cream while he hopped from foot to foot with his arms outstretched.

That night he watched YouTube Kids while I finished all the bottle in the fridge. Then I uncorked something special, organic and spumante I'd saved specially for the holiday. The evening darkened, the boy fell asleep. I picked up the phone.

'No, this time I'm going to ask you some questions!' I was on the grainy bedspread, in déshabillé, *dishevelled* if you like, white flesh exposed to nobody, hair tangled in saltwater, a cone of melted ice cream tipped over on the bedside table. The boy slept on like a little angel. I drank the wine down to its last few vinegary droplets and flopped back, laughing, and waves crashed on my skull.

Trouble Again

1. Pleasure

'What do we do now?' she says.

'We get a mediator,' he says.

'No, what do we do now?' she says advancing towards him with a digital pregnancy test.

They are two storm-faced parents, man and woman, in a semi-detached pebbledash in a quiet neighbourhood not close to town. The month is January, 2021. Tuesday, mid-morning. They are still in the clothes they slept in. Margaret charges; Sergio stays in his corner, where he's recently installed his desk and his machines.

What the disagreement is about, neither of them will remember. But for one thing, Margaret isn't normally allowed to just walk into the bedroom. They have agreed as much in their sessions with Joan. They have agreed she is only to enter for an urgent reason, or if she needs something from the room, and the same applies to his entry on her side of the partition, the box room where she works on her documents and sometimes sleeps, if a row has been left unresolved. Posing questions from doorways is no longer acceptable, not normally.

She stands above him. Sergio draws back, then swivels around to study the test. And as he reads the tiny words in the results window – PREGNANT 1–2 weeks – his face softens and his eyelids fall. Up through the floorboards come the merry sounds of three children, the two big girls and one little boy, unsupervised at play and school. Today's lesson: burn six pieces of toast under the grill, and a new swear word.

Sergio gets up and kneels before Margaret, taking both her hands in his. He tells her he is sorry, so sorry, and she bows her head, wrapping her arms around his neck. 'Sorry,' he says and she shuts her eyes and smiles. The word, it always pours over her like a fresh spring, quenching a thirst she has been rasping on for days.

A knock on the door, and they both get up and put the test away. They have to get back to their work; number crunching, or home-schooling in a dressing gown. He returns his headphones to his ears and they protect him, like a helmet. In the full-length mirror, she belts her gown again. Her eyes blue and brilliant with the lightness of her news.

Although. *Mediator.* That's new. Neither of them has yet threatened such a practical consideration in their demise. *Mediator* is new. But PREGNANT 1–2 weeks. If PREGNANT 1–2 weeks doesn't beat *mediator*, then she'll never win a fight.

—

Three days later, she sits cross-legged on the floor on her side of the partition. Next to her, a piece of burnt toast and her phone, open at a page of information on the HSE website. The new legislation has only quite recently come into force, and she hates to think it will be her it benefits. As she reads, she sips a large cocktail of Campari with freshly squeezed orange juice, one orange segment and two ice cubes knocking about. It is Friday night.

Friday nights still hold a stubborn remnant of excitement for some adults. Tonight they were supposed to have a Chinese takeaway with Margaret's brother, Fran, who they have recently asked, with unspoken desperation, to join their bubble. A takeaway had been the plan, but in the late afternoon Sergio had come downstairs and begun his tidying. Unfortunately, Sergio had told Margaret the whole place was in a mess. And unfortunately, Margaret wasn't going to take any shit from anyone.

Sergio had walked the rooms with an open plastic bag, whipping up the items from the floor. Hair clips, gel pen, half a comic book. She hated it when he did the thing with the open plastic bag. 'Please can you put away …' she said. Whip whip – colouring pencils, loose playing cards, Nerf bullets, an apple with just one bite taken. She went up to the bedroom, shut the door behind her and pressed her back to it, thinking, this. All over again.

This – it was less a thought than it was a feeling. A sliding, shutting feeling. Or the evaporation of all feeling. The feeling it has all gone wrong, all over again.

And the rest of the evening, gone. Stony silence, hushed fight with the door closed, voices rising, shrill pleas. The heavy clicks of doors deliberately not being slammed, the cancelled guest. All over again. The cancelled takeaway, the overfilled glass, another night top-to-tail with the four-year-old to look forward to.

2. Despair
All fights are the same, with small variations, new insults shed. New lows. Fresh promises. Each party brings in something unexpected every time, from the first sparks of contention to the inevitable timorous and bedraggled resolution. And by the end they have both said such hurtful things as to become strangers to themselves and to wish only for forgiveness and to be chastened and be tamed.

A year or so before this came the last fight. She thought it had to be the last. It was late at night, and just as she thought he might hold her in his arms, he instead glared through her. She followed him downstairs. In the kitchen, he tore the cork off a bottle of grappa and swallowed a mouthful. He had never done that before. It was maybe twelve thirty at night.

'I, am, just, so, tired,' he said, very slowly.

'You have to go to sleep then, you need rest,' she said.

'Oh, I'll go to sleep alright.' He gave a bizarre, high-pitched laugh. 'That's what I'm going to do.' And he swerved past her into the garage.

'No,' she said.

'Yes.' He locked the door behind him.

The minutes passed. Twenty, thirty minutes. When she couldn't think of anything else to do, she pressed her father's number and she told him to come quickly.

Her father brought Fran, who is a little taller than him. The three men stood in the kitchen talking in guarded voices while she threw some things into a bag, took her sleeping son out of his cot and strapped him with her in the back of the car. Waiting in the cold outside, she went over the items in the lumpy cloth bag at her feet. Bunched t-shirts and socks, Pampers, bananas, a carton of milk, two pizza bases from the fridge and a jar of tomato sauce. They would have to eat the next day wouldn't they? Three books, two notebooks and a snakes-and-ladders board, without dice or pieces. Her father drove them home and they stayed seven months.

One problem back at the house where she grew up was the bedrooms were all taken. There was her father, Fran, her sister Caroline and her husband, their toddler and baby; and in the attic conversion, a Brazilian chef named João.

A bedroom was devised in the living room, the room where, as a teenager, Margaret watched TV and ate Pringles. The accommodation was welcomed but not very suitable. There were no wardrobes – it was a TV room – only cabinets packed with old wedding photographs and porcelain plates and champagne glasses and dust-coated tureens and gravy boats for dinner parties though Margaret had never once seen these ornaments used at any party.

On the first morning Margaret woke at dawn to the sound of wind chimes. She thought it must be wind chimes, or a little toy xylophone or music box. Her son was not beside her. She pulled herself up and looked around the half-dark. She crawled off the bed, and there he was, cross-legged at the foot of his mattress, smashing crystal champagne glasses against one another.

She wasn't sure it was a good idea to go back into her childhood once again. She didn't like it all that much the first time, or the second or third time. She was thirty-seven now, and she had been home so many times it ceased to be a home, became more of a glorious shelter that kept her, perpetually, a child. In the mornings, Caroline made porridge for the children, while Margaret crept past her father in his room to take a shower in his en suite, and then she cycled her boy into playschool. And then came home to try to clean up the living room.

Their clothes and books were stored in stacks. Every time she took a book out of the book stack, or looked for a t-shirt in the clothes stack, the order was disrupted. And when her little boy got home and messed up the stacks, chaos swept the room. It was a problem, not having wardrobes, for an adult and a child. But to do something about it would be to accept this for what it was.

Back at home with Sergio were his girls, Giorgia and Angelica, also their childminder, a human-resources manager named Bruna. Every day, Margaret went back and forth between the houses to drop her son and collect him and also do some laundry and light house-work and check the toilet wasn't blocked again. No one ever asked that these tasks be attended to, and it was probably preferred that she would not keep coming back like this. She just really wanted to clean her house. The bathroom was in need of renovation and the wood was rotting underneath the tiles; before all this, she'd wanted to do renovations. Now she just went back and forth between the houses. Twice a day, sometimes in the rain, or wet winds or hailstones, with the boy on the back seat falling asleep. Only once, it was hailstones, but almost every time, he fell asleep on their convey-ance. His upper body lolled sideways, and drivers rolled down their windows and yelled out: 'The child!' and she yelled back: 'I know!'

It was an existence that gave her continual black amusement, though no one shared the joke. Her sisters thought she should make a list of pros and cons, light some candles, make a choice. But Margaret could not think of anything so permanent as choice. Sergio Fantasia was her fiancé. They were engaged in Capri. Margaret wore his ruby solitaire on a chain around her neck, as the band needed resizing, and the claws had come undone, and the stone moved in the setting – but she couldn't commit to these repairs.

Between them they had three children. Any final parting would wrench siblings from each other. And his girls, they had lost one mother: they should not lose two.

Sometimes, cleaning up the kitchen with her father, she would say: 'I'll go mad!' or: 'Why me? Why has everyone forsaken me?' and he would look distraught and wait for the outburst to subside. He seemed to be looking on uselessly, leaving her alone to figure out these problems. She was a nuisance to him, to all of them. She resented how he shirked from her predicament. Then one evening, her father came to her with a piece of paper, and said there were three options. He had written down the options in his neat spidery handwriting:

1. You keep going like this.
2. You separate.
3. You work on it.

Beside option 3 was the number of Joan.

3. Confinement

They met Joan for the first time on a January night in her creaky Baggot Street practice and agreed a price for six sessions. Joan was a pale and wiry woman of fifty-five, silk fuchsia scarf knotted around her neck, pearl teardrop earrings, and the candles in the room were always unlit.

Joan wasn't the first or even the second woman. She was the fourth. But they began to feel at ease with her as they related both sides of their fairy-tale romance, the whole fiasco, her gaze switching between their dejected faces. And there emerged, in the expensive stillness, the most profound respect they'd yet encountered.

The next time, Joan asked if she could read a few questions to the broken couple. 'Because you know,' she said, 'we don't want anything to happen to you of the kind we're seeing every day on the news.' Margaret swallowed. Margaret wanted never to be on the news.

Joan asked them to answer: 'Never, Seldom or Sometimes'.

'Do you find you can share problems with your partner?' she read, glancing up.

'Do you ever feel ignored by your partner?'

'Does your partner use alcohol in a way that has caused problems?'

'Do you or your partner ever throw things?'

'Do you or your partner ever yell or shout during arguments?'

'Do you or your partner ever push or slap or spit?'

'Do you ever argue with children under eighteen within earshot?'

'Do issues of culture, religious beliefs or values cause difficulties between you?'

'Do you experience closeness or affection with your partner?'

'Do you ever pressurise your partner to have sex with you?'

'Do you ever touch or grope your partner without their consent?'

'Do you ever bare your genitals at your partner without their consent?'

'Do you or your partner feel there is secrecy around money?'

'Never!' They were both saying. 'No!'

'Sorry, Joan, those questions are disturbing me,' Margaret said.

'Actually, spitting, go back to spitting. Yes to that,' said Sergio, massaging his thighs with spread hands. Margaret gasped at the betrayal, dazzled with rebuke. It happened once, and she'd never been so sorry – they argued for a moment.

Joan made them take three deep breaths and then released the couple from the room.

At the third session, she suggested they breathe out an emotion, anything they felt in their bodies. 'What do you feel?' Joan asked.

'Fear,' said Margaret.

'Pain,' said Sergio.

'That's fine, breathe it all out. Now. Try this. Breathe in peace. Peace,' said Joan. She fluttered her hands a moment, as if sprinkling the room. 'Now this time, I want you to breathe in something else. Close your eyes. I want you to remember the first time you met. I want you to breathe in love. Breathe in love. Breathe out peace.'

Afterwards, Margaret said: 'You shout like a military commander!' and Sergio said: '*Fa la primadonna!*' and banged Joan's money down on the table. Joan loosened her scarf.

Margaret left.

At the fourth session, Sergio discussed the way self-absorption, in relationships, can set about a kind of decay. And Margaret had apparently made no effort to learn Italian.

'I have downloaded the app, I'm paying the subscription, and the settings are too complicated!' she countered, raising her voice.

Joan said, 'Easy, easy. Shush. Now I want to you to look at each other. Look in each other's eyes. Breathe in love,' she told them. 'Breathe out peace.'

They breathed in love, for the next few weeks, and it tasted like fumes. Margaret breathed out the fumes of hate.

'I think you're too hard on the girls,' she said.

'I think you've been spoilt by your parents and you're much too soft,' he said.

'I am soft on them because they are afraid of you,' Margaret said. They sat in silence, drained of the people they once were. The hour was up, six weeks had been completed.

That night they said goodbye to Joan and found their way out to a black, drizzly sky.

'It's over, isn't it,' Margaret said.

'It's over,' Sergio said. 'There is nothing more we can do to salvage the crumbs of our ruined affection.'

Margaret got on her bike and put the news in her earphones. The radio voice said that thirty-seven people had now tested positive, the National Public Health Emergency Team had made their recommendations. 'Stay tuned for the announcement,' the voice said.

At nine o'clock the Taoiseach told everyone they had to stay at home and stay safe. Margaret could not understand what this meant. Only that she had to pick a home.

True, she had been to-ing and fro-ing, breathing her microbes all over the place. It was deemed safer, by everyone, to return to the house they had abandoned. She would go home to him, and there, she would have Bruna to help her with the children while she maybe wrote a novel.

The next day, she and her boy returned through the empty streets with a car full of suitcases, some borrowed furniture, and her computer perched in the front seat like a third passenger.

The following week Bruna found a flight to São Paulo. João from upstairs in her dad's found a flight also. Maybe it was the same flight. The children milled around. Margaret and Sergio began a new six-week course online with Joan and every Tuesday, at 8pm, they would sit in the kitchen at the laptop and watch Joan's long face peer down, while the girls crept in and out, pretending they were hungry. The sessions entailed some bad times. But Margaret believed, even during their most fractious of Zooms, that they could go on together.

For the next year, they saw few others in their bunker and though it was an atmosphere of coughing and distrust and paranoia, plunged together as they were, she loved family life and its possibilities for security and fun. Margaret started thinking about new fabrics. This was their first home, bought together, and it meant something to have fallen in love and had such dreams. She dropped the one-parent family benefit, drew the PUP, and the more pandemic money she saved up, the more she thought of all the soft furnishings money could buy.

She stood in masked queues and picked up paint colours and tile samples from bewildering warehouses.

She ordered swatches for curtains and Blu-tacked them to the windows to see how they performed in every light of day. Cooking became plentiful and obsessive. Loaves of sourdough would puff up in a Dutch oven, casseroles and ragu were made in almost horrifying quantities. Heavy saucepans spat with red oil and meat would be ladled into tubs and into trays upon trays of lasagne, though Margaret and Sergio were vegetarian, and the children sometimes decided they didn't like lasagne anymore.

The day after the cancelled takeaway, Margaret and her brother break the rules with a bottle of beer at his garden table. She does not tell him she is pregnant, but asks him what he thinks she should do about the fights. Fran suggests a three-strike system. Three and it's over: 'If he can't learn to handle his emotions it could be one, two, three and you're done,' Fran says and he smacks the table. It is winter 2021 and Fran is enjoying the sociability.

Strike #1 Becoming a stepmother was difficult but the girls never rejected Margaret and she became protective of them. Over five years they developed shared interests. Picture books, unicorn stickers. Not beading – beading had upsetting consequences, every time. Now, they bake cakes and biscuits and read stories and sit with boxes of Lego – Giorgia follows carefully the instructions and Margaret puts the arms and hands on the minifigures, while her boy looks for rare pieces he can sneak into his pockets.

Sergio is tearful when he comes into the little playroom to see how well they all get along; it was he who introduced his daughters to this craft, and it's he who orders all the Lego on his paydays. Giorgia started with purple-coloured Lego Friends but now she doesn't like girl things; soon she's doing 16+ Star Wars. She is twelve, her sister ten. She gets lost in her new sets, spending days alone in her bedroom and stamping her foot, clenching her fists and wailing if something goes wrong. She wants to have her own channel and become an internet sensation. Margaret listens, spacing out, as Giorgia tells her things she didn't know about palm oil, microplastics, the multiverse, or a game she is designing that brings in all these topics.

Now, their bonding is tested in their isolation and home-school. Margaret wonders. Is it possible to want to marry someone whose cologne you find offensive as its floral reek travels the house each morning in a swirl of shower mist? He apologises, says he'll throw it away, then hides within his padded headphones. Margaret resents caring for his daughters. Studiously, she does not say this aloud. But any meal cooked, any Lego played, accrues points only she keeps a record of, knowing there will come a day she may need to produce this evidence of her superior commitment. Days are long and difficult. Angelica can't organise her own Zooms. She walks the house singing, talking, dancing up the stairs, draws hearts on the walls. She adores arts and crafts; pieces of clay get everywhere. She makes beautiful cut-out snowflakes to stick on windows, and leaves the paper clippings all over the floor, white confetti speckles every surface. Asked to clean up, she looks insolently at her stepmother. 'In a while,' she says, and leaves the room.

One night, Angelica smears a fingerful of Margaret's sourdough batter along her computer screen as recrimination for having been told to go to bed. Hell opens, glittering like a bead curtain, and Margaret knows she could easily wander on in there. She is lucky, she knows, that she always has her father and brother and sisters, and her meditation app, and her legs to take her for a walk in their green suburb; these items in her artillery of privilege will save her from injuring a person. The moment recedes. They light a fire and watch half of a Netflix original family film, before the younger two fall asleep, and Sergio carries each one over a shoulder up the stairs.

Giorgia, she always stays awake reading, or tiptoeing around, late into the night. She lies awake in the dark, staring at her ceiling.

She has been described by her principal as having 'an intelligence that is not inconsiderable', in meetings arranged to address her disruptive behaviour. She rejects the home-school curriculum. She falls behind in Maths and Irish, she is offered special tutors. When forced to attend her Zooms she appears diligent, stationed at her laptop, but when Margaret checks one day she finds she has her camera switched off and her profile picture is the face of a gerbil.

Then all she wants to do is build her 18+ Chewbacca Lego, a birthday present from her father which Margaret hadn't fully approved of, as it carries a gun.

'It's a crossbow,' the girl corrects her. 'Sometimes I think you don't know anything. It fires arrows, can I show you?' and she finds the video on Margaret's phone of Chewie firing a rigid shot.

Over one weekend the sleek creature is built, sloping brown-fur piece by sloping brown-fur piece. Her father helps her to assemble the weapon. Last of all, father and daughter each stick on a peeping little eye, then display it on the kitchen shelf. Nobody is fighting, and another film has been earned.

Angelica talks absolutely all the time.

'Hi!' she'll say on the stairs.

'Hi!' in the kitchen.

'Hi!' while Margaret lies in bed reading Dickens, or reading Amazon customer reviews or just looking at pictures and videos of her son.

Margaret lectures the girl on her excessive greeting style and forbids her to bother her at all after 8pm. Angelica still has questions.

'Hey, what day is it?'

'What time is Daddy taking us out?'

'Can I please have a pancake?'

'When are you getting me new markers?'

'Hey. How are you?'

Margaret says: 'Would you stop asking me questions.' Snapping like this has a nasty aftertaste. But from working with Joan, she believes she has the tools to apologise sincerely, and to explain that her mind gets tired having to think of answers to questions.

'Can I ask just one more question. I promise it's the last,' the girl says.

'OK.'

'What's the point of life?'

Very soon after 'PREGNANT 1–2 weeks', mornings became nauseating sea journeys. This time, Margaret experiences continual seasickness, without the purge of vomiting. Just a continual stay in a cabin, thrust around the ocean. In the afternoons, the TV goes on by appointment, and the *Loud House* theme tune booms up the ceiling into Margaret's side of the partition. One afternoon she hears silence and comes downstairs. Silence should never be trusted, she's learnt – she dreads another fort they've gone and built and fallen off and hurt themselves. She opens the door and sees something else instead. Teddies are lying all over the floor. Dogs, wolves, unicorn pigs, like the scruffy victims of an ambush. 'What's happened?' Margaret asks. Angelica and the boy stand silently before the TV. Margaret takes the remote, turns on the telly and sees all the colours flow together like a rainbow of spilled petrol. The screen has been cracked by the glass eye of a stuffed wolf.

Sergio comes downstairs to make his coffee, passing them in the TV room. He asks Angelica what happened. Margaret walks out and blocks her ears. She comes back for her son, picks him up and fastens him inside the buggy he has almost outgrown. 'Mama, why?' he protests, but becomes placid once the hood goes up and they are out the door. They walk to the supermarket, they walk through the dairy aisles. Here again, she thinks. Ah, yes, this. She knows this place so well. Blocked ears are just a part of life. Hiding in bedrooms is part of life. Sitting on a bench in an emptying shopping centre, that happens sometimes too. Walking home past the bridge by the shopping centre and imagining dropping down into the passing cars, that's every day.

'Do you live in your own head a lot?' Joan asks her at one time. 'Well,' she says, 'I do.' She thinks, I really do. All the time. It's not detachable from my body, yet it takes me anywhere I want to go.

4. Confinement, Continued

Margaret sits at the kitchen table with a cold ginger tea and a packet of cream crackers. The children, off school for a lifetime, crash about. At intervals, she tries to make toast. At the start of their most recent captivity, she'd tried to make a piece of toast, but the lever sprang back up. The toaster appeared to have broken. It was a very fine-looking yellow toaster with a retro design, one of Sergio's indulgences – he loves to buy her kitchen things, cards and chocolates, a new phone, earthenware mugs, the best-quality eggbeaters for Mother's Day.

She had tried to order a new toaster, but it didn't arrive. It never arrives. Every so often she receives an update from the Royal Mail, or conducts a heated phone call with customer service, because their new toaster has been warehoused in the confusion of the new Brexit laws. They turn the grill up high to toast six pieces of toast for three irritable children, then run off to do something else, and something else, and finally fish out the black toast from under the grill. She curses, loudly, thinking how much happier other people are.

She eats the crackers, watching eight seasons of *Mad Men* on her laptop while the girls shout at each other and have physical fights. She watches her episodes in bed at night, and Sergio watches his programmes downstairs. Margaret likes the parts where Don Draper goes to meet a woman, the parts where he walks into a room and removes his fedora with a bashful smile. The parts where he is having sex with one of his mistresses in an unusual position. She rewinds, replays them. Her desire for a fictional construct must remain a secret. The baby is another secret. She wonders if everyone else lives above this seeping marsh of secret wishes, secret loathings, jealousies; can only hope they do. Her tears, as time goes on, remain a secret. Tears in bed, or at the kitchen table. Tears wetting the blue paper mask in the parked car outside her father's house. Tears because they just can't get along, she and Sergio, and the ring, she removes from the chain around her neck and returns to its little box.

Strike #2 When the children do return to school and playschool some time in spring, Margaret lies on in bed nursing her fatigue. The girls run in and out of the room to borrow socks, or to ask for homework signatures or coins for the book sale.

'Mama, where's my schoolbag, Mama, where's my lunchbox?' asks her little boy, one morning. 'Where's playschool?' he asks.

The next time she opens her eyes the house is very quiet. She knows immediately she fell back asleep. She sits up, pleased to have had the extra few minutes. Downstairs the front door hangs wide open.

Margaret calls out her son's name. She goes out to the front garden, then around to the back garden, calling his name. Nothing. *Where's playschool?* She runs around checking all his hiding places – under the bed, under the sofa, on the shelf by her computer; the garage, the treehouse. The door swings open bringing in the breeze from the street, from the roads, from the perilous main roads. *Where's playschool?* Both Sergio and Margaret run out of the house and she goes one way, he goes the other. She runs across the road to Jean and Alex; they both run in opposite directions too, calling his name. Margaret rings the police.

'Is he by any chance wearing his shoes on the wrong feet?' the cheerful sergeant asks. 'Yes, we have him here.'

When Sergio returns from the Garda station, he walks past Margaret into the house without a word. The boy sits crying in the back of the car, realising what he has done. In the bedroom, Margaret buries her face in some more tears. Sergio asks her if she realises the consequences of getting the police involved – in Italy we never, ever, get police involved *che cazzo*! Or some other profanity, she never understands.

The mood has changed again and it's back over to her side of the partition, top-to-tail in the single bed. From her pillow, in the box room, she can see a street sign: NO THROUGH ROAD. It bores her to have words like NO THROUGH ROAD bunged together outside her home, for what will be the rest of her life. To be told so frequently that her house is balanced at the mouth of a dead end. She spends a huge amount of time in that room, reading her novel in the poor light of a hedgehog shade.

She reads, again, the website. Making a decision like this is not what she wants – not what any woman could ever want, Margaret now appreciates. A baby was what she wanted those nights she reunited with her lover, both of them optimistic and carefree and foolish in their isolation. Now, she wants it back out again. To Joan she bawls that she wishes the baby would be taken naturally so as to avoid having to choose to put an end to it – it is a miserable thing to think, and she is glad she's said it aloud, just as I am glad enough to have written it down for her here.

The first time Margaret got pregnant she recorded all the strange things that happened in her journal. She wrote about the mysteries of her condition, she wrote about her emerging hostilities with Sergio following on from the brief affair she had with a used-car salesman (that's what he was). And she wrote about how Sergio's wife became very sick and died.

Now, as her stomach swells for a second time, the story she wrote appears in a serious magazine. She receives her two complimentary copies in the post, brings a copy to her father, and Margaret's life is gingerly passed around the family.

'Has Sergio read this? It's just so damning,' says Caroline.

'Sergio loves it.'

Margaret's father clears his throat. 'It's an assassination,' he says with a touch of pride. 'I would maybe wonder, why you would want to publish it. It seems very personal.'

All she wants in life is to impress her father and everything depends on his approval. But this is – yes. Personal. This is too much information. She looks for the words to persuade him that it is worthwhile, that she is going in some sure direction. 'I got six hundred euro for that,' she stammers.

5. Delirium

Margaret's father and she only meet these days on walks between their neighbourhoods, and he stays a fearful two metres away from her. 'Darlings, the world wasn't meant to go on indefinitely!' he tells his daughters in the early months of viral panic. 'What one of us will probably find,' he says, 'is that it's not the virus that'll get us. It'll be cancer.' Bravado, as it turns out – he is petrified of the virus and lives to avoid it. He stays upstairs in his bedroom for the first few weeks and Caroline brings him his meals prepared with sterilised pots served on a sanitised tray. To come downstairs for his walk, he keeps a torn piece of paper on the hall table, on which he leans rather than touch the contaminated surface of the banister. Some days into the siege a squadron of fat brown moths begin multiplying by his bedroom window. 'It's an infestation of twenty, thirty moths,' he WhatsApps his children. He disinfects his wardrobe, orders lavender-scented mothballs, washes all his clothes and deep cleans the wood to get out all larvae and eggs. He doctors a kitchen sieve into a swatting weapon, and counts the moths as he exterminates them. 'I think I'm flattening the curve!' is one of his few jokes. He admits to his children over Zoom that he is feeling down. 'It's the isolation,' he says, 'and it's the moths, too.' He is lonely, left to brood. Their mother is gone a year. Her clothes and coats still hang around the house, her bursting smile imprisoned in the photographs, and nothing else left of her. He does everything he would have done when she was here – he cooks to the opera strains on Lyric FM, sits by the fireside, reading books so big they crush his legs.

A year passes. Restaurants and shops reopen. By April 2021, the family are sharing a fireside in the evenings, and Sunday lunches, because he has decided life is short. He buys rotisserie chicken and vegan rolls and takeaway pizza and has as many of them as want to eat lunch, laying the table in fine style and opening wine. His vaccination is booked. Then one day he goes into hospital for chest investigations.

On a Zoom call from his hospital bed he tells his children they have found a tumour on his lung. 'Well, I love you all,' he says, before the meeting ends.

Margaret is unspeakably happy, to be having a little baby. Sergio, who wants for her to succeed, rearranges her study, rewires her machines, punching cable ties into the wall, replacing the keyboard and mouse. Margaret's perch by the NO THROUGH ROAD when she hides from the noise and tension looks very neat at least. In life, the scattered distribution of her things has been a scourge for her. She leaves her stuff all over the place and yet, for some reason, she resists affectionate portrayal. Perhaps it's that she shows herself so much love, not many other people have to.

But Sergio loves her. Sergio tidies all her things and unblocks the paper jam in her printer and fixes it up. On weekends, to give her a break, he takes all three children out to forests and playgrounds and makes spaghetti. Margaret's fatigue passes, she takes long indulgent cycles along the Grand Canal and comes home late with the basket of her bike stuffed with sushi rolls and steaming dumplings.

Under Joan's instruction, they try to see one another's point of view. 'It hurts me when you criticise me for leaving crumbs on the kitchen table,' Margaret says and feels like an idiot, she wants to be shot. She spots Chewie, staring at her from the kitchen shelf. This plastic creature, and the Lava lamp next to it, neither would have been her chosen kitchen ornaments.

Uncle Fran comes to mind the children and he lets them beat him up or takes them for a walk. Margaret and her lover fill out hospital forms together, they go for a twelve-week scan, grin at the legume shape encased in the picture. They have a sandwich in a café in the park, take a selfie with their ultrasound picture. Margaret turns up beaming at the clinic, to see the midwife. The midwife takes her urine sample, blood pressure, asks Margaret to lie back while they push around at her abdomen.

Then facing her from down by her feet, the midwife reads through a list of routine questions. 'And now sorry about this one,' she says. 'Do you feel safe at home with your partner?'

In the ultrasound department of Holles Street a sign reads 'please do not sit here coronavirus COVID-19' in one unpunctuated monotone. Margaret is here to have the big ultrasound, the one where they show you the four chambers of the heart, the lungs and suchlike. And though she pulses with fear she is not thinking, at this moment, about the baby. That baby is of no concern. Texts flow in from her father. 'Food hateful. Fellow inmates moribundi. No joke here kids this is double pneumonia. I've got the priest in. We're looking at 100bp and 90 on the oxygen stats else its blast off.'

The previous Friday morning, Caroline and Lisa had decided he was not himself as he sat quietly on the sofa, turning white. His hands shook. His breath became short, then he struggled to breathe at all. Paramedics treated him in an ambulance, and on arrival at the hospital he was set up with an oxygen tank. He has been on the respiratory ward for a week by the time he meets the chaplain for blast off.

In the waiting room of the maternity hospital, Margaret's phone rings. Lisa says: 'I don't want you to worry, but we think maybe he has become delirious.' Outside, Sergio walks the length of Merrion Square in accordance with the rules. The baby is scanned in Sergio's presence. The baby is perfect, and Margaret and Sergio leave holding hands.

Over the next week, her father sends a regular report on the WhatsApp group. They are not allowed to visit him, and notes on his condition come fast, with blood-pressure (BP) and blood-oxygen levels, medications taken, itemised info on lunch and dinner. 'One dessertspoon cereal mixed with milk, half a sliced kiwi, twelve grapes, boiled egg.' Practical household tips ('For lawnmower try five stabs rather than three of the red button'), abrupt sign-offs ('Sorry folks, BP critical, need to focus. Over and out.'). He begins making bank transfers, requesting documents – marriage cert., house deeds, planning receipts, perpetuity receipt from the cemetery. He just wants to make everything easier for them. His children are still not allowed visit him, he is not sick enough. They all know what it means if someone tells him they are allowed to visit him.

On the Sunday morning, her father rings Caroline to finalise his affairs. They talk for forty-five minutes while she transcribes his concerns and wishes on the back of one, then two envelopes – details of his estate, tips for the funeral, books he has to give back to their owners, people to thank, places one might find the receipt for the Woodie's bin house they never assembled, email addresses, legal problems, club membership dates, account passwords.

His children are told they are allowed to visit him, one at a time.

Once Margaret reaches the hospital, he's got everything off his chest. She has one job, to give him Sunday lunch. The vegetarian options in the hospital are limited, dried-out victuals straight out of supermarket packets. Margaret has made her father something called tofu moussaka, with roasted aubergines and a pine-nut cream. Cooking for her father makes her feel more useful than anything she's ever done.

By the time she gets through the security guards, fills out the safety protocol forms, and reaches the correct blue pencil pleats, what she finds is a man formerly her father. Thin as a rake, white as a winter sky, tubes coming out of his nose and hands. He tells her in a small crackling voice all about what happened to him. He'd been given too much sleeping medication and he had lain as if in a straitjacket, thrashing inside to get out. The night enveloped him in a bad dream. It was the worst dream he'd ever had. He and the other men in the ward – they both looked around the ward, from the obese man to the horizontal dying man – he and the men around him were being packed into coffins and sent off on their journey. The nurses were drugging him with barbiturates to make the passage easy, he'd caught them at it. He woke up thinking he was dead, refused breakfast, and waited for Judgement.

'But I do seem to still be here,' he says, with eyes popping from grey hollows. Margaret clutches a bony hand. What is left of him is here indeed. 'That dream!' he continues. 'It was like a Beckett play.' He relates his dream with fresh and ghastly shock. He defies his daughter to believe what he is telling her, about the dream, the horror to which this dream, this nightmare, subjected him – 'because I really thought it was the end'. She marvels too. She nods at him, in shared disturbance, but thinks, let's not offer any consolation. This nightmare was true to life. It was like running for a train. He missed his train; now he just has to wait for the next one.

She serves her father a piece of tofu pie on the saucer of his tea mug. He takes a forkful of this repast. 'Wow!' he says. She grins at him. He asks after Sergio and each of the children. 'That relationship was only just beginning really,' he says. Margaret tenses, then understands he is talking about his own relationship with Sergio. Her father sees what is noble and interesting in everyone. 'What we really all must do,' he said to her once, 'is improve the quality of our conflicts.' She believes he will help her to resolve hers too, the conflicts in her home and in the corners of her mind. Margaret has no peace. She oscillates from one outrageous and perverse longing to the next. Even today. Part of her thrills at the thought of his death. She wants to speed up his end so that they can have a funeral and everyone will come and celebrate with them and sympathise with Margaret and finally respect her – that she would even think these thoughts. She frightens herself.

They are both masked now, but distance is only theoretical. She holds her father's hand, trying to soak in the life underneath his pallid skin. The man facing them on the other side of the ward is very evidently dying. His cheeks have gone right in. His eyes look out from a place of kindness, goodness, decency. A nurse comes with oral morphine and the man closes his eyes and sucks back the syrup from the plastic syringe like it is honey and wine. Her father's eyes are shutting too, and she has to leave him.

After the rehearsal for his death, Margaret's father improves. His oxygen levels improve, he begins to breathe independently. His strength improves, he does his physio, tries the hospital stairs, tries washing ('*Mirabile dictu*! I took a shower!'). He even gets out of hospital. He will renew his passport and take a trip to the Canaries. But he has stared death in the face. Death stared back at him and it slipped inside him that day.

Strike #3 One hot, cloudless Monday in June, a tiny silver Mercedes scales the side of Margaret's car going around a roundabout off the M50. The doors of the two cars meet in a long and painful scrape. The driver is from Moscow, in her sixties, bronzed and shimmering, wearing a slinky white-gold dress, her neck and wrists strung with costume jewels. She has a particular aesthetic. 'What the hell? Look how dumb you drive!' she screams as they stand breathless on the side of the road. Margaret and the woman stare at each other accusingly, then study the red paint stains that have come off on the woman's perfect car. Neither is ready to admit they are the one at fault.

That afternoon Margaret lies on the double bed. Nervously, she tells Sergio all about it. When the woman's husband phones her up demanding money from her, Sergio takes the phone and says, 'Hello sir, I am Margaret's husband. Aha, Russian? *Privet,*' and gives his full name with military title. Margaret is always amazed by the ease and bombast with which he speaks to strangers. By the end of the phone call, everything is forgiven. The man is apologetic even, and Margaret and Sergio laugh, kissing each other goodbye at the bedroom door.

Sergio goes off to collect the children while she sits relaxing on her side of the partition with her documents and editing tools. Outside, the sky is brilliant blue like something you could jump right into. Sunlight casts the quiet street in this bright stillness. She sighs and looks back at her document. This one, it's a short story, and it's been going on the longest time. Words, there are just so many of them. She thinks that it might never end. The key turns in the front door and the house floods with Sergio and the children, tumbling in from school.

Loud crashing sounds come up from the floorboards. Methodical blows that rise in a crescendo of little pieces shattering. Much louder than usual. Margaret thinks, they must be having a really good time. She pulls her chair tight into her desk and tries to read a sentence.

'Again!' she hears him shout. Silence follows. 'Once more!' One, two, three blows, then a longer silence. Footsteps, and she looks out the window to see him carrying something in armfuls to the black bin on the street. He elbows open the lid and drops it all in, bangs down the lid – the lid pops back up. But why are Chewie's arms and legs and head in pieces? How about that for weird. She returns to her screen.

It is Monday, and the rubbish truck is late. As her heart speeds up, it occurs to her that she could go outside to the bins and reverse something of what has happened. Then the rubbish truck arrives to take the bins away.

'Giorgia was bold in school again and now she's going to have to pay for it. I mean this time she was REALLY bold. That child is causing a DISRUPTION, she is CAUSING CHAOS. She is PREVENTING OTHER CHILDREN FROM DOING THEIR WORK so yes I have dismantled HER HARD WORK to show her how that FEELS I have sent her to her ROOM she DESERVES NOTHING. DON'T PAMPER HER.'

He's trying to pass her on the landing. It doesn't make sense. *That doesn't make any sense.* She doesn't say this, simply, she lets him pass, into the bedroom and she retreats into the box room, squeezes into her desk and blinks at her document. Her heart beating so hard she feels the pulse beat in her neck and it's so loud she can hear it.

Here again. Right back here. This time, it's like she's swallowed poison. Her neck throbs, her limbs don't want to move at all. She drapes back across her office chair, impaled, and shuts her eyes. Breathe in love, she remembers, sneers. A long intake of mindful air pollutes her lungs.

Her door opens, Angelica comes to her. 'This is the worst day ever! You'll never guess what!' she starts; but Margaret can't piece together what Angelica is trying to say, and now the boy is jumping on the bed so she has to stop him, but – her limbs still don't want to move. She takes out her phone but thinks of no one she can call this time.

She stands up, frail and watery. She feels her way across the landing and knocks.

'Don't pamper me. I deserve nothing—' Giorgia is talking quickly, cross-legged on the floor, black tendrils of hair in her face, arms flying up and down. She is ripping books in half. 'My favourite books. Look, I won't need my favourite books anymore, I don't deserve anything I like,' and she gets to her feet and tips into her wastepaper bin a bundle of colourful paperbacks ripped up from their spines.

Margaret knocks on Sergio's door.

'You know,' she tells him, in the bedroom where he fills the desk and chair, 'that is the last strike. I told you, remember, this is a strike system, we had a system. This is where it ends for me.'

'Perfect opportunity,' he says, and closes his ears with headphones. Margaret nods. She stands, nodding. Returns to her office chair, and there, she remembers, and puts both hands to her stomach. Six months along.

6. Sorrow

As it happens, that evening she is going to her father's for a takeaway. He's invited all his children. A nurse from the palliative-care team came around to the house and he seems to want to mark the occasion, to begin the end in style. 'What'll we get?' he earlier asked on the phone. 'Pizza? Thai? Indian? I don't know, I hate them all.'

They decide on Indian and Margaret arrives late off her bike and pokes around the containers. Her father says: 'And how was your day?'

'Not the best,' she says. 'Drove into a Merc on the motorway.'

'Oh no,' everyone says. Margaret holds out her glass which her father fills with white wine. 'Did you do any damage?'

Margaret begins to cry. 'No,' she says, blocking her eyes. 'And that wasn't even the worst thing.'

'Oh?' her father says. Five faces turn in expectation to the one person who can't speak. She tries to speak, can only articulate sounds, and tears flow down her face. 'Tell us what happened,' her father says.

After dinner, Margaret and her sisters sit around their father's bed. Caroline has persuaded him to watch another episode of the *Olive Kitteridge* adaptation – she and her family still get to live with him while they try to build their house. Margaret is always envious of their box sets as her sister has his company all to herself. But tonight they are a father and three daughters on one bed, Frances McDormand playing Olive in the background. Two sisters have been paid a visit by the clandestine hairdresser; Margaret's grey roots push through in stripes. None of them are watching the programme. Margaret describes again what happened, and they close in on her: their fixed looks of concern. They make suggestions, and Margaret stares out of the room, into the past, to a speculative future mingled with last night's dreams and recurring, stupid epiphanies, recurring desires, impossible plans. It is getting late and she is very tired; she wishes to be carried on a stretcher rather than cycle up the hill, back to that house. The baby zips through her. 'Can I ask a favour?' she says. 'Don't ever let me tell you everything is fine.' She also asks her sisters if they will be able to help her with the baby when it arrives.

Returning that night, she finds the door to the box room has been left ajar, and she cranes to see him sobbing on the single bed.

The next morning, she sits folding his t-shirts. She has a pile of laundry to get through and she isn't about to extract his things out and ask him to fold them himself. She could ask him, he would probably prefer that. But she won't. That would be to relinquish her hold over what is his. Anyway he would do the folding wrong. She sits folding his shorts and sweaters and dad-rock t-shirts into untidy parcels with the *Loud House* theme tune coming up the floorboards and this thing, this creature, twisting through her insides.

Tomorrow, their new picnic table is arriving. Somebody needs to assemble the table and benches and it will not be Margaret. There are a lot of things to do around here. Everyone is making holiday plans and having small numbers of people in for barbeques. The laundry, the tumble dryer, the school collections, the filling of the car engine, the problem with the windscreen-wipers, the greeting of the neighbours all demand a certain kind of approach.

This is how the days go on. Clothes are folded and put away, the kitchen is left clean, the best sound of all is the dishwasher, whose chutes and waterfalls crash around in perfect containment, every evening, the children all in bed at last. The household revolves as normal, pulling her back into the churn. The white noise of their life together lulls her with a forceful calm.

For weeks she meets him only in the kitchen, looking pale with ringed and testy eyes. One or two discussions: he is very sorry, won't happen again. She tells him to stop spraying that sickly cologne, he doesn't; she throws away the bottle. With this, he doesn't argue. Avoids her, assembles garden furniture. The girls and he go out for hamburgers. Two new Lego sets are purchased, a Rebel Base and another, identical Chewbacca; that one stays in the box unbuilt. Margaret hides it in the garage.

The day she finds him on the landing, lining up three suitcases in a row she feels a rushing of affection for him, for everybody. He has booked flights to Italy for himself and the girls. They're going to stay all summer with Mamma, sort everything out, see Don Mateo, his spiritual guide, and he will walk the forests that surround the hamlets of his birthplace. She knows he will stock up with cans of olive oil, with wine and pasta, great blocks of salty sheep's cheese, balsamico; maybe he'll bring truffles and small, broken fruit tarts in a baker's box. They will live together in this close nest of forgiveness and of love. She wants to throw her arms around him. She wants to follow him to Italy and be, again, the daughter of his soft and tentacled mamma. She could book flights today, open her Italian app. Instead, she looks at him from across the kitchen. And tells him never to come home.

7. Pride

For her father's last birthday, he asks for a pair of decent slippers, a pair of light pyjamas and a dressing gown, as he still wears his dressing gown from boarding school.

He is sitting up in his hospital bed, tinkering on a laptop with his will, Margaret eating pecan halves from tinfoil in her handbag next to him. His requests seem strange as presents normally annoy him and he hands them straight back. He explains it to her. 'If I'm going to be spending all my time with whitecoats, I'll need to look respectable too.'

'You look fine!' she says, but he clears his throat.

'I look.' He stares at his daughter. 'Like a ghoul.'

The palliative nurse comes in, a woman of fifty with a neat amber bob and gleaming eyes. She busies herself around the bed, discussing how to build strength through nutrition and physiotherapy, recommending pineapple juice. This angel of death has a plucky, upbeat disposition, though sometimes she says absolutely nothing, and her green eyes flash very gently. Margaret feels this woman is trying to entice her father over the precipice, into the abyss – she's trying to push him over. She dislikes this woman's ease with something so infinitely terrible, and distrusts her entirely.

Her father asks: 'About how long would you think I've got?'

'Oh, I would be thinking months,' says the nurse. *Months* – she says it in a tone of wonder, as if months were a long time. *Months, oh, really? You don't mean months!*

Her father tells the nurse about Margaret's baby, and they all talk about blood sugar levels. He pours water from the jug into his glass, and sips it with urbane appreciation, wincing only as he swallows. When the nurse is gone he turns to Margaret. 'I'm not sure you can wait months, can you?'

She isn't sure she understands what he is saying. Though she has some idea. Shame fills her. There should be no exchange for his life. She clutches at his fingers, stroking his soft hands and talking too quickly – 'But you made such a miraculous recovery in the summer and there's this new drug—' He clears his throat again, shutting his eyes with the discomfort. And he tells her, 'I have lung cancer at stage four. You get an infection, they blitz you. You get another infection, they blitz you. My dear children don't need this anymore.'

As she is getting up to go he hands her his debit card to buy the birthday presents.

Two days later, she receives a letter from a solicitor, and quickly looks online. Her bank balance has changed to a figure so absurd and unfamiliar it is almost hypnotic. Money she hasn't earned and has no understanding of. She pays off her credit card bill, pays her sisters back a bit of money she has borrowed. She makes a large transfer. From his childhood bedroom in Casalgrande, Sergio finds a small flat in a new development near the Dublin Mountains; after a short virtual tour he places his deposit. At home, she writes an advertisement for a childminder, and then she finds the number of the woman they've been waiting for – highly recommended, with almost forty-years' experience – the mediator.

—

What she does next, she is advised against. She does it anyway, urgently, compulsively; she can't help it. It's all been upsetting her too long. Not just the dated kitchen but the old bathroom, and left alone with her ideas she decides, yes, now is the time. We still have a couple of months before the baby arrives. .

Mornings, when the boy is at camp, she sits on a donut cushion in a traffic jam to collect the boxes of tiles from the tile warehouse in the industrial zone, then the tins of paint from the home-decor centre. She thuds though the house with a tape measure. She wonders in bed at night about Milky Way slumber downs and new mattresses; and in her dreams she sees the paint colours being laid on the walls – Azure Cool, Nordic White. Days are spent on Roman blinds – linen, cotton, duck egg, spun gold, tropical birds and flowers, three kinds of nautical stripe. An afternoon bent over, rooting though wallpaper bargain bins. She stands in queues in the Marks & Spencer's bedding department, moving from foot to foot, developing a haemorrhoid.

A call comes in from an unknown number. It's a long time she has been waiting for him, and now he's returning her call. Thady has a rich, sing-song voice as he lays out his set of skills. He is one of two carpenters readily available to tile their bathrooms. Two carpenters, ready to tile.

They come early one morning and pull up the floor to source the problem. A quotation is supplied, on paper headed by the name of a different business, one no longer trading; she looks it up. But the men have a van and they are willing to start. 'Get the husband to have a look at that and we'll be back some time tomorrow,'

Thady says. They leave the old floor pieces in the front driveway and head off. A week passes.

8. Agony

She is lying on the bed with her feet resting on the bed-post and her ass elevated on a pillow to drain the blood back out of the haemorrhoid. Around the house the children fight and squeal, making a stop-motion Lego show on an app. The summer is over and the bedroom floors are awash with open suitcases, spilling clothes and presents. The walls are freshly painted, the girls' bedroom wallpapered with seahorses. Sergio enters, calls the two girls inside. He will be leaving the house for a little while. He announces this calamity there in the bedroom, which is being stripped of his office fur-niture and clothes to become a nursery, and sick bay for Margaret. In one corner, a cluster of folded-up desk, cardboard boxes and bulging Tesco bags-for-life, intended for his one-bedroom flat.

The girls both nod, then begin to cry in their father's arms, one long-legged girl on each bulky knee. They cry with a kind of obedience, knowing an emotion is expected of them. He pulls both of them in close and Margaret turns away.

Over the following days she tries a walk. Coming in from the pharmacy the bottom of the bucket of Epsom Salts cracks and salt crystals rain down the stairs and get into the floorboards.

The haemorrhoid has a punishing quality, like a biblical snake, or a penknife being turned in her. Her backside throbs and stings after she's removed the fro-zen peas, which have fully defrosted, soaked the sheets.

Why, she wonders. Why has such revolting evil come to me this close to the end; I had been doing so well. We have all been doing so well.

Her phone beeps: help. But it isn't. It is her Italian app in the shape of a cartoon owl with blinking eyes. A speech bubble from the owl's beak says:

Aw, you left me all alone.

Beside the owl, a link for her next vocabulary lesson, and she flings the phone across the room. She writhes around the bedclothes, the haemorrhoid having thrombosed in its rage. On the floor, next to her discarded phone, two mounds of laundry wait in baskets. No school lunches are made, the toilet is lying in the front garden, and someone needs to take the boy to his first day of Junior Infants.

On the phone in a waiting room at Holles Street, in dread of yet another rectal exploration, she hires a woman with a soothing voice to move in and help her with the children.

Sergio doesn't like his flat and comes back every Friday to be with his family, his laundry in a bulging Lidl bag-for-life. He stays the weekend and on Sunday roasts a chicken before going back to his place to play cards online with the *ragazzi* back in Casalgrande.

One Sunday night before he sets off again, he comes to her on the sofa.

'Could I ask you if I could feel the baby move?'

'Of course.'

He kneels down, rests his hand around her stomach and brings his ear close to it. She breathes in his scent, closing her palm around his cheek. His cheek is warm and golden, smooth, padded. He was the one she loved most, for him she would do anything. She closes her eyes, drifting back, succumbing, and in the seconds that pass she feels, not affection, but a horrible sting in the back of her throat. Heartburn.

She wants the baby out and wants to be alone.

For a few moments they remain in each other's arms, and for the last time.

The leaves fall crisp and golden on a street cast in sunlight, and through the house goes an electric drill. But she would not go outside even if she were able. Home improvements have developed into full structural works, and the upstairs bathroom now looks like the inside of a skip.

When the men first returned to get down to the tiling, they seemed like steady workers. Thady is a twinkling, retirement-age character with broad shoulders, a bit of a lad still. Margaret has to drop his envelopes of cash up to The Jolly Roger where he can be found socialising, weekday evenings, with other local friends and tradesmen. Thady does the talking and negotiating, Joe is more careful when it comes to words, and seems to harbour strong suspicions generally. He keeps watch at the threshold to the house, tipping his ash on the front step.

Vans back into the driveway with boxes of tiles and tubs of grout and adhesive, the men hack and drill, creating piles of construction waste. The toilet needs to be ripped out, the shower replaced. One morning, coming in from the school run, Margaret faces Joe at the porch where he stands, fag in the side of his mouth, contemplating something grim, it looks like. He is wearing a weathered t-shirt with a Bad Santa in sunglasses across his chest. He eyes her as if she might insult him.

'Joe,' she says. 'What do I do with all of this?' They both consider the heap of rotten wood, broken floral tiles, the shower base.

'Recycling centre,' says Joe.

'Recycling centre,' she repeats.

He nods. 'Fifteen euro for a carload.'

She walks back into the house and clutches the end of the banister. Step by step, she heaves her weight up to the bathroom and stands back against a peeling wall. She holds her stomach in her arms like a bowling ball as she looks around. The floor is still gone. What she sees is a shredded hieroglyph of dated workmanship, splintered rot, DIY gone wrong. These men have worked hard, they have exposed the crust of the earth and found it to be diseased.

During the day she watches them carefully. The moment she finds them laying fresh plasterboard over the disease she kicks up. They are disguising the problem, covering up the fungal undergrowth instead of thinking of our future! 'Four children are going to be living in this house!' she tells them. 'Give it a year, or less, before the damp and mould come back.' Bending down to press the wood with her palm to show them how wet it is, she feels a shooting rumble in her farthest depths. She grabs hold of the sink and waits, breathing out, until it passes. Leaning frontways, her bowling ball sways in the room.

The next evening, everyone asleep, she is rewatching the first episode of the first season of *Mad Men* when she starts to feel strange. But it's not due for a week, she thinks. And I have to get four boxes of 20 x 20 white ceramic tiles from Right Price Tiles tomorrow. The men will be back at 8am. The bathroom is a cemetary.

She writes to Sergio, then feels her way upstairs and goes in to check on her little boy but is seized, on entering, and has to get down on his bed and breathe in love. She breathes out peace on the pillow they share. The boy sits up and squints at her. 'Oh,' he says.

He is always keen to have a chat.

'Did you know the great white shark is the size of a school bus?'

'No, that's interesting.'

A few voluptuous minutes pass, and she comes to again.

'Do polar bears have eyebrows?'

After a while his eyes close. A gust of wind comes through the windowpane, talking quietly in her ear. We try our best, but it's never possible to be alone.

Acknowledgements

Sarah Davis-Goff and Lisa Coen, two fire-starters, you lit up my world. Thank you for your belief in this book and for providing such close and thoughtful editorial guidance, while doing everything else as well.

To my agent, Marianne Gunn O'Connor. You asked me to write a love story, and look. Thank you for your generous and steadfast enthusiasm.

To the talented Fiachra McCarthy, for your cover; to Marsha Swan for typesetting, and to Sióbán Devlin for proofreading, thank you all.

Brendan Barrington of the *Dublin Review*, you printed my first ever story and this changed everything for me. Eimear Ryan at *Banshee*; Niamh Campbell at *Belfield Literary Review*; Danny Denton at *Stinging Fly*, thanks, each of you.

John Patrick McHugh, I am so glad I scrubbed up and went into town the night I ran into you, as it led, if indirectly, to this book. And thanks Dublin.

Matilda Culme-Seymour and Ruth Lyons, I am so grateful to you both for reading drafts of these stories and sharing your wise thoughts. Philip Ó Ceallaigh, my friend in Trouble, thank you.

Conversations with a multitude of people helped this book along in different ways, thank you. All my aunts, and Kyran. Barbara FitzGerald. Ronan Molony. Lesley Caplin. Ciara Considine. Anna Farmar. Sheila Armstrong. Sophie White. Professor Francis Leneghan. Maya Kulukundis. Isabelle Vallet Dunne. Mary McCarthy. Rosita Sweetman. Rob Doyle. Amy Stephenson. Dr Michael Murray. Eoin Tierney. Donny Mahoney. BQ. Handsome Paddy. Luke Sheehan and his handsome father, Ronan. Jennie Taylor. Simon Ashe-Browne. Donal Flynn. Eli Diamant. Daniele Idini. Enrico Fantasia. Rory McArdle.

Richard Lalor, accountant to the stars and social misfits, thank you.

Hourican sisters, it's been a delight and a cacophony knowing you.

Dr Rachel O'Dwyer, you're a terrible influence, and thank you for that.

Ruth Hegarty took me seriously when there was no need, and Colin Murphy tolerated me for years in his garret – anything has seemed possible since knowing both of you, which I hope is a good thing.

Frankie and Beatrice, it's not that you helped with this book. But you are the reason I try and the beats of my heart.

My siblings, Katie, Frank and Grace, three obelisks, I owe you more than I'd like to imagine, this book is for you. But you don't have to read all of it. Okay?